A TIMELESS Romance ANTHOLOGY

blind date
collection

A TIMELESS Romance ANTHOLOGY

blind date
collection

SIX ROMANCE NOVELLAS

ANNETTE LYON

SARAH M. EDEN

HEATHER B. MOORE

VICTORINE E. LIESKE

RACHEL BRANTON

SARIAH WILSON

Mirror Press

Interior Design by Cora Johnson
Edited by Anna DeStefano and Lisa Shepherd

Cover design by Mirror Press, LLC
Cover Photo Credit: iStock #58498420
Cover Photo Copyright: PeopleImages

Published by Mirror Press, LLC

ISBN-13: 978-1-947152-46-5

Table of Contents

Three Historical Romance Novellas

Three Contemporary Romance Novellas

The Promise
That Katy Did

ANNETTE LYON

Chapter One

Midway, Utah—1884

KATHERINE DIDDLE—KATY, to pretty much everyone who knew her—offered a handful of coins to the girl behind the counter at Bonner Brothers Mercantile in exchange for a jar of ointment.

"Have a good day," Margaret Bonner said.

Katy gave what she hoped was an approximation of a smile in spite of her heavy heart. Today had been a difficult day, and it would continue to be far less than "good." She headed home, across Main Street before turning west, walking quickly as she cradled the precious container. Hopefully the salve inside it would ease Sue Ellen's cough and make breathing a little easier in her final hours.

The walk wasn't long, yet it seemed to stretch into infinity. Midway was a small town of farmers and miners tucked into the Rocky Mountains. In spite of not wanting to watch the one person who was most like family pass away, she hurried along so she would be there when her spinster friend needed it.

How long have I been gone? Katy had slipped out after Sue Ellen had fallen into a fitful sleep after a night filled with coughing, wheezing, and growing weaker by the hour. Katy would have preferred to ask one of the Wilson children to run the errand, but she and Sue Ellen were guests at the Wilson household.

Permanent ones, but guests all the same. The family had

been generous enough. They'd paid for the doctor and even offered the closet off the kitchen as a private place instead of sleeping in whatever corner they could find for her in the small house. For too many years, that had meant the girls' rooms, because there simply was no other spot.

The tiny room off the kitchen barely fit a narrow mattress, a chair, and an old milking stool Katy used as an end table. But it had a door, and therefore meant sought-after privacy. The closet shared a wall with the stove, so the space stayed warmer at night. Over the last week, Katy had spent most of her time caring for her dear friend, who was old enough to be her own grandmother. They shared no blood relation—Katy was a distant cousin of Mrs. Wilson, and Sue Ellen had been a long-time friend with no living family. Even without being blood relations, Katy felt closer to Sue Ellen than anyone.

Consumption was not an illness to take lightly in anyone, but for a spinster of seventy-five—already bent from age and a life of work and service—the diagnosis did not bode well. Not for the first time, a glimpse of what the future likely held came to Katy's mind in stark relief. After Sue Ellen passed, Katy would be the only outsider in the household. And what a lonely, bleak life that would be without someone like Sue Ellen to share it with.

Be grateful, she chided herself. *You have a roof over your head and hot dinners every day.*

The family never mistreated her nor Sue Ellen, who had largely been left to themselves. Sometimes they were grateful for the lack of attention, but they'd often felt ignored. Having Sue Ellen as a friend had softened the edges of what would have been lonely days and nights. Katy couldn't find fault with the Wilsons, who had opened their doors. The family didn't have to take the women in. Heaven only knew that they already had enough strain on their lives with their own seeming multitude of children and accompanying duties.

The house came into view, but it appeared blurry in

Katy's vision. She blinked away the tears burning her eyes. Her free hand swiped wetness from one cheek, and then the other. She slowed her pace and tilted her face skyward to help the tears dry up. This was not a time to be showing sadness or weakness. Sue Ellen needed her to be strong and hopeful. Happy.

I will not go inside with any trace of grief, or she'll know the truth, Katy thought, blinking furiously to dry her traitorous eyes. When Sue Ellen first fell ill, the doctor told Katy in measured tones that he'd consider it a miracle if Sue Ellen lasted a week. That was two weeks ago. Katy knew that her friend's time on earth could likely be counted in hours. She prayed that between the ointment and the new bottle of laudanum Dr. Crockett had delivered that morning, Sue Ellen would be comfortable during her passing.

Eyes dry, Katy stepped from the corner, crossed the street, and headed for the drive at the side of the house, intending to go in through the back as usual. But when she reached the gravel, the front door squeaked open.

Odd. Only occasional guests used the front entrance. Katy turned to peer at the departing visitor; dirt and rocks crunched beneath her feet. The last person through there had probably been the minister last winter when the family hosted him and his wife for dinner. Neighbors knocked on the back door, whether dropping off extra fruit from their trees or simply paying a visit. Even peddlers knew to go around back. Now, a man with graying hair stepped onto the porch and pulled the handle until the latch clicked.

Did no one see him to the door? Who is that man?

He set his hat in place, and as he moved toward the steps, Katy came to herself. Unwilling to be caught watching him, she picked up her skirts again and hurried along the drive.

"Miss?"

She stopped in her tracks and held her breath. Drat the noisy gravel, and drat the visitor's curiosity. Couldn't he tell by her haste that she had urgent business? She heard his heavy footsteps. As he drew nearer, she could feel her cheeks burning hotter, as if she were a child caught in misbehavior. She slowly turned around, unsure what to expect. His trousers were clean and pressed, his shirt starched, his dark red cravat tied impeccably. His starched and pressed clothing juxtaposed against the leathery, brown skin of his face. He'd clearly dressed up for this visit.

"Excuse me," he said, "but . . . are you . . . Katherine Diddle?"

"I am," she said cautiously. "May I ask who you are?" An edge of the jar bit painfully into her palm; she willed her fingers to relax. Her jaw tensed instead, as if her unease needed someplace to settle.

The man removed his hat. "Heinz Balmer," he said with a small bow. "I recently moved to town with my daughter and her family."

His speech, while clear, had the softened vowels and distinct consonants she'd grown up hearing from many older Midway residents. She tended to forget that they were Swiss immigrants; to her ear, that's simply how most elderly people sounded.

Was his daughter's family new to Midway? Or were they long-standing residents, and Mr. Balmer had simply joined them? If the latter, then his daughter might be a neighbor Katy already knew.

You'll have time to pry later, she told herself. *But now, you need to get back inside.*

"A pleasure to meet you, Mr. Balmer." Katy bobbed at the knees then glanced at the house. Her curiosity got the better of her, so she added, "Did you have business with Mr. Wilson?"

"No. I came to visit an old friend." He glanced at the house, and his face seemed to light up, but just as quickly, it faded into an expression of melancholy. "To say hello, and, it appears, to say goodbye."

He knows Sue Ellen? How?

Sue Ellen hadn't emigrated from Switzerland, yet how else would this man know her, when she'd lived in Midway for decades? What had brought Mr. Balmer to Midway now?

And how did he know my name?

From Sue Ellen, she realized with relief.

"It was nice to meet you, Katherine," Mr. Balmer said with nod.

"Most people call me Katy," she managed in something resembling a croaking whisper. "I mean, if you were to ask for me around town using my full name, most people wouldn't know who you meant. But I should go inside because—" She cut off before she could say Sue Ellen's name. "I need to get back."

He seemed to understand. He nodded, staring at the pockmarked drive, and swallowed hard. "She is a good woman. Thank you for caring for her."

Before Katy could reply, he was crossing the street. She watched until he reached the far corner, expecting him to turn back or explain or—she didn't know what else. She gripped the jar, and the sharp corner reminded her to hurry back to Sue Ellen.

Katy slipped through the back door in a bit of a haze. She rushed to the closet but then stopped at the threshold to look at Sue Ellen before entering. She meant to watch for the rise and fall of Sue Ellen's chest—and to try not to wake her. But no sooner did she reach the door than a very awake Sue Ellen spoke.

"Katydid, there you are." The old woman sat propped against an additional pillow.

"Did you sleep well?" She almost said how good Sue Ellen looked. Her cheeks had color in them again, and she smiled in a way Katie hadn't seen in weeks.

"I certainly did, for once." Sue Ellen chuckled, which set off a coughing fit.

Katy set the jar on the milking stool, sat on the edge of the bed, and gently held Sue Ellen's fragile frame in her arms, patting her back to help loosen the phlegm, or at least offer a measure of comfort. When the spasm ended, Sue Ellen sat back again, looking tired but still wearing a smile as she drew a handkerchief across her mouth. It came away bright red. If not for that, Katy's hopes for a miraculous healing would have flared, but the doctor had made it clear that such a symptom was dire indeed.

"I brought an ointment to soothe your cough," Katy said. She resettled Sue Ellen on her pillows and tucked her beneath three heavy quilts, then pulled up the chair. "Here, let me rub some onto your chest. Margaret insists it'll open your lungs right up."

Sue Ellen submitted as Katy offered her most tender touch, smoothing the ointment on just as Margaret had instructed. "There," she said, screwing the lid back on. "Need more laudanum? Dr. Crockett brought by a full bottle earlier."

"Yes, please. Thank you, Katydid."

She smiled at the old nickname. Had her family lived, she would have been known by *Katherine* instead of *Katy*. Sometimes, though, she liked to think that her parents would have come up with the idea to call her *Katydid* as Sue Ellen had. As Katy stood to fetch the medicine bottle, Sue Ellen grasped her arm. The wrinkled, bony fingers held Katy's wrist with surprising strength, so she sat back down, worried.

"What is it? Where do you hurt?" Her gaze tracked from the top of Sue Ellen's gray hair to the lumps that were her feet at the base of the bed.

"Katydid," Sue Ellen said evenly—and so quietly. Quieter than a whisper.

"Yes?" She leaned in, wanting to hear every word, wanting to keep Sue Ellen talking for as long as possible. Because then she would still be here.

"After I—"

"Shh." Katy shook her head sharply. "Don't talk like that."

Sue Ellen smiled, and Katy braced herself for another

chuckle—and coughing fit. But this time, Sue Ellen rested her hand against Katy's cheek. Katy placed hers over Sue Ellen's chilled one, hoping to warm it. "We both know my time here is almost gone."

The tears Katy had been fighting for two weeks, tears she'd deliberately left behind on the walk home, broke through the dam she'd built and spilled over. "Don't go. Please."

"I don't want to." Sue Ellen's voice wasn't nearly as strong as it had been a moment before. "God willing, you won't be alone for long."

"I know. The Wilsons will keep me company."

"Not the Wilsons." Sue Ellen shook her head and squeezed Katy's hand with surprising force. "You've been my solace for years, and I thank God for that. You were a light when my life became dark. I spent many years regretting . . ." A coughing spasm interrupted. Katie helped Sue Ellen sit up to help clear her lungs, then patted her back until the fit passed. Sue Ellen eased onto her pillows again, and Katy wiped more spittle and blood from the corner of her mouth.

"There." Katy set the handkerchief aside. "Much better."

"Family," Sue Ellen said in almost a whisper.

"What was that?"

Sue Ellen's eyes were closed, her breathing labored. "Family." As she continued, she took a breath between words. "I want . . . you to have . . . a family . . . husband . . . children."

"That would be nice," Katy said vaguely. "You rest now. I'll warm up some beef stock, and—"

"Heinz," Sue Ellen said. "Promise me you'll talk to Heinz."

"I don't know anyone named Heinz."

"Speak with him."

Katy took Sue Ellen's hand and did her best to soothe her friend, who seemed to be slipping into a state of delirium. Katy had heard of such things happening when the end was near.

7

Sue Ellen likely meant a long-dead cousin or childhood neighbor.

"Tell me about Heinz," Katy said, unsure how else to comfort Sue Ellen. "What is he like?"

"He left a moment before you came in." Sue Ellen suddenly sounded alert, and anything but delirious. She looked intently at Katy, as if trying to tell her that this Heinz person mattered terribly. "You must have seen him leave. He wore a red cravat."

The man outside had worn a red cravat. His given name might have been Heinz—the meeting had gone so quickly, she didn't remember. "I met a Mr. Balmer."

"Yes, that's him." She closed her eyes and nodded, the hint of a smile back again. "Talk to him."

"Very well," Katy said. If Mr. Balmer spoke to her, she would certainly reply. Why in heaven would Sue Ellen insist that a young woman have a conversation with an elderly man?

"Promise me that you'll talk to him—privately." Sue Ellen's voice sounded tight, and her hand trembled between Katy's.

Sue Ellen might not know what she was saying—or possibly who she was saying it to. The idea that Sue Ellen might no longer recognize Katy made a thick lump stick in her throat.

She's not delusional. She remembers her visitor, Katy thought, *including what he wore.*

"Promise," Sue Ellen said again. "Promise you'll speak with Heinz—and that you'll listen to what he has to say."

Mr. Balmer might have changed completely since Sue Ellen last saw him. What if he was senile? Or dangerous? The idea of a private meeting with an elderly man made Katy anxious. Yet the pleading in Sue Ellen's eyes softened her heart.

"I promise," she said. "I'll speak with Heinz privately, and I'll listen to everything he has to say. You have my word."

Sue Ellen closed her eyes and breathed easier. "Thank you, Katydid." Her body relaxed, and she drifted into unconsciousness.

Talk to Heinz Balmer. Katy stroked the back of Sue Ellen's hand.

What an odd promise to exact from one's deathbed.

Chapter Two

Two Weeks Later

HELPING GRANDPA HEINZ into the wagon turned out to take more effort than Barrett Eversoll expected. His grandfather put most of his weight on Barrett's arm as he slowly stepped up, then steadied his balance before settling on the bench.

"Thank you," he said, patting Barrett's arm. "I'm fine now."

Only then did Barrett let go and round the wagon. He hopped up on his side, but before sitting, he picked up the wildflowers Mother had bound with ribbon. He handed the bouquet to Grandpa, who rested the flowers in his lap.

"Off we go," Barrett said, flicking the reins and clucking at the horse. "You'll have to remind me how to get to the cemetery."

He got a simple nod of agreement in response. As the horse reached a canter, Barrett licked his lips, eying Grandpa Heinz from the corner of his eye. He wasn't frail yet, not by a mile, but he did show signs of aging, and seeing those things always tipped Barrett's world askew. This was a man who had always been strong as an ox and busier than bees—always working, rarely at rest.

After a few minutes of rolling westward in silence, he opened his mouth to ask a question, but Grandpa's pensive expression made Barrett close his mouth. Grandpa looked lost in thought, with a melancholy mix of emotions registering on his face: sadness at remembering the past? Barrett could only guess what someone in their last years thought about. He often wondered what lingering regrets he'd carry. Maybe decades from now, he would be the one looking somber for that very reason.

At least Grandpa still had his mental faculties. He didn't forget things that had just happened or ask questions that had already been answered, as their neighbor Mrs. Miller had done back in Salt Lake. She no longer recognized her own children.

As the street came to an end, Grandpa pointed to the left, and Barrett guided the horse and wagon that way. Grandpa kept adjusting his grip on the bouquet as if he was distracted. Barrett eyed the burlap-wrapped stems bound with pink ribbon. Grandpa still wasn't speaking. Another sign of age? Or was he remembering something from his younger days? This visit was for Grandpa to pay his respects to an old acquaintance who'd died soon after the family moved to town. Thoughts of that friend surely brought back many memories.

Did his wistful eyes mean that he was pondering words said he now wished to take back? Did the slight crease between his brows hint at words *unsaid* that should have been spoken? Did that expression speak of deeds done . . . or undone? Actions he wished he could be forgiven for?

They reached a crossroads, and Barrett slowed, waiting for his grandfather to indicate which way they should go. They came to a complete stop, and Barrett turned to ask. Grandpa's eyes looked red and watery. Barrett envisioned the young man Grandpa had once been, once at a crossroads of decision. Perhaps now he looked back and realized he'd chosen the wrong path.

You know of no such thing, Barrett argued with himself. *You're putting your own worries onto Grandpa.* That was plenty true; Barrett worried about his future, never sure of which opportunities to grasp, so he hadn't grasped any. What decisions—or lack of decisions—would he one day regret?

Everyone experiences doubt. Everyone has some amount of regret. They must.

If such feelings weren't universal, Barrett, at least, understood them. At twenty-five, he'd long-since passed the age when a proper young man found a wife and settled down. All of the boys he'd played with in the schoolyard were now husbands and fathers, but not him. Barrett wanted a family, and plenty of young women had appealed to him over the years. Still, doubt always crept in, and he always found a reason to walk away from every girl he'd ever considered courting seriously.

As Barrett thought of such times, Grandpa gave directions to the cemetery by pointing, not saying a word. Now he indicated right, so Barrett obeyed. Too bad life didn't have such simple guidance.

He could have used such a guide with Cassandra Wentworthy. He'd courted her for several months, only to surrender to the nagging fear that he might be making the wrong choice. He couldn't bear the idea of binding himself to one person, only to discover her to be a fetter. For months, he'd worried that Cassandra mightn't be the right woman for him, or that *he* might be wrong for her. That she didn't love him. That he didn't love her. That she'd say no if he were to take a knee and ask for her hand.

So many fears and doubts and worries. *Something* had always stood in his way, and in the end, when he hadn't proposed, she cut him off and started going on rides with Owen Amundson. Soon after, they married.

Barrett hadn't said a word to stop it. When Owen took her out for their first drive, Barrett was uncertain whether she'd accept a proposal from him instead. And if he was being entirely honest, his continued silence was because if he did ask for her hand and she said yes, he'd never know if she'd married him to avoid hurting his feelings, or whether she really wanted to be with him.

The cemetery appeared in the distance, and as they

approached, Barrett slowed the wagon until it stopped at the entrance. Grandpa Heinz sniffed—the closest thing to crying that Barrett had ever seen in his grandfather.

They both gazed out over the headstones, and Barrett noted the newly dug grave on the far side. It already had a visitor: a woman standing at the foot, her head slightly bowed. The shadows cast by her hat obscured her face; at that distance, he couldn't make out her features at all, not even to guess at her age except to guess that she wasn't elderly. Peering closer, he noted strawberry blond hair trailing down her back in a thick braid. She was a younger woman, then. Older women tended to keep their hair up.

She dabbed her eyes with a handkerchief. She bent toward the mound, kissed two fingers, and pressed them onto the soil. Watching the private moment felt somehow disrespectful; he hadn't meant to intrude.

"I'll get out here," Grandpa said, looking resolute.

Barrett had to blink to return to the moment. "I can drive you closer."

"Getting out here."

After climbing down, Barrett tied the horse to the gate. He rounded the wagon to help Grandpa down, but before reaching up, Barrett looked over his shoulder at the girl. "Who is she?" he whispered, realizing only after hearing his own voice that he'd spoken the thought.

Grandpa reached for Barrett's hand and smiled knowingly while being helped down. A look of amusement made the old man's eyes sparkle; Barrett felt his cheeks warm. *A man of his age shouldn't have such keen hearing.*

"She, my dear boy, is the reason for our visit today." Once on solid ground, Grandpa tilted his head toward the visitor by the grave.

"I thought the woman buried there was the reason." He looked again at the flowers, which hung, petals downward, from Grandpa's hand. Was the bouquet intended for this young woman instead?

14

"Sue Ellen—may she rest in peace—had a part in this," Grandpa said. "Wait here. I'll be back in a jiffy." Without further explanation, Grandpa headed through the cemetery gate and walked toward the oblong mound of soil that marked the fresh grave.

Barrett stayed behind. Not knowing what else to do, he removed his hat out of respect and waited on the wagon bench. When the young woman saw Grandpa, would she leave? If so, she'd walk right past the wagon. Barrett looked down at his work clothes and wished he'd worn something nicer.

The young woman looked up and saw Grandpa Heinz walking toward her, holding out the flowers. Barrett squinted to see her reaction, but shadows made it impossible to tell much beyond the fact that her posture and bearing didn't seem startled or wary. If he'd come upon such a view on his own, he would have assumed the two already knew each other. But Grandpa was as new to Midway as Barrett was.

The woman took the flowers and held them to her face, as if smelling them. Barrett concluded that the bouquet had always been intended for her, and not the newly departed, but then she bent and placed the bundle onto the grave, laying them beside a handful of wildflowers she'd probably brought herself.

After a moment of quiet reflection, Grandpa Heinz would return to the wagon, and they'd head home. Or so Barrett assumed. But for some time, Grandpa and the young woman talked, sometimes gesturing toward the grave. He noted a moment of laughter and had the oddest desire to know what it was about.

The sun beat down; Barrett was heating up and wishing for a glassful of his mother's lemonade. He wiped his brow with his sleeve. The young woman turned from Grandpa and peered toward the cemetery entrance.

At me?

He froze in place, one hand resting on top of his hat in

his lap, the other gripping the reins as if the horse were ready to bolt, rather than being an ancient nag that could barely manage a trot.

Can she see me? Probably not. What is Grandpa saying? They're both looking at me.

Grandpa Heinz pointed directly at the wagon, erasing all doubt about Barrett's being at least a part of their conversation. He did his utmost to act casual, as if his ears hadn't heated up so much that they could probably burn holes through his hat if he were to put it back on.

At long last, Grandpa gave a small bow and returned— oh, so slowly, it seemed—to the wagon, leaving the young woman still standing at the fresh grave. His walk back afforded plenty of time for Barrett's thoughts to invent increasingly crazy reasons his grandfather would be talking to a strange young woman at a new gravesite—and more, why they would discuss *him.*

Maybe it was the old nag they were talking about. Maybe the woman wanted to buy it. Barrett wished he could believe the ludicrous idea. He couldn't give away a horse so old that it might drop dead on the road at any moment.

When Grandpa reached the wagon, he said nothing, just wore an oddly mischievous smile. Barrett's middle felt as if a swarm of bees were stinging his insides, and they could be calmed only by knowing what mischief Grandpa was planning. Yet he couldn't be frustrated with the old man, not when his entire demeanor had changed from melancholy to mischief over the course of a simple visit to a grave.

Barrett helped his grandfather into the wagon then climbed on himself and got the old nag moving. With the cemetery a block behind them, Grandpa's smile widened into a grin—an odd reaction after visiting the grave of a newly departed friend.

"What's so funny?" Barrett asked.

"Nothing at all," Grandpa Heinz said. "Nothing at all is *funny.*"

"Then why are you smiling like a cat that caught a mouse?"

Grandpa clapped a hand onto Barrett's shoulder. "Because you will be attending the dance at the social hall tonight."

"No, I'm—wait, what?" He nearly ran the wagon off the road, then reined in the horse harder than intended. The wagon lurched to a stop.

"And," Grandpa continued, ignoring Barrett's contradiction, "you'll be escorting Miss Katherine Diddle."

"Do you—I mean how—why—" The myriad questions refused to take sensible form, leaving Barrett stuttering senseless. He turned in his seat to look at the young woman, wondering if she still stood at the foot of the grave, but he'd driven too far to see her anymore. "Was that Miss Diddle?"

"Let's get home." Grandpa Heinz nodded toward the road.

Barrett reluctantly clucked at the horse, and they continued their journey, but he felt as if he were in a fog. "That is Miss Diddle, isn't it? How do you know her? Why am I escorting her to a dance? I haven't been to one in ages."

"All the more reason to attend one in your new hometown." Grandpa stared forward as if the wagon were still moving.

Barrett sat in stunned silence. "I'm not good at making conversation with strangers."

"All the more reason to get out there and meet people." Grandpa laughed and gave Barrett's leg a few hearty pats. "Practice."

Barrett tried to form a response, but his mind and mouth refused to cooperate. How did one contradict one's grandfather? He took a big breath, let it out, and managed, "Just tell me who she is and why you've committed me to a social event without my consent."

"All in good time, my boy." Grandpa gestured toward the

horse and added, "Let's get home before she falls over dead in the heat."

Barrett flicked the reins. "Remind me to never drive you anywhere ever again."

"We'll see about that." Grandpa chuckled again.

And this time, Barrett couldn't help but crack a smile of his own.

Chapter Three

WITH THE WILSON family's laundry hung out to dry, Katy went to the kitchen to finish preparations for canning Mrs. Wilson's famed tomato soup. She peeled and chopped onions while the Wilson girls got ready for the dance upstairs.

All kinds of muffled sounds made their way to the kitchen: excited tones, giggles, hopes for who would ask whom to dance, speculation over whose dance card would be filled first. And this was after lengthy debates over which gowns to wear. Not that the girls had wardrobes full of dresses to choose from. But they did have several "best" dresses. The Wilsons were well enough off, though not extremely wealthy, or so Katy always heard. To her, they were as rich as kings.

Her eyes brimmed with tears she tried to blink away. Mrs. Wilson entered the kitchen, noted her emotion, and went to Katy's side. "Let me finish with those onions. This year's crop must be extra strong."

Katy surrendered the knife and stepped aside, glad to hand over the chore, and not wanting to mention the real reason for her crying.

As Mrs. Wilson took over the chopping, she tipped her head toward the stairs. "Katy, why don't you go get ready for the dance?"

"Now?" she asked, butterflies jumping to life in her stomach.

She had no desire to continue chopping smelly onions, but she wasn't so sure about primping for the dance with the Wilson girls. Her nicest dress was broadcloth, not silk, in what she had once considered to be a pretty pale blue. Over the years, she'd come to wish for more—a shimmering satin dress in gold, green, or pink, like so many other girls had. Maybe one of silk. She'd attended a number of events at the social hall, but she'd always come a little late, having finished chores for Mrs. Wilson before getting ready. She didn't mind arriving after most of the other guests; on the contrary, she enjoyed time in the house, alone, with the quiet of only her own breathing and footsteps instead of the entire brood of Wilson children and the chatter of family.

Family that wasn't hers. Family she might never have. Sue Ellen was right; in spite of being surrounded by the Wilsons, and though they tried to be kind, Katy felt very much alone.

"I can get dressed after Rosalie and Scarlett are done," Katy said, walking to the sink of pots and pans. "I'll help down here a bit longer."

"You'll do no such thing." Mrs. Wilson walked over to Katy and stood between her and the sink, folded her arms, and gestured at the clock on the wall. "Mr. Balmer's grandson is calling for you at seven. You scarcely have an hour. We can finish the rest of this in the morning."

"But—"

"You've worked so hard today. And every day since Sue Ellen's passing. You deserve a night out. Enjoy yourself."

"Very well. Th—thank you." Katy stepped away from the sink, and the butterflies went crazy, as if trying to escape her middle. The only way to calm them seemed to be to avoid thinking about the dance—a nearly impossible feat while dressing for it and putting her hair up with combs.

At Katy's delay, Mrs. Wilson stopped chopping and a put a hand to her hip. She pointedly watched Katy's retreat until she began climbing the stairs, and only then did the sound of the knife on the cutting board carry to Katy's ears. With each step, she wondered if it would be better for her to lie down for a spell. If she happened to fall asleep and never got dressed, perhaps she'd be able to avoid going to the dance after all—in which case, her heart rate would stay at a reasonable level, and she wouldn't worry about passing out at any moment. As it was, she had to stop on the landing, gripping the banister, and catch her breath. She didn't mind dances; she typically enjoyed them. But she had a specific caller coming for her—someone she didn't know. And *that* changed everything.

She faced taking a mile-long walk to the social hall with the young man. Having to dance with him. Needing to talk with him during the ball. Then walking back—and talking some more!—all while feeling awkward. Maybe she could plead feeling lightheaded and ill, and have Mrs. Wilson relay Katy's regrets to the Balmer grandson.

But no. I promised Sue Ellen. The reminder gave her the push she needed to take the last stairs, though an argument went on in her mind over precisely what she'd promised.

I already spoke with Mr. Balmer at the cemetery. That was what I promised. It was at the foot of your grave, which certainly counts as private. I never promised to be escorted to a dance by anyone.

Katy walked through the girls' room, where they chattered and buzzed. She continued past them, to the short entrance that led to the attic storage area. She unhooked the latch, swung the door open, and stepped inside. The evening sun filtered through a small window, showing dust swirling in the air above the mattress, where she slept in the warmer months. The attic room gave her a little privacy, and she didn't intrude on the Wilson girls' space here. At eye level, Mr. Wilson had hung a bar on a chain, and it was on this bar that Katy kept her own clothing.

She sat on her mattress, fully intending to lie down to catch her breath, but her blue dress seemed to stand out from the line and mock her. In spite of her nerves, she went to the bar and lifted the dress off it. White lace at the neckline, embroidered hem. The dress wasn't ugly or worn out, but it wasn't all that pretty, either. It didn't have the bustles that were all the rage in the mail-order catalogs, or the layers of overskirts with gathers and ruffles. Someday she'd own something nicer.

You spoke to Mr. Balmer, but you didn't seek him out. The thought hit her hard, and it felt as if Sue Ellen were speaking directly to her.

Katy argued against the thought. *But it* was *in private.*

You also promised to listen to Heinz.

Katy's fingers gripped the dress around its hanger; she felt as if Sue Ellen were intruding on her private life.

"I *did* listen to him," she whispered as if Sue Ellen could actually hear her. "Why else would I be attending a dance with his grandson?"

Some of Sue Ellen's final words returned to Katy's mind. *God willing, you won't be alone for long,* and, *I want you to have a family, a husband, and children.* Katy wanted the same things, but she didn't dare hope for them.

And then it hit her. Sue Ellen and Mr. Balmer had discussed his grandson and this very dance. How had Katy not seen the truth before? Her friend had deliberately planned this evening before she passed away.

"I'll go because I promised to," she whispered, hoping Sue Ellen, wherever she was, could hear. "Just remember the telegram that arrived today. I won't be here much longer." Whispering to an empty room wasn't the same as curling up at the bottom of Sue Ellen's bed and talking into the wee small hours of the morning. Katy had a deep desire to do so one last time—but of course, never would.

Her eyes grew misty as she walked to the old, warped mirror leaning against one wall. She held the dress before her, and not for the first time, she thought that the blue brought out the color of her eyes. Through unshed tears, she found herself chuckling at the idea of Sue Ellen using her last minutes on earth to plan this night.

"You do beat all, Sue Ellen Pettit."

Chapter Four

BARRETT LEFT THE family's new home at half past six—plenty of time to walk to the Wilson house, and then some. He'd wanted to delay his departure, but Grandpa wouldn't hear of it.

A young man is always prompt, he'd said, gently urging Barrett out the door, but only after approving of his freshly pressed suit, clean collar, and new tie, which Grandpa himself had purchased at Bonner's for tonight.

But "prompt" and "arriving much too early" were two entirely different things, so as Barrett reached the corner before the Wilsons', he slowed his step until he stopped entirely. He pulled out his pocket watch to check the time—ten minutes to seven, even though he'd walked extra slowly to avoid getting dust on his suit. As he slipped the watch back into his vest pocket, he felt a piece of paper inside, and pulled it out. It was a torn section of newsprint, with words penciled into the empty margin.

Knock on her door at two minutes after seven. You'll be on time, but not too early for her if she's not quite ready on the hour. —Mother

She must have slipped the note in after pressing his suit. Smiling at the advice, he folded the note and replaced it, glad that his instincts had been correct. But being right meant waiting twelve minutes instead of ten. And at the moment, every minute felt eternal.

He spent the next twelve minutes pacing along the side of the block, out of sight from the Wilson house. His mind spun in a hundred different directions, none of which calmed him at all. Grandpa had acted so sure, so intent, on this evening, as if Barrett's entire future depended upon it. Too bad Grandpa seemed to have forgotten how many times Barrett had avoided making any decision that would change the course of his life. Such choices were downright terrifying. Stringing along Cassandra was only one of several badges of shame Barrett still felt weighing him down. Having his grandfather's hopes raised for the success of this evening regarding a future between Barrett and Katherine Diddle only made that weight heavier.

At long last, his watch read two after the hour. Barrett strode around the corner, along the front walkway, and onto the Wilson family porch. He paused, pulling out his handkerchief—something his mother had trained him to bring along on nights like this—and dabbed nervous sweat from his brow. Only after tucking the cloth back into his pocket did he straighten his posture, put on a smile, and knock.

A moment later, the door opened, and a middle-aged woman appeared. "Good evening. I'm Sarah Wilson. I assume you are Barrett Eversoll?" She held out a hand, which Barrett took as he bowed slightly.

"I am indeed," he said, releasing her hand.

"Come in, and I'll fetch Katy for you."

"Thank you." Barrett took off his hat, wiped his feet on the mat, and stepped inside the parlor. As he waited, he couldn't help but wonder at Mrs. Wilson's phrasing. Did Katherine prefer the nickname of Katy, or had the family imposed it upon her? He could almost hear his mother posing the question. He decided to ask; Mother would be pleased if he showed that kind of courtesy to a young lady.

Soon three young women appeared, two with elegant hairstyles and fancy dresses—although he didn't know enough about either to be able to describe them—and a third young woman behind them, wearing a far simpler dress. She, too, wore her hair up, but hers wasn't adorned with baubles or shiny ribbon, as the others were. She blushed and lowered her face, revealing a sprig of baby's breath tucked into the side of her loose bun.

I'll never see baby's breath the same again, he thought, amazed at how the simple flower made her look fresh and beautiful—and real—in a manner the other two girls did not possess.

Mrs. Wilson entered the room after the girls. "This is my eldest daughter, Rosalie," she said, rounding the group and pointing to the pretty blond in the shiny green dress. "And this is her younger sister, Scarlett." Her dress was gold, with accents befitting her name.

"Pleased to meet you," Barrett said bowing to each. He felt his face flush with relief that neither of these painted, faux beauties was his partner for the evening.

"Oh, and this is Katy," Mrs. Wilson said, backing up a step as if the young woman he'd come for was an afterthought. The slight bothered Barrett, but Katy didn't seem to notice it.

At first, her gaze seemed latched onto the wood floor, but she finally lifted her face to his and managed a slight smile. "A pleasure to meet you, Mr. Eversoll."

Barrett wanted to correct her, to ask her to use his given name, but his mother's face appeared in his mind, and he stopped himself. He'd mention using his Christian name later, though not in front of the Wilsons. "It's my pleasure, I assure you, Miss Diddle," he said, holding out his arm.

She stepped forward, and, after what appeared to be a moment of shyness, she slipped her hand into the crook of his elbow.

"Shall we?" he asked, and glanced at the door.

Katy nodded but said nothing as she followed him out. Mrs. Wilson waved goodbye, wished them an enjoyable evening, and closed the door behind them. As they reached the street, Barrett made the mistake of looking over his shoulder. Mrs. Wilson and her two daughters peered out the parlor window, clearly giggling. After being caught, they dropped the window sheers and fled. He blushed hotter, glad that in a moment, he and Katy would soon turn the corner and be out of sight.

"Do you prefer to be called Katherine or Katy?" he asked, only then remembering how some well-bred ladies took offense at being referred to by their given names. He rushed on before she could answer. "Unless, of course, you prefer Miss Diddle. I didn't mean to presume to take liberties while we're only acquaintances."

Katy glanced over at him with an expression he couldn't quite read—quizzical, perhaps? Amused? Probably, but not in a mocking way. She shook her head and smiled, looking down the road as she answered. "No one has ever asked me that," she said with a shrug. "At least, not that I can remember."

"No one?" Barrett's step slowed, and it was his turn to look at her incredulously.

She slowed too. They paused in their walk, as if under mutual agreement, just long enough for her reply. "Before my parents died, they called me Katherine. My younger brother used to call me Kathy."

"Used to?" he repeated.

"He passed away about six years ago. Whooping cough." She reached over and rested her other hand on the one tucked into his elbow. The gesture felt friendly, intimate, as if she were holding his arm. He hoped she'd keep her hands right where they were for some time. He contemplated what he could do to encourage that very thing.

"I'm so sorry about your brother—and your parents." To be an orphan, alone in the world at such a young age . . . he couldn't imagine the challenges she'd faced. Yet his effort at compassion sounded hollow, no matter how sincere his intentions.

"It's all right. I was fortunate enough that my uncle's family took me in. I've lived and worked with the Wilsons for several years now."

"And they call you Katy," Barrett filled in. "Were they the first, or had that become a schoolhouse nickname?"

"They were the first," she said. "I didn't like it initially, but I was too young to protest, and I didn't want to seem ungrateful. They offered me their home, fed me, and clothed me. Who was I to complain about how they shortened my name?" She walked along in silence. Barrett felt an unreasonable frustration toward the Wilsons for not even asking her preference on her name, yet she seemed at peace with her station in life.

"Besides, something good came of it," Katy said suddenly.

"And what was that?" Barrett felt as if he were unearthing pieces of treasure, and he wanted—needed—to find more of it.

"The Wilsons also took care of Sue Ellen Pettit—your grandfather's friend."

"Of course," Barrett said with an exaggerated nod. "The two of them schemed this evening into being."

Katy smiled as she looked at her feet, showing a dimple in her cheek, which he had an almost irresistible urge to kiss. *Almost* being the operative word, fortunately.

"Sue Ellen was quite a character," Katy went on. "She gave me a new nickname, and thanks to her, I started to like *Katy*. She was a remarkable woman."

And another person lost to Katy. His throat tightened at the thought of his family dying, of his being taken in by a distant relative. In the brief moment he'd interacted with the Wilsons, he'd sensed that they were kind enough toward Katy, but she clearly wasn't one of the family. What would it feel like to fall asleep every night, never feeling as if you belonged under that roof?

"Sue Ellen used to encourage me to do things I thought were scary or hard—reciting poetry at the school's year-end production, singing a solo at church, quizzing me on multiplication tables before tests at school, teaching me how to play a difficult piece on the Wilsons' piano, even being patient with me when I could not seem to get the hang of knitting and wanted to hurl my needles out of the window." She laughed at the memory, a musical sound so contagious that Barrett laughed too. "But she never let me quit or give up. She insisted that success was only a matter of time, so I might as well think of myself as the girl who'd already done whatever hard thing I was facing. And *that* is how she came to call me Katydid."

"As in the insect?" Barrett asked, raising his brows. He hadn't expected that type of nickname.

"Exactly. She used to say, 'Remember that a katydid always looks like it's praying. And that's the key. Prayer is what makes hard things possible.'"

"Wait, isn't a—" Barrett began, but she cut him off.

"I know what you're about to say, and you're right. Sue Ellen confused the praying mantis with the katydid." She shrugged and lifted her head a little higher, as if the memory was such a happy one that the inaccuracy meant nothing. "Honestly, I like katydids—they look like leaves, so they blend in with bushes and trees. They don't draw attention to themselves. I'm . . . well, I'm a bit that way myself. So the name fit."

He looked over at her serene countenance. Miss Sue Ellen had intended to give her young friend a name that referred to her spirituality and faith. And that act alone meant far more than the fact that she'd gotten the insect wrong. Something about that made him respect Katy all the more. He read between the lines to what she hadn't said: she'd seen hard times in her young life, but she'd overcome them through faith, through prayer. She clearly cared about those around her, and their motives mattered to her.

"Katydid," he said, trying the name. But then he remembered how it had been used only between the two friends. He quickly glanced at Katy for any signs of displeasure. Her face registered no annoyance, only a sudden neutrality—but even that seemed to be a subtle sign that she didn't like hearing the name from a virtual stranger.

As the social hall came into view, along with the line of couples in finery lined up outside, he brought the conversation back to his original query. "What would you prefer me to call you?" He had his suspicions, but he wanted to hear it from her.

She lifted her hand and waved it in the air; he immediately felt the loss of the delicate weight on his arm; at least her other hand still rested in the crook of his elbow. "You may call me whatever you wish."

"Not good enough," he said, keeping his tone light. "What do *you* want?"

Katy licked her lips in thought, and her grip on his arm tightened slightly as she opened her mouth. "What do I want you to call me?" She shook her head, lifted her eyes to his then quickly lowered them again, before managing, "I—I honestly don't know."

An awkward silence passed between them, and as they reached the line of attendees waiting to get inside, Barrett decided to avoid the subject of names altogether. Instead, he asked about her hobbies. Soon she was laughing over some scandalous story the older women in town had gasped over during the last quilting bee, all of which centered on a supposedly inappropriate book.

"I expected Mrs. Adams to faint cold right there on top of the quilting frames," Katy said, laughing. "And I didn't have the heart to tell her that the story was written by William Shakespeare."

"No," Barrett said.

"Oh, yes. Granted, it actually *was* inappropriate—the Bard could be quite bawdy at times—but Mrs. Adams almost reveres him as a saint."

"Then you did the right thing by not revealing the author of the heinous work," Barrett said, trying to keep a straight face but utterly failing.

They continued to talk easily as the line moved, and through it all, he couldn't help but sense that there was more to Katy's life than she spoke of. Something about it, oddly enough, reminded him of Mrs. Miller, before her dementia. She'd served everyone around her, never expressing a wish, need, or opinion of her own.

He had no memory of the woman ever appearing happy. Worse, her family all behaved like spoiled children, demanding her prompt action any time they desired anything.

Barrett hoped that Katy hadn't lived a portion of such a life, but he suspected otherwise. The thought made him uncomfortable, and his protective instincts rose inside him. He wanted to take Katy away from that life and give her so much more—she deserved that. He wanted to keep her away from anyone who wanted to use her goodness as a parasite would. He wanted to see that wide smile and hear her unfettered laugh.

A tendril of understanding—and with it, a twin tendril of sadness—had reached into his chest and touched his heart. He'd known this young woman for only a few minutes, yet he'd already learned more than he'd ever suspected possible. Katy was intelligent and hardworking—and pretty, though he doubted she knew the latter, or that many people in town noticed her finer qualities. Her features weren't the flashy kind, and she didn't carry herself in a way that asked for stares and admiration, unlike the Wilson girls, with their satin dresses and rouged cheeks. Much of Katy's beauty rested in how she seemed to care about others and hope for good things.

Except those around her take advantage of her goodness. She won't even tell me what she wishes me to call her.

Yet he knew she had a strong opinion on the matter. As an orphan relying on the charity of others, she'd probably learned not to ask for what she wanted. But to instead be grateful for having the necessities of life. So she kept her opinions to herself.

She has probably never asked for a slice of her own birthday cake, he mused, but then a sobering thought hit him. *What if she's never had a birthday cake? She deserves a birthday cake. A big one, with fresh whipped cream and strawberries and . . .*

"Barrett?"

Katy's voice pulled him out of his thoughts, and he realized he'd missed her last anecdote. "Oh, I'm so sorry," he said with a shake of his head. "I got distracted for a moment. Won't happen again."

She eyed him with concern. "You seem . . . preoccupied. Is something the matter?"

Nothing aside from the anger he felt toward those who thoughtlessly mistreated her and took advantage of her. He wanted to make this night different for her, bring a little light into her life tonight. And that laugh was a start.

"I have a question for you," he said.

"And what's that?" she spoke easily, comfortably—so different from how she'd looked and sounded in the Wilson front room.

"What is your favorite kind of cake?"

Chapter Five

"I ENJOY ALL kinds of cakes," Katy said.

But the look on Barrett's face said he wasn't pleased with her answer. Her fingers tightened nervously around his arm, something she didn't realize until he reached up with his other hand and placed it over hers. The weight and warmth of his touch had a dual, paradoxical effect, simultaneously calming her nerves and jolting her heart rate into beating faster than the pounding of a horse's galloping hooves. He glanced her way and smiled slightly; she found herself smiling in return, and felt a blush come to her cheeks as she shyly looked away.

A more experienced girl wouldn't be so foolish as to blush when a strange man does nothing more than look at her.

If he looked over again, her cheeks would surely turn crimson. Yet she quietly hoped he'd do just that, even if it would mean blushing as dark as a poinsettia. The setting sun cast long shadows ahead of them. She finally mustered the courage to say something.

"So what am I to call *you?*" she asked. "Mr. Eversoll, perhaps?" She couldn't help but glance over, even as she tried to hide an amused smile.

"Oh, don't you dare!" Barrett chuckled, lifting his face to the sky and laughing. She bit her lower lip at seeing the very reaction she'd hoped for. His laugh had a deep, warm quality, like the cellos in the orchestra she'd heard last winter. "Mr. Eversoll will always be my father. Most people call me Barrett, but close friends call me Barry. Not that I have any close friends in Midway . . . I mean . . . we're still new here . . . I'm sure I'll have close friends . . . just . . . not yet."

Katy laughed quietly at his stammering, relieved that she wasn't the only one feeling a little nervous.

"Forget I said any of that," Barrett said, "and pretend instead that I'm dashing and have a silken tongue." He shook his head and rolled his eyes at himself, seeming to fix his gaze on the sidewalk and his boots, intent on *not* looking at her.

She didn't think his neck had been pink before, but now his skin was flushed, and the color crept above his starched collar. What had caused him to blush? Being so near a handsome young man had muddled her mind enough that she had to think through the conversation again. Oh, yes— she'd asked what she should call him.

Close friends call him Barry.

Would he prefer her to call him Barrett? As friendly as they'd been over the last few minutes, the reality remained that they'd known each other for less time than it took to milk a cow. Considering herself a "close friend" would be the height of presumption on her part.

Unless . . . Did he miss being called Barry? Maybe he mentioned it because he wanted her to use it. *But he didn't say how I should address him.*

Then again, I didn't exactly give him a satisfactory answer when asked the very same question.

She debated the ramifications of using either name. If she hoped to see him again to continue—or, rather, begin—a courtship, then using "Barry" might be best. But did she want that?

I don't know what I want. Sue Ellen, why did you arrange this?

Normally, in as small a town as Midway, seeing Barrett in some capacity would be inevitable, no matter what kind of relationship a couple might have beyond a single social event. If the evening went poorly, awkward encounters would be impossible to avoid entirely. She knew girls who'd stayed home from church socials, quilting bees, and more to avoid the inevitable gossip of the older ladies, who always latched on to fresh, intriguing rumors as a dog on a piece of meat.

I've never come close to being the subject of such a conversation, she thought. For years, she'd been both horrified at the idea and somewhat disheartened that such a thing was about as likely to happen as Mount Timpanogos suddenly vanishing one morning.

Here she finally was, being escorted to a dance by a handsome young man—perfect fodder for the next quilting bee—yet she wouldn't be around to hear any of the gossip or try to avoid the young man in question should the evening go south. She thought of the telegram tucked beneath her mattress, of the message it contained, offering her a position to begin as soon as she could arrive. She'd arranged a ride with Mr. Winn, a dairy farmer who would be taking a wagon of cheese to Salt Lake day after next.

Nothing can come of this evening, she thought. *I have no need to be anxious about what I do or say around Barrett Eversoll, because I won't be in town much longer.*

The knowledge was reassuring; she couldn't remember the last time she'd gone to a social event without worrying over her appearance. Her dresses were always several seasons out of fashion. Her hair never more than a simple twist, possibly with wildflowers tucked into one side—never feathers or a mother-of-pearl comb or a silken ribbon. No necklace or simple pearl earrings. Freshly polished but worn boots.

"I won't call you *Mr. Eversoll*. Promise."

Tonight, on one of her last in town, she had a dance partner, and therefore had no need to worry about filling her dance card with the names of partners who were only offering charity. Katy stood a bit straighter as they approached the steps leading into the social hall.

"I suppose we'll simply have to figure out what we feel most comfortable calling each other as the evening wears on," Barrett said.

"Agreed," Katy said, deciding to do everything in her power to avoid ever having to refer to Barrett Eversoll by name. If they remained in close proximity, she might never have to use a name when speaking to him.

Out of the corner of her eye, Katy glanced at Barrett. Now his cheeks were slightly pinker than before; they matched the shade of his neck. She didn't dare believe her eyes, however; the idea of a man such as Barrett Eversoll blushing over her— Katy Diddle—was nothing more than wishful thinking.

The line stretched past the next house around the corner. The hall doors must have only recently opened, as the line was slowly moving forward, snakelike.

When neither of them had said anything for several minutes, Katy couldn't stand the silence. "So . . . what is Salt Lake City like?" she asked. "I don't plan to stay in Midway forever, but at the same time, it's all I know. This is a nice town, and the valley is beautiful, but I've always wanted to see what lies past the mountain." She nodded toward Mount Timpanogos, beyond which lay several cities and the tens of thousands of people living in them. "I've never seen a train station—only the single rail line that goes up to Heber from Provo, and that hardly counts. Main Street never has more than a few carriages or wagons, even at the busiest of times." She sighed as she imagined Salt Lake City. "What it would be like to have the choice of mercantile stores, and restaurants, and, oh, someone once told me that the city has gas lamps that light up the big roads at night. Is that true? What is the city really like?"

She ran out of breath and suddenly realized that she'd blathered on, spouting off question after question, without letting Barrett get a word in. So entirely unlike her. She'd probably said more in the last ten seconds than in the previous sixty minutes combined.

Yet the topic had her excited today—she'd been thrilled to pieces ever since deciding to take her future into her own hands, to not stay in this valley, but to move to the other side of Mount Timpanogos and find a new life for herself there.

Barrett didn't answer right away, and his hesitation made her regret the sudden rush of words. "I'm sorry; I shouldn't have gone on so," Katy said. "I'm sure you miss home. I shouldn't have poked at such a fresh wound."

"No need to apologize—really. I just had to ponder on how to answer, is all. Yes, Salt Lake City has gas street lamps, although only on the busiest streets. As for what it's like . . . it's bigger. Much bigger."

"Bigger?" Katy repeated, drawing the word out in the hopes that he'd elaborate.

"How big depends on what you consider to be the city," Barrett said. "Salt Lake Valley has many settlements, and they all kind of blur together. But no matter how you slice it, there are a *lot* more people there than in Midway. You could live your whole life without meeting everyone." He took a deep breath and looked around them as if admiring the view. "But Midway is nice in a lot of ways. I do miss the theater, though. And the department stores. I didn't realize how noisy the streets were back home until we got here." He gestured toward the people around them. "This is the most people I've seen in one place since we moved here."

"And it's probably the most you'll see until the next social event," Katy said. "Please, do tell me more about Salt Lake. I want to know as much as I can because . . ." She bit the inside of her lip.

They took a few more steps, and when she didn't continue, Barrett said, "Because . . . ?"

She squeezed his elbow and decided to tell him her secret. After all, who would he blab it to? Certainly not the Wilsons. "Because I'll be living there soon."

"Really?"

Katy nodded excitedly. She eyed the couples ahead of

them in line, making sure no one was paying her words any mind. Not even the Wilsons knew what she was about to reveal. She took half a step closer to him and lowered her voice. "Last week, I secretly sent a telegram to the *Deseret News*, stating my interest in working as a housekeeper or a nanny."

After all her work she'd done for the Wilsons, she was more than qualified for both positions. She'd considered adding "cook" to her list of possible positions, but in the end, decided that her culinary skills hadn't quite advanced yet to the level of managing an entire kitchen.

"Really?" he said again, sounding impressed.

"Yes. But oh, I've been so anxious about telling Mrs. Wilson."

"Why? Would she be cross?"

Katy put a hand to her middle to quiet the butterflies at the thought of telling Mrs. Wilson. "She'd be disappointed, I think. She might need to hire a girl to do the extra work. Or maybe she'd expect her children to do more—and her daughters wouldn't take kindly to that."

She sighed. "I keep telling myself that I have no reason to feel guilty about leaving. It's not as if I have close family here. I've worked hard to pay for my room and board, but I don't want to live off of charity forever. I have a feeling that Mr. Wilson won't miss the burden of having one more mouth to feed." She'd paid for the telegram with egg money from her own chickens, so no one would know about her advertisement.

"Have you gotten any offers yet?" Barrett asked, sounding as if he really believed that she had no reason to feel any guilt. "Or is it too soon for that?" He sounded as if he had full faith in her ability to make a new life for herself. The only other person to ever speak to her that way was Sue Ellen.

They'd reached the hall's main doors, where they stepped up and walked inside. The ceiling was high, and the wood floor had a design made with various shades of inlaid wood—

one almost purple. The effect looked exquisite and expensive. She'd attended events here before, but somehow hadn't noticed just how beautiful the interior was. Everything looked prettier tonight—even Mount Timpanogos, when she pointed it out to Barry.

Barrett, she corrected herself. She inadvertently thought of him as a friend rather than a mere acquaintance. Except that Sue Ellen had trusted Mr. Balmer's judgment; Balmer hadn't been a stranger to Sue Ellen.

What was Mr. Balmer to Sue Ellen? What is Barrett to me?

He led her to the far side of the room, where a refreshment table stood, and he ladled some punch for her. "So," he said, handing her a glass. "Have you received many replies to your newspaper notice?"

"Two," she said, holding her drink in both hands because if she didn't, the excitement might make her spill. "I've visited the telegraph office every day and personally fetched the mail, just to be safe. I wanted to be the first to know."

Barrett took a thoughtful sip of his drink. "Do you think you'll take either offer?"

"Definitely. The first was as a housekeeper for a hotel in downtown Salt Lake, which would be fine, but the other offers higher pay, fewer hours, and better accommodations: I get to be the tutor for a wealthy family of six children in a city called . . . *Sugar House,* I believe."

"That's part of Salt Lake City; it's a very nice neighborhood," Barrett said. "Have you accepted the position?"

"I did just today. I must find a way to tell the Wilsons soon, because I leave day after next."

"Congratulations," Barrett said, all smiles.

Their conversation was interrupted by the conductor of the band, which was set up on a platform in the corner. "Ladies and gentlemen," the man called. "Welcome to this evening's event! We will start off with a reel. Couples, please take your places."

Barrett set his glass on the table and extended one arm toward the dance floor. "Shall we?"

"I'd be delighted." Katy placed her glass beside his, took his hand, and followed him to the floor.

Moments later, the music began. The fiddler's bow moved so fast it became a blur. As the figures began, every dance step Katy had ever learned fled her mind. Yet thanks to Barrett's gentle yet confident way of leading, her feet somehow remembered where to go and how to dance right when they needed to. The next thing she knew, she and Barrett were dancing right along with the rest of the couples, one dance after another. After four straight dances—each nearly ten minutes long, and each better and more enjoyable for her than the last—the band took a break.

She caught her breath as she applauded the musicians, and as the noise died down, Barrett leaned in. "Would you like to go outside for a spell?"

"Definitely," Katy said, wishing it were ladylike to wipe one's brow with the back of one's hand as men could. "I could use some fresh air." She'd enjoyed herself thoroughly so far, but she wasn't used to so many people, so much sound, in one place. It was all rather overwhelming.

"Come," he said, and took her hand in his warm, strong one.

The touch sent a zing through her—up her arm, down her back, then to the tips of her toes and back up to the crown of her head.

Silly, she thought, following Barrett through the milling crowd. They'd been in almost constant contact since she'd stepped out of the Wilsons' front door, whether resting her hand in the crook of his elbow, or while dancing. Yet the feel of her hand nestled inside his sent her stomach dipping and spinning deliciously.

This felt different. Intimate. Deliberate. Not simply gentlemanly behavior. If he'd meant to show nothing but good breeding, he'd have simply offered his elbow again instead of taking her hand in his.

Perhaps he liked her—really liked her.

Or perhaps I'm a fool.

But if so, what was the harm? She could still enjoy the evening. Only two more nights in Midway, and she'd be heading off for Sugar House. It wasn't as if anything could come of one night's flirtation.

As they passed through the hall doors and reached the welcome evening canyon breeze, Katherine Diddle could not contain her broad smile. Indeed, she had no desire to, especially when Barrett shot her a wide smile of his own and winked as they rounded the corner.

Chapter Six

THE COOL NIGHT air washed over Barrett, making him sigh with relief; his suit had made the hall stifling. Plenty of other couples clearly had the same idea, as the lawn in front of the hall seemed practically covered with young people, and he'd much rather have some privacy with Katy.

"How about a walk around the block?" he suggested.

"Yes, please," she said emphatically.

After reaching the sidewalk, they strolled in silence until the murmur of the guests on the lawn dimmed and was overtaken by the sound of crickets chirping in the darkness. Plenty of other couples milled about, but the quiet of the night provided a sense of privacy. Katy took a deep breath, and as she let it out, her shoulders lowered and her very essence seemed to relax.

"Dancing was very fun," she said. "You lead very well."

"Why, thank you."

"But I'm glad we're outside now." She lifted her face to the dark sky, seeming to admire the constellations spread across the celestial expanse. "It would be a pity to waste such a night, don't you think?"

"It would be a pity indeed," he said quietly.

The waning moon was still bright enough to light up her face as if a silver lamp shone down from above. He didn't look up at the stars in the sky; he was too busy admiring Katy's profile illuminated by moonlight, which made her look like a wood nymph from one of his mother's bedtime storybooks she used to read to him.

They walked and walked for at least an hour—far longer than they'd danced—circling the same block over and over, then walking down Main Street one direction and then the other. The music carried several blocks each direction; the social was clearly still under way.

Dancing with Katy *had* been very fun. She might well have been the best partner he'd ever had, Cassandra included. But he didn't mind missing the rest of the dance if it meant he could hold Katy's hand a little longer. He hadn't released it since first taking it on their way out of the hall. Better yet, Katy seemed happy to keep her hand there.

And through it all, they talked and talked. They compared preferences in music and books. She brought up politics—something he'd never known a young woman to discuss before—and turned out to know more than he did about what was happening in the Utah territory and even in the States. She expressed well-thought-out views he'd never considered, and he admired her sharp intelligence and keen wit.

Eventually, the sounds of the band stopped, and the two of them paused to look in the direction of the hall. Barrett reached for his pocket watch and checked the time—one o'clock in the morning. Dances were known to go later, but this one had clearly ended. Rosalie and Scarlett would arrive home soon, and Katy would need to do the same.

"I suppose I should walk you back," Barrett said reluctantly.

"I suppose so." Katy's voice carried the same reluctance—an encouraging sign.

They turned toward the Wilson home, though neither seemed to be in any hurry. In fact, Katy seemed to slow her step ever so slightly. As they approached the house, Rosalie and Scarlett appeared with the young men who'd accompanied them, laughing and chatting as they went. Katy's step paused, and Barrett followed suit. They stood in the shadows of a nearby tree as the girls said goodbye to their beaus and went inside. The front door shut with a thud, but Katy waited several more seconds before nodding and continuing forward.

Instead of leading him to the front door, however, Katy walked to the back of the house, perhaps to avoid any prying eyes from the front windows, which he appreciated.

At the back door, she turned to face him. "Thank you for a lovely evening." Resting her hands on his shoulders, she went on her toes, leaned forward, and pressed the briefest of pecks on his cheek. Then she froze, as if she'd shocked herself by the action, and they stood there, unmoving, cheek to cheek. His pulse sped up at her closeness, and he didn't want her to pull away. Before reason could seize control and ruin the moment, his hands settled around her waist. He waited for her reaction. She leaned in closer, sending a thrill bubbling up inside him. Once again, he didn't allow himself to think; he just acted. He shifted his face, pulling back the slightest bit so instead of their cheeks touching, their lips hovered a hair's breadth apart.

Katy shivered in his arms, and her breath seemed to catch. She glanced down—at his lips, he thought—then looked into his eyes again. Interpreting the motion as permission, he closed the remaining space between them and pressed his lips to her warm, soft ones. She seemed to melt into his arms—and kissed him back with an energy he hadn't suspected she possessed.

At last they broke apart, and their foreheads rested against each other as they caught their breath. When she pressed her eyes closed, he worried that he'd overstepped his bounds after all. But her unrestrained smile wiped away his concern.

She finally opened her eyes, smoothed his shirt with both hands then stepped backward. "Good night, Barrett," she said before opening the door and slipping inside.

He didn't have time to answer before the latch clicked shut.

Heart still pounding in his chest, Barrett slipped his

hands into his pockets and moseyed on home, taking his time. He wanted to commit every moment of this evening to memory, even if it did mean getting only a couple of hours' sleep before he had to wake up to milk the cows.

❦

The day after the dance felt like pure torture for Barrett. The cows refused to cooperate—one going as far as kicking over a full pail of milk. As the day wore on, every chore seemed to complicate itself, with frustrating problems springing up from out of nowhere like night crawlers after a storm.

Deep down, he knew why the day felt so miserable, but he didn't want to admit to the fact that he wanted to court Katy, to see if they could have a future together. He'd never met anyone he felt so comfortable with so quickly, someone so intelligent on a plurality of topics, someone he danced so well with. Not even Cassandra had made his heart pound the way Katy did.

Remembering their kiss made him break out in goose-flesh, even under the hot summer sun. But every time he thought of kissing her—how she'd leaned in, how he'd wrapped his hands around her waist, how soft and eager her lips had been—his spirits came crashing down again at the dismal reality: tomorrow, Katy was leaving for Sugar House.

Why couldn't she have taken a job there *before* his family moved here? Fate certainly had a cruel sense of humor.

The summer sun had dipped below the horizon when Barrett went inside. He took a long drink of water from a tin cup then dropped into a chair before the cold fireplace. Grandpa Balmer sat in the other chair, staring at the bricks covered in soot from winter fires as if deep in thought. At first, Barrett was glad that his grandfather appeared lost in thought; his own sour mood didn't lend well to conversation. But Barrett's mounting frustration spilled over, and he found himself breaking the silence.

46

"Grandpa, may I ask you something? I need a serious answer."

"Of course." Grandpa intertwined his fingers, rested them on his lap, and turned his attention from the cold fireplace to his grandson.

"What was last night really about?"

Grandpa tilted his head to one side. "I'm not sure what you mean."

"The dance. Katy Diddle and me. Your little scheme with Sue Ellen Pettit." Barrett leaned forward, hands clasped tightly, as if he were trying to squeeze blood from a turnip. "Why did you two plan for us to attend a dance together? That doesn't sound like a particularly fitting deathbed promise. And I assure you, the consequences have been rather unpleasant."

Rather unpleasant being the greatest understatement of his life. The day had been pure misery for him. No matter how hard he'd worked, thoughts of Katy kept coming to mind—things she'd said, her laugh, the way she followed the slightest lead on the dance floor as if she were a feather, the magical look of her face lit up by the silver moon. He'd been tortured by the fact that she wouldn't be part of his life. He might never see her again, unless she returned to visit Midway, but by then, she'd probably have a husband and several children. And he'd still be pining after her.

"Hmm." Grandpa crossed his legs and rested his chin on one hand. "I'm sorry to hear that. We thought you'd complement each other. What specifically did you not like about her?"

"Nothing whatsoever," Barrett said miserably. When Grandpa looked befuddled, Barrett raked his fingers through his hair and went on. "Katy is remarkable. She's pretty and smart, and we even danced well together. We spent much of the evening outside, simply talking. With anyone else, that could have been dull beyond words, but I'll forever count it as one of the most enjoyable nights of my life."

Grandpa's expression changed from happy to confused. "So you found her compatible, then? You like her?"

Like? Such a pedantic word for an ethereal evening. "I didn't think I would, but yes. I . . . like her . . . very much."

"Then what is the problem, exactly?" Grandpa's bushy white brows drew together.

"She's leaving for Sugar House in the morning. She found a position there."

"I see. That is quite a pickle." He leaned back in the chair, steepled his fingers, and gazed once more into the cold fireplace as if puzzling out the problem.

Barrett stood with a sigh. "I'm going to bed. Good night."

"Sit down," Grandpa said suddenly, and his terse tone brooked no argument. Barrett obediently took his seat again, but he glanced around the house. Family members were usually about, yet he and Grandpa were somehow alone.

"You and I are far more alike than you think," Grandpa began. Barrett wanted to ask how—and many other things— but held his tongue. "When I was your age, I was afraid. Of failure. Of success. Of not finding the perfect girl. Of letting the perfect girl get away. I was afraid of so many things. Not that I would have described it that way to myself back then."

Wonderful. Grandpa thinks I'm a coward.

"Once, I courted a wonderful young lady—pretty, kind, smart, talented. Everything I could possibly want in a wife. And I loved her—oh, how I loved her."

"But?" Barrett could sense the word hanging in the air.

"But we argued—I don't even remember what the row was about anymore. Only that I refused to give in. I was so convinced that she should apologize and beg my forgiveness. I was afraid that if I were to be the one to bend and ask for her forgiveness, well, that would make me look weak, and then she wouldn't respect me as a man. Word would get out, and I'd be a laughingstock." He shook his head. "So I didn't go to her, though I was in the wrong. And when she didn't come begging for my forgiveness . . ." He held out his hands helplessly. "I lost her."

"Did she marry someone else?"

Grandpa chuckled sadly as if Barrett should have figured out the rest by now. "No, son. She moved away with her parents, and never came back. *I* married someone else, and I grew to love your grandmother very, very much. I want you to know that. I have never for a moment regretted marrying her. But that doesn't erase the fact that as a young man, I was an utter fool to let fear stand in my way." His stare seemed to bore into Barrett's heart, making him squirm in his seat.

"Why are you telling me all of this?"

"Because the dance was an attempt to right that wrong of so long ago."

Now it was Barrett's turn to furrow his brow. "I don't understand."

"The woman I let get away. She was Sue Ellen Pettit."

Understanding slowly came over Barrett, as if a sunrise were illuminating his mind. "You two decided to arrange a meeting between Katy and me . . . But now she's moving away."

"Just like Sue Ellen did."

"I hardly know Katy," Barrett argued. "We haven't had any kind of row."

"Yes, but you've allowed fear to hold you back before, haven't you?"

Barrett sank back into the chair. "Cassandra," he breathed.

"Cassandra," Grandpa repeated. He reached across the gap between their chairs and rested a hand on Barrett's knee, then waited for him to look up. "Don't repeat my mistake. If you want to be with Katherine—even if you only hope to be right now—then tell her."

"But—"

"No buts." Grandpa lifted a hand to cut him off. "Tell her, or you'll always wonder what would have happened. Trust me;

you don't want to live with 'What if?' going through your head year after year." He leaned forward and pushed himself to his feet. "I should retire. My old bones are aching."

Long after his grandfather had gone to bed, Barrett stayed in his chair, staring at the empty fireplace. Grandpa was right; Barrett had let fear hold him back before, and if he didn't act quickly regarding Katy, he would wonder "what if?" for the rest of his life.

But how to act? What to say? He couldn't very well beg her to stay behind and continue to live on charity, not when she had the chance to be independent.

A tiny voice whispered that perhaps, if she stayed, she wouldn't live at the Wilsons much longer. That she wouldn't need to be entirely independent because she wouldn't be alone.

She might have me.

He fought the urge to quash the hope the idea brought, and instead began pacing the room. When that didn't ease his mind, he went outside and walked the streets of the city, drawing ever closer to the Wilson home and then walking past it, then rounding the block until there it was again.

When night had at last surrendered to dawn, Barrett's mind felt muddled with fatigue, and he wondered if Katy would think he'd gone mad.

Katy. The thought of her name, a buzz of happiness shot through him. *She's leaving today.*

Smoke rose from the kitchen chimney, and early morning noises reached him: indistinct voices, clomping boots, a slamming door. Barrett found a nearby stump and sat on it, figuring that Katy had to be leaving soon. Sure enough, a wagon pulled up and stopped. It was filled with rows of milk cans and large, round shapes wrapped in paper—aged cheeses, most likely. Dairy farmers taking their wares to sell in Salt Lake were one of the more common modes of transportation in Midway. This was the dairy farmer Katy had arranged her ride with.

The driver noticed Barrett and nodded a silent greeting, which he returned. The back door slammed, and Barrett quickly returned his attention to the house, his body humming with anticipation and nerves. He stood, waiting, until Mr. Wilson and one of his sons appeared, each holding one end of a trunk they carried. Coming from behind was Katy in a conservative traveling dress, which looked far plainer than her gown from the dance. That made no difference. She seemed all the prettier, framed by the drab material.

She marched along easily, but suddenly, the stones under her boots crunched hard as her step came up short and she gaped at Barrett. Her mouth hung open slightly. She snapped it shut, bobbed at the knee, and nodded toward him. "Good morning."

So formal—after I've kissed those lips, I can't bear to hear her sound so distant toward me.

But answering her would be almost as difficult. For a fraction of a second, he considered walking away to save his dignity, but his grandfather's words held his feet fast. He stood a little taller and pulled back his shoulders.

"May I speak with you a moment?" he asked.

Katy looked at Mr. Wilson, as if he were the one who needed to give permission, but Barrett didn't want to hear from that man, only from Katy. He kept his eyes fixed on her.

After a moment, she nodded and walked over to Barrett. By the time she reached him, twin blooms of pink colored her cheeks. A good sign, he hoped. He reached out both hands and waited, holding his breath, until she took them both with her own. "Barrett, you look as if you've seen a ghost," she said, searching his face. "Are you ill?"

He shook his head. "I had to speak with you. To say . . . to say good-bye."

Not what he'd come to say.

"No, I mean . . ." He cleared his throat and tried again. "I don't want you to move away."

"You . . . excuse me?"

"It's an incredibly selfish thing to wish for—I'm fully aware of that. But I like you—very much. More than I would have thought possible after spending a single evening together. But Sue Ellen and my grandfather—" He cut himself off. "That doesn't matter right now. What does matter is that I couldn't let you go without telling you that I've come to admire you greatly, and that if I were to be fortunate to be given the chance, I would be most grateful for the opportunity to . . . to *court* you."

There. He said what he'd come to say. A weight lifted off his shoulders at the same time another landed in his stomach as he awaited her response.

Katy looked over her shoulder at Mr. Wilson, his son, the farmer, her trunk. She looked back at Barrett. He didn't dare say more. She bit her lower lip, seemingly deep in thought. Then she turned on her heel and walked away from him. He'd imagined many possible reactions from her, but this one had never crossed his mind.

Had he hurt her? Said something that gave offense?

She marched right past the wagon, past her trunk, Mr. Wilson, and his boy, and turned up the drive. Barrett watched her go, confusion building in his chest. Should he leave?

At the edge of the house, she turned her head and jerked it, indicating something at the back of the house. Then she flashed him a smile—oh, praise the heavens!—and quickly walked away, disappearing behind the house. Did she want him to follow?

Not willing to leave the situation to chance, he ran past the Wilsons and the farmer, hurrying after her, calling, "Katy!" He rounded the house, searching for her, only to find her right where he'd left her last night—by the back door stoop. "Katy," he said again, slightly out of breath from running while anxious.

She took his hands and drew him closer, then closer still. His heart seemed to be pounding right out of his chest. She stepped onto the stoop, which gave her a better vantage point for gazing into his eyes.

"I was hoping you'd come. When I saw you standing there, I was afraid I was dreaming."

"Really?"

She nodded. "I don't want to leave. And I don't have to go. Plenty of other girls applied for the job, so I won't be leaving the family in a lurch."

Barrett almost forgot to breathe.

"But there is one important thing I need to say if you're going to court me." The glint in her eye seemed to belie her words.

"What is it?" he asked. His knees threatened to tremble.

She wrapped her arms around his neck, pecked his cheek as she had the other night, and she whispered into his ear. "Call me Katydid?"

He pulled back ever so slightly, one eyebrow raised. "Really?"

"Really... *Barry.*" She pulled him closer. "Now stop arguing and kiss me before those men come around to see what's going on back here."

She didn't have to ask twice.

Annette Lyon is a *USA Today* bestselling author, a four-time recipient of Utah's Best of State medal for fiction, a Whitney Award winner, and a five-time publication award winner from the League of Utah Writers. She's the author of more than a dozen novels, even more novellas, and several nonfiction books. When she's not writing, knitting, or eating chocolate, she can be found mothering and avoiding housework. Annette is a member of the Women's Fiction Writers Association and is represented by Heather Karpas at ICM Partners.

Find her online:
Blog: http://blog.AnnetteLyon.com
Twitter: @AnnetteLyon
Facebook: http://Facebook.com/AnnetteLyon
Instagram: https://www.instagram.com/annette.lyon/
Pinterest: http://Pinterest.com/AnnetteLyon
Newsletter: http://bit.ly/1n3I87y

A Lady of Sense

SARAH M. EDEN

Chapter One

London—1817

MARRIAGES OF CONVENIENCE are seldom convenient. Engagements by force tend to be equally miserable. Eleanor Sherwood, though only twenty years old, understood these truths quite well. She simply could not convince her parents to be similarly enlightened.

"Mr. Broadstead has £8,000 a year," her mother said over breakfast the day after informing Eleanor of her impending engagement. "He claims connections to many of the most important people in the kingdom. You are fortunate he is agreeable to this arrangement."

Eleanor had met Mr. Broadstead. "Fortunate" was not the word she would choose.

"He is so pompous," she countered. "He speaks of little other than himself and looks down on absolutely everyone. He is precisely the sort of gentleman with whom no lady of sense could ever truly be happy."

"A lady of sense would not turn her nose up at such a beneficial connection."

Her parents had married for the same type of benefits: financial improvement and securing their status in Society. Her desire for affection and tenderness in marriage truly mystified them. Perhaps one particularly glaring disparity would appeal to their more practical natures.

"Mr. Broadstead is forty years old," she reminded her mother.

Mother, however, was unimpressed. "You, Eleanor, are twenty. *He* can still be particular about his choice. *You* cannot."

Father entered the breakfast room. "Broadstead is coming this morning."

"This morning?" Mother turned wide, anxious eyes toward him. "Before calling hours?"

"He means to make his assessment of Eleanor," Father explained. "He prefers to do so without an audience."

"He means too look me over like a horse at Tattersall's?"

"Please dispense with the dramatics." Mother took a sip of tea. "A gentleman has every right to make certain his potential bride meets with his approval."

"Shouldn't a lady be granted the right to determine the same thing about her potential husband?"

Mother folded her hands on her lap and assumed the posture she always struck before delivering a long and tedious lecture. Eleanor quickly turned her attention to her father who had, on occasion, shown Eleanor some degree of sympathy.

"How well do you know Mr. Broadstead," she asked, "beyond his income and connections?"

Father's brow pulled in contemplation. "Not overly much," he admitted. "He is generally regarded as a gentleman, with few rumors of unsavory behaviors or tendencies."

"*Few* rumors?" How terribly reassuring.

Father dismissed her concern with a wave. "One often hears talk of gambling and such things connected with any number of gentlemen. Indeed, I cannot imagine there is a single gentleman of the *ton* who has not placed a wager on a game of cards or a horserace at one time or another."

"And do all of them have gambling rumors swirling about their names?"

"I did not say he was a paragon," Father insisted. "But I do believe him to be acceptable."

"Could we not make absolutely certain before moving forward?" Eleanor pled. "He need not be perfect, but we ought to at least know whether or not he would prove an embarrassment to our family honor."

Her parents couldn't always be convinced to make decisions with Eleanor's welfare in mind. But preventing a mark on the family name had at times been impetus enough to cause them to inadvertently make their daughter happy.

"Broadstead doesn't consider them officially betrothed," Father said to Mother. "Perhaps a bit of caution would not go amiss."

"Dearest"—Mother had a way of using the endearment that made it sound like an insult—"she cannot possibly hope for a better match. We would be inexcusably foolish to risk it."

Risk it. Those were two *very* promising words.

Could Eleanor give Mr. Broadstead enough pause that he would delay this connection? With a bit of time, could she manage to convince her parents—her father, at least—to not force this engagement upon her?

She would be walking a fine line. Should her parents suspect her strategy, her hopes of receiving any consideration from them would disappear. Further, should she take her efforts too far and convince Mr. Broadstead that she was utterly unfit to be a gentleman's wife, he would no doubt spread that information far and wide. At twenty years of age, having never made a splash in the social world, she could ill afford to undermine herself. She didn't want to marry Mr. Broadstead, but that didn't mean she was decided against marriage itself.

I will simply give him enough pause to delay this a few days, time enough for me to think of a way out.

When Eleanor's would-be suitor was announced late that morning, she found herself perfectly able to face him. Though her worries hadn't entirely abated, she was no longer in a panic. Her confidence swelled under the influence of her quickly-laid plans.

The expected pleasantries were exchanged between her parents and Mr. Broadstead. Eleanor pasted a somewhat vacuous smile on her face and prepared to commence with her battle strategy.

"Mr. Broadstead," Father said, "I believe you know my daughter, Eleanor."

"Miss Sherwood, what a plea—" He drew the first syllable of the word out as his silver-streaked brows arched up in surprise. "Are you feeling unwell?"

She settled a look of innocent confusion on her features. "As well as I ever feel, Mr. Broadstead."

He eyed her ever closer. "Is that so?"

She nodded pleasantly.

He turned toward Father, and lowered his voice, though she could still hear him. One of her earliest impressions of the gentleman had been his propensity for unnecessary volume. "Does the girl suffer from a liver complaint?"

Oh, the effort needed to keep a smile of triumph off her face! Yellow was supposed to be all the rage this Season, thus Mother had insisted she have a dress made in the fashionable shade. Unfortunately for Eleanor, wearing yellow rendered her countenance positively sickly. The effect was not enough to make one think she was on the verge of death, only that she was, perhaps, not of a strong constitution.

"Eleanor is quite healthy, I assure you," Mother said.

Mr. Broadstead did not appear entirely appeased. "I, myself, am considered quite hale and hearty, though I would not go so far as to say I enjoy perfect health. I do enjoy a stronger constitution than most, owing to my insistence on taking expeditiously good care of myself. One cannot ignore one's well-being and then expect compassion for suffering the ill-effects of their own indifference."

What an insufferable egotist, to excuse himself from all human compassion by judging those plagued with poor health to be deserving of their suffering. She had rightly guessed that he would take such a position. Appearing before him with even a hint of an ailment had, as she'd hoped, planted a seed of a doubt in his mind.

"One cannot overestimate the importance of a healthy disposition," Mr. Broadstead continued. "Many of my acquaintance have applauded me for my robust health regimen. Sir Thomas Howard has even commented on it recently."

"A baronet," Mother whispered, her voice filled with awe.

"In fact," Mr. Broadstead added, "Sir Thomas asked me for the particulars of my methods, so he could experience the same positive results for himself."

Eleanor had only been in Mr. Broadstead's company on a handful of previous occasions. Yet during those interactions she had sensed that his subtle, self-directed compliments were offered in the hope of receiving more in return from those around him.

Mother and Father were quick to add their voices in support of the baronet's evaluation of Mr. Broadstead's admirable constitution. They asked which other impressive members of Society shared Sir Thomas's opinion and were impressed with the names they were given. When everyone's attention shifted inevitably to Eleanor for her turn to speak on behalf of his hardiness, she undertook the second part of her strategy.

"I remember a man," she said, "in our small corner of Herefordshire—a tenant of one of the neighboring estates, I believe—who always enjoyed excellent health. I have often wondered if strong constitutions are more prevalent than we generally assume them to be."

She offered an expression of deepest pondering, as if she were truly contemplating the matter. If Mr. Broadstead thought she was sincere in her question, rather than undermining his claim, he would be far less likely to guess at her purpose.

"Prevalent?" He blinked a few times, the heaviness of his eyelids rendering the movement almost painstaking. "I assure you, Miss Sherwood, mine is not a 'prevalent' disposition. Why, practically everyone comments on their amazement at my robustness."

"People are impressed by interesting things, are they not?" Eleanor wandered a bit away and sat on a spindle-backed chair near the fireplace.

That was the third and final aspect of today's efforts. A tiny lapse now and again in her expected behavior as daughter of Mr. Broadstead's host and hostess would make him wonder if she would be a negligent hostess herself. She didn't mean to push any bounds of propriety nor act in a truly ridiculous manner. She would simply fall short a small handful of times.

Mother shot her a look of quiet reprimand before returning her attentions to their visitor. "Please do be seated, Mr. Broadstead."

He accepted the offer and, with a glance in Eleanor's direction, chose a seat near the fireplace as well.

"I have heard wonderful things about your estate in Derbyshire," Mother said. "I understand you have made a number of improvements to the house."

"I have, indeed." Mr. Broadstead straightened his wide cuffs. "Though I don't personally think I have done anything any responsible estate owner wouldn't have done, my neighbors have said they are quite in awe at all that has been accomplished on the estate. Indeed, Broadstead Manor is quite the finest house in all the area and, some have said, all of Derbyshire."

"Is not Chatsworth House in Derbyshire?" Eleanor asked innocently, knowing his home could not possibly be considered more grand than that famous estate.

Mr. Broadstead's gaze narrowed a bit on her. "I am only relaying what others have said, Miss Sherwood. You would do well not to question the opinions of those you have not met. Brash young ladies are not generally thought well of."

"I had not meant to give offense." Eleanor poured herself a cup of tea without first offering any to Mr. Broadbent.

Mother rectified the oversight after another of her quick, scolding glances.

Mr. Broadbent eyed Eleanor with more than a hint of uncertainty. That little bit of doubt was all she needed. She would spend the remainder of his visit not drawing further attention to herself. Nor adding to the slightly unfavorable impression she'd given, while at the same time not fully redeeming herself.

She slipped slowly at her tea, doing her utmost to appear as though she wasn't listening to the others. In reality, she paid very close attention to the gentleman her parents had chosen for her.

He spoke often of the many flattering things his various friends and associates said about him, his estate, and his intelligence. The only phrase he uttered more often than "people say…" was "you likely wouldn't understand." The second was generally directed at Eleanor, alongside reminders that lady's opinions, knowledge, and views were inferior to those of gentlemen. He further insisted that, given time, she would learn when it was best to remain silent and allow gentlemen to discuss important matters uninterrupted.

"It has been my experience," he told her parents some ten minutes into his visit, "that young ladies are at a disadvantage in matters relating to logic and deduction. They simply haven't the mental capacity."

Ah. So it was not her battle strategy that had made him think so poorly of her. It was that she was young and female. He would have made the same evaluation even if she had been on her best, most proper behavior. Would her efforts that evening prove fruitful at all? If he already thought so poorly of young ladies, would behaving in a way that only confirmed his presumptions change his interest in marrying her?

A welcome glimmer of hope, however, arrived at the time of his parting.

Father asked if he meant to call again soon. Mr. Broadstead answered in only the vaguest of terms. He, then, was not entirely determined to move forward immediately with the match.

Eleanor allowed herself the smallest bit of relief.

She and her parents had not been free of their visitor more than mere seconds before Mother spoke. "That was quite an interesting display, Eleanor."

"I haven't the first idea what you mean."

"Mr. Broadstead might not yet know you well enough to realize you are not as vapid as you led him to believe you are."

Father's expression was less harsh than Mother's, though no one seeing it would mistake his reaction for empathy. "You are this determined against the match?"

"I am concerned," she corrected, "that we have taken insufficient time to know if he is, in fact, a good match."

Mother was quick to respond. "He has—"

"—£8,000 a year, I know."

"Do not use that insolent tone, Eleanor."

"Can we not allow a bit of time for being certain?" She directed the question to her father. "We ought to at least explore our options."

"What options does a girl of your age have?" Mother scoffed.

"That is precisely what I would like to know."

Father's furrowed brow eased a bit. "Is that what this protestation is about? Options?"

"To an extent," Eleanor said.

He nodded firmly. "Well, then. I shall see to it you have options."

That was the last he said before leaving the room, shoulders firmly back, chin up. Eleanor knew her mother's lecturing posture well, but she was even more familiar with her father's demeanor of determination. He had a plan, and that, to be perfectly honest, worried her more than the prospect of an unwanted marriage.

Chapter Two

PETER HAVENSHAM HAD missed a few things about London in the three years he'd been away. Tedious musicales featuring the inept daughters of the *ton* were nowhere on that list. He enjoyed music when performed relatively well. He enjoyed the company of others, even when cramped into such small quarters as the Garrisons had provided. This night, though, the room was full to bursting with both ill-played selections on the pianoforte and matchmaking mamas and pushy papas, nearly all of whom had made a point of introducing him to their eager daughters.

The marriage mart. He certainly hadn't missed that.

As soon as he was able to make his escape without insulting his hostess, Peter did so, and with all possible haste. Why was it so utterly impossible for a gentleman to meet a young lady with whom he might strike up a tender association without having to endure such misery? That did not seem such a strange request to make.

He was alone in the world. His father had died three years earlier, and his brother the year after that. Peter had no other family, his mother having passed on when he was too young to truly remember her. He had only an empty estate and a house filled with silent rooms. He'd hoped, by returning to London, to renew old friendships and, if fate proved kind, to meet a lady he could love and with whom he could live a happy life. Someone to bring joy back to the corridors of his home. He'd forgotten how wretched Society insisted on making the process.

He entered his club, questioning his own intelligence. What had convinced him that London life during the Season would have changed at all in the past three years?

Peter went directly to his favorite room: the library. He'd spent many an evening here, quite often in the company of his closest friend, Robert Carlton. This late at night, however, the library was empty. He took some solace, despite missing Robert's companionship, in the quiet peacefulness that enveloped him. He dropped into a leather armchair and leaned his head back, staring at the ceiling.

One pleasant evening spent in enjoyable conversation with a young lady. Was that truly such an unattainable goal? He'd never thought so before the past few weeks.

"Havensham, isn't it?"

A gentleman, vaguely familiar, and, judging by the generous amount of grey in his hair and the lines on his face, more of an age with Peter's late father than with himself, had stepped inside. He made his way to the chair nearest Peter, whose peace and quiet, alas, had not lasted long.

"I was sorry to hear about your father." The new arrival sat. "And about your brother."

Peter had learned to respond with a simple nod when receiving expressions of regret over his recent losses. The pain was not as fresh as it had once been, but the reminders, constant as they had been since his return to Town, had brought much of the heartache back.

"Have you grown tired of Society so quickly?" the gentleman asked. "We are a mere few weeks into the Season, and here you are hiding at the club."

"I simply have too much respect for Bach to hear any more of his works destroyed by unskilled musicians."

The gentleman smiled slightly. "A musicale, was it?"

Peter nodded. "Undertaking the social whirl is a dangerous thing when one is a single gentleman of some standing."

"You would prefer a simpler approach to finding and courting a young lady?"

"Does not every gentleman?"

The new arrival turned a bit in his chair and faced Peter more directly. "I knew your father, though I realize you and I are not well acquainted. Gregory Sherwood." He held out his hand, and Peter shook it. "He was a fine gentleman, your father. I suspect you are very much like him."

"I try hard to be," Peter said, puzzled by the direction of their conversation.

"In deference to him and in recognition of how insufferable the marriage mart truly is, I would like to invite you to join my family in our box at the theater tomorrow."

The invitation was a surprise, to say the least. "Your wife won't mind?"

"She won't. Neither will my daughter."

Ah. The mystery was solved. Another ambitious father.

"I appreciate the generous offer," Peter said, "but I am not—"

"This is not an attempt at matchmaking," Mr. Sherwood said. "We are not concerned over her future. I simply thought you might enjoy an evening away from the pursuit of very determined young ladies and their families."

Peter tried to imagine such a thing. He hadn't in the three weeks he'd spent in London enjoyed a single evening free from the company of those who saw him as little more than a potential income and home for their daughters. Though it would likely be awkward, spending the evening in the company of a young lady to whom he'd not yet been introduced, her father had assured him that the family wasn't desperate for a son-in-law. Peter could for once simply enjoy a night at the theater.

The evening might prove to be a fine one after all.

Given the three weeks he'd just endured, the fates owed him a bit of good fortune.

Eleanor was convinced the fates disliked her. Far from abandoning the plan to marry her off to Mr. Broadstead and allowing time for her to find her heart's desire, Eleanor's parents had issued an ultimatum under the guise of "giving her a choice."

They had chosen one alternative to Mr. Broadstead, selected by her father. He had chosen a gentleman whom she'd never met and had only the vaguest recollection of ever hearing about. The near-stranger would, in fact, be joining the family in their theater box tonight. She was charged with coming to know him, deciding her feelings, and choosing to marry either this stranger or a gentleman she disliked more by the day. She had tonight's meeting alone in which to make her decision.

The fates must positively despise her.

She and her parents were alone for now in the family box, but the evening's performance would soon begin. With each passing moment, Eleanor grew more uneasy.

"What do you know of this Mr. Havensham?" she asked her father.

"Very little." He had been short with her ever since Mr. Broadstead's visit. "He is near in age to you. In my brief conversation with him, he said nothing unkind about any specific person and didn't say a single flattering thing about himself. As those are your primary objections to Mr. Broadstead, I assumed this new gentleman would meet with your approval."

She was absolutely certain her father knew more of this potential suitor than he was admitting. His requirements were far too specific for such a haphazard selection. He had, however, taken to mirroring Mother's campaign of mockery, belittling Eleanor using her own sincere words of concern.

Was it so ridiculous of her to long for a husband who was respectful, and who would treat her with gentleness and dignity? At times like these those wishes seemed more than outlandish; they felt pointless.

"Does Mr. Havensham know why he was invited this

evening?" Her heart lodged in her throat as she waited for the potentially humiliating answer.

"No." Father left his response at a single syllable.

That short word, however, was enough to give her hope.

She and this man could make one another's acquaintance without the pressures of a settled understanding. She would be far more likely to meet the real him rather than the façade so many put forward when they were aware that they were being assessed.

Perhaps the evening would not be an utter disaster after all.

Chapter Three

MR. AND MRS. Sherwood politely welcomed Peter when he arrived in their family box. They gave every indication of being pleased to have him there, yet an odd tension permeated the box. Had Mr. Sherwood neglected to inform his wife of the invitation he had extended? Perhaps she didn't approve of the intrusion on their privacy.

Before Peter could formulate an admittedly confused apology, Mr. Sherwood motioned him further inside.

"Havensham, may I introduce you to my daughter." Mr. Sherwood indicated a shadowed corner of the box. Someone stood there, though Peter had not before noted her.

"Eleanor," Mr. Sherwood continued, "Mr. Havensham."

Peter bowed. Miss Sherwood curtsied. She remained tucked in the dimly lit edges of the small space, neither stepping closer nor asserting herself. Nearly all of the young ladies with whom he had interacted managed to latch on to a gentleman within moments of an introduction. Either she was more subtle in her approach or disinterested. Either way, his enthusiasm for the evening grew. He might truly be able to relax.

"I thank you for the invitation." He directed his gratitude to Mr. and Mrs. Sherwood. "I have not been to the theater since returning to London."

"You are very welcome." Mrs. Sherwood's tight smile contradicted her words. Her husband's posture did as well.

Peter glanced in Miss Sherwood's direction, hoping for

some indication of the truth of the situation. She had not yet emerged from her quiet corner.

Was she bashful? That would explain her parents' hesitation. They were likely nervous, not knowing if he would be patient and understanding, not knowing if she would spend the entire night in awkward silence.

Peter had known many people in his life who were quiet and reserved, some of whom were painfully shy. His good friend Robert's younger sister had always been bashful, as had a schoolmate of theirs. He'd found those with more reserved dispositions were often the very best of company if one was willing to make the effort to know them. Miss Sherwood, he hoped, would prove to be a similarly agreeable acquaintance.

"Do you attend the theater often?" He kept his tone light and gentle so as not to give the impression that she was required to respond if she was not yet comfortable doing so.

She surprised him. "We do come fairly often. Personally, I prefer the opera, though I do enjoy the theater as well."

Hers was not an overly boisterous nor loud voice, but neither had she proven too bashful to answer his question. What, then, kept her to the shadows?

"What is your opinion on musicales?" he asked.

"That depends entirely upon the music, does it not?"

His lips turned up in genuine amusement, something that had not happened often during his recent years of loss and loneliness. "You speak as one who has attended a few too many painful musical evenings."

"As do you, Mr. Havensham."

Mrs. Sherwood inserted herself into the discussion. "Eleanor, do allow the poor gentleman to be seated. We must not keep him standing all night."

The reprimand was offered in more harsh a tone than necessary.

"Forgive me, Mr. Havensham," Miss Sherwood said. "Do be seated."

He accepted the offered chair, one directly in front of him. Mr. and Mrs. Sherwood sat to his left. The only seat yet unclaimed was to his right. Miss Sherwood took a single step closer, no doubt meaning to sit. The movement brought her, for the first time, into the light.

She did not appear to be so young as most misses making their bows to Society. That, alone, would be a welcome change from much of what he'd experienced in Town. He'd been given few opportunities to converse with ladies closer to his own age. Having passed through so much that was difficult and soul-aching these past three years, he'd returned to London to find he now had nothing in common with misses of seventeen or even eighteen with very little experience of the world. Conversations with them tended to be painfully inane.

"Have you been to London often?" he asked.

Her smile was subtle and the tiniest bit impish. "Is that your indirect way of asking how old I am?"

Not only had this unexpectedly intriguing lady managed to bring a smile to his face, she'd now made him laugh. "I was attempting to be delicate."

"Then allow me to be delicate in return. I have come to Town enough times to be considered a failure but not so many as to have been placed permanently upon the shelf with the old maids." Her dancing gaze remained on him but a moment longer before slowly shifting to the stage.

"That was your version of delicate?" He was enjoying this conversation.

"Perhaps I missed my mark." She folded her hands in her lap and assumed an extremely prim posture. With her next words, she adopted a demure tone. "Why, Mr. Havensham, we mustn't discuss such things. Please, let us speak instead of the weather or the latest fashions."

Peter nodded solemnly. "Much better, Miss Sherwood. Much."

Her smile slipped a little. "Do you ever grow weary of it,

the constant requirement to speak of a hundred little noth-ings? The purpose of the Season is to allow people to meet one another, to forge friendships. Yet, no one is ever permitted to speak of anything even bordering on important. How is anyone to ever know another person if not allowed at least some personal discourse?"

"Eleanor, please." Mrs. Sherwood once more employed a harsh tone of rebuke.

Miss Sherwood set her attention on the stage, though it was yet empty. She sat with no slump to her shoulders, and not even the first hints of defeat in her expression. A quick glance at Mrs. Sherwood told Peter that she was convinced that her daughter had conceded. He didn't believe that in the least.

He began to understand a bit of the puzzle this family presented. Mrs. Sherwood was a touch dictatorial. He sus-pected her husband was as well. And Miss Sherwood was not one to be so easily subordinated.

He had stepped into a quiet, polite feud.

"Tell me, Mr. Havensham," Miss Sherwood said, as inno-cent as anything. "What are your thoughts on the weather?"

His grin returned on the instant. Miss Sherwood would be the victor in her family's battle of wills, he had no doubt.

"I have often found *the weather* to be an unavoidable difficulty. One might be enjoying a lovely conversation, for example, and quite without warning, *the weather* casts a chill over the experience."

He saw her bite her lips closed. With obvious effort she held back a smile. Not only did she have backbone, the lady was quick-witted, having realized his veiled reference to her mother's interruptions of their discussion.

The remainder of the evening passed much as the begin-ning had, with witty and enjoyable conversation. He learned a little more of Miss Sherwood's likes and dislikes and gained small insights into her character.

What he knew of her after only a few hours' acquaintance, he liked. Indeed, he liked her enough to feel a strong inclination to know her better.

As he prepared to leave at the end of the performance, he turned to Mr. Sherwood. "Might I be permitted to take your daughter for a ride in Hyde Park tomorrow?"

"Of course," Mr. Sherwood answered.

Peter dipped his head in a show of gratitude, then once more faced Miss Sherwood. "Until tomorrow."

She offered the expected curtsy and even favored him with a smile. She was delightful. And witty. And fiery.

Too many in Society were not what they seemed. Too many put on a front as a means of gaining an advantage. How he hoped that did not once again prove the case.

Chapter Four

ELEANOR PACED THE length of the drawing room. She'd hardly slept the night before.

A brief few hours were not nearly enough to know someone's character as thoroughly as was necessary to decide upon a future together. Yet, she had been given no other choice. She knew Mr. Broadstead better than Mr. Havensham, but that knowledge had only given her information enough to realize that she could not be happy with her parents' choice. Mr. Havensham, without knowing he was being assessed as a possible matrimonial candidate and, therefore, less likely to be misrepresenting himself, had in his and Eleanor's brief few hours together claimed a bit of her affections.

She liked him, and she was convinced that he was a far better choice of husband than the arrogant and mean-spirited Mr. Broadstead. But how did one go about explaining such a thing to a gentleman whom one had only met the night before? She needed to make the explanation herself as her father was unlikely to do so in a manner that accurately portrayed Eleanor's position and opinions, and she wanted Mr. Havensham to understand both. The undertaking was best accomplished by her, no matter how overwhelming she found the prospect.

She heard his knock. Her heart skidded to a halt behind her ribs. She straightened the cuffs of her carriage dress, then fiddled with the buttons at the wrists of her gloves. What would he think of her? Would he even listen, or would he simply dismiss the situation as complete nonsense? And what if— She tried to breathe through the broken thought. What if he refused?

"Mr. Havensham," the butler announced.

Mr. Havensham was there in the very next moment, somehow even handsomer in the light of day and in the less formal clothes meant for driving. She had spent a portion of her long, sleepless night thinking back on the moment he'd first arrived in her family's box at the theater. He had struck her as very appealing, but not, she'd come to conclude, due solely to his outward appearance. He had the air of one who defaulted to kindness and gentleness, rather than the smug arrogance so common in a gentleman of means. He put a person at ease.

After a bow in acknowledgment of her curtsy, Mr. Havensham greeted her. "A pleasure to see you again, Miss Sherwood." The smile in his eyes spoke of sincerity.

Unlike Mr. Broadstead, he did indeed seem to enjoy her company. Oh, how she hoped he would not dismiss her plea out of hand. She couldn't bear to think on the misery that otherwise awaited her.

"You seem troubled." His light tone had turned heavier, his expression shifting to match. "Has something happened?"

She had hoped to delay this discussion until after their ride, but that seemed increasingly less likely and, admittedly, less wise. He deserved to know the whole of the situation, if only she could summon the courage to lay it all before him.

"Mr. Havensham, may I please speak candidly?"

His brow pulled a little, but otherwise he showed no sign of concern. "Certainly."

She pulled in a fortifying breath. "You were brought to the theater last night under false pretenses."

Some of the humor left his blue eyes. "I fear you will need to be a bit more specific."

"My parents did not tell me that you would be joining us last night, and they did not tell you that they have all-but promised my hand to a Mr. Broadstead."

His nose wrinkled up, even as his mouth twisted in displeasure.

"I see you are acquainted with him."

"I am." Those two words spoke volumes of his disapproval of the gentleman. "But what has he and your near-understanding to do with me being deceived last evening?"

His words were quick, to-the-point. An air of wariness had settled over him. She missed the easy conversation they'd shared at the theater. And yet, she'd known this would ruin it all. But she pressed onward. He was her only source of hope.

"I have expressed to my parents my distaste for Mr. Broadstead, as well as my prospect of nearly unrelieved misery as his wife. They offered me only one alternative."

He watched her closely, intently, but without indication of having solved the riddle she'd put before him. There was nothing for it, but to speak the words out loud.

"I am to choose either Mr. Broadstead or—" Her voice caught in her increasingly thick throat.

Heat stained her face. Her pulse vibrated through her entire body. Every reassurance she'd offered herself as she'd rehearsed this speech in the dark of her bedchamber fled on the instant. What she was proposing was madness, and she knew it.

"Oh, I see." The look of surprise, of almost horror, on his face told her he did, indeed, see. "Either Broadstead or me."

She nodded, unable to do anything more.

"That is why I was invited to join your family last evening." He paced away, his posture rigid and angry. "Not, as I was assured, as a gesture of kindness in memory of my late father, or as an acknowledgement of my years of loss and subsequent loneliness. I was brought to be evaluated and decided upon, quite without my knowledge."

"Please, sir. Do not be angry with me. I was not made aware of my father's invitation, nor of my parents' intention to issue this decree."

He stopped at the far windows, though she would wager

hc wasn't truly gazing at anything beyond the glass. "Did you know before I arrived last night?" he asked through a tight jaw.

"Very shortly before, yes."

He turned enough to look at her once more. To her surprise, he did not seem truly angry. He appeared more disillusioned than anything else. And who could blame him? He'd been played an awful trick.

"Was any of it sincere?" he asked. "The personable conversation? The levity?"

"It was all sincere," she insisted.

"You will forgive me if I struggle to believe that." He was upset, that was clear, but his temper didn't flare, and his manner remained calm, not resorting to insults nor unflattering evaluations of her. How very different he was from Mr. Broadstead, even now.

"My family has not been forthright with you," she acknowledged. "Your distrust is more than warranted."

Mr. Havensham resumed his pacing. "Your father accepted my request to call on you today. Why would he do that, if you were promised to another? Or very nearly promised?"

She twisted the button on her left glove, hating that she was forced to lay bare the difficulties in her family. "His intention was to force me to make a decision."

"And have you made one?" he pressed.

"I have."

She hadn't thought Mr. Havensham's expression could grow more guarded, but it suddenly had. The remainder of the speech she had rehearsed died unspoken in a moment of utter clarity. The true nature of what she was about to do became clear. She had fully intended to play upon his sympathies, to appeal to the code by which he lived as a gentleman, and to attempt to convince him to enter into a marriage he neither wanted nor had sought. She had stepped into this room with the express purpose of treating him little better than her parents had treated her.

She could not do such an unfeeling and reprehensible thing.

She would not.

"You have known enough of sorrows, Mr. Havensham. You deserve happiness, and that is not to be found in a forced union." How well she knew that. "Your kindnesses to me last evening meant more to me than you likely know, and I thank you for that. I only hope that you can look back on our brief acquaintance and not think too ill of me."

He stood, still and silent, watching her with a disbelief that pierced her heart.

She took refuge in the manners that had been infused in her since birth. "I will not keep you, but rather wish you a good afternoon and a pleasant remainder of your Season."

He did not immediately seize the escape she'd offered. Instead, he continued his study of her. "You are choosing Broadstead?"

Her lips turned in that odd semblance of a smile that often precedes the tears of heartbreak. "I am choosing to have integrity."

Mr. Havensham remained only a moment longer before slipping from the room. As soon as she was alone again, she allowed her shoulders to droop and her head to drop forward. She pressed her hands over her eyes, willing the tears to remain at bay.

She had made the right choice; she knew she had. Pushing a good man into a marriage through coercion or guilt or pity would have made her little better than her own parents. He would have been unhappy, and she as well.

At least by choosing Mr. Broadbent, only she would suffer. Somehow she would find solace in that.

Somehow.

Chapter Five

MISS SHERWOOD HAD cried. Peter had looked back for a brief moment after leaving the Sherwood's drawing room. A week had passed, but he could still clearly recall how her expression had crumbled, her hands flying to cover her tear-filled eyes. He had not, no matter the effort he employed, been able rid his mind of that sight.

He'd been impressed by her willingness to not plead with him to rescue her from her difficult circumstances. He had been taught all of his life that a gentleman did not abandon a lady in distress; that he should dedicate himself to relieving the suffering of one so defenseless. But what else could he have done in such an impossible situation? One evening's acquaintance was no basis for a marriage, not a happy one at least. Had she implored him, he would have been hard pressed to find a satisfactory resolution for them both.

She had proven herself honorable and brave and far too good for the likes of Broadstead. The gentleman was nearly old enough to be her father. Setting aside that mismatch, the man was arrogant and mean-spirited. She had shown herself to be witty and thoughtful, two qualities Broadstead would likely never appreciate. Even on such a short acquaintance as Peter's and Eleanor's, he felt certain the marriage she now faced would become one of utter misery.

How was it that her situation haunted him still, when he'd known her for so short a time?

He truly liked what he knew of her. He'd even imagined that maybe, depending on what more he learned of her and whether or not he found they got on well over the course of more meetings in a variety of circumstances, there might be reason to consider a future together. His past three years had been filled with deep mourning and overwhelming responsibilities, leaving no time for romantic entanglements. Prior to that, he'd been too young for thoughts of matrimony to enter his mind. And being a younger son, he'd always been a bit unsure of his prospects.

In one brief evening at the theater, Miss Sherwood had turned his thoughts to the possibility of no longer being entirely alone in the world—only to slam that door shut once more the very next day. Lud, he was tired of the games Society forced them all to play.

Still, stepping into the Strudwicks' ballroom and seeing the crowd gathered there made being alone seem less of a terrible predicament. The space was full to bursting. He'd not intended to make an appearance at this particular gathering, but Robert Carlton had indicated he would attend. Peter hadn't seen him since coming to Town. Robert's company would be ample reward for enduring such a crush.

At least it wasn't a musicale.

Miss Sherwood, Peter mused to himself, would have laughed over their shared distaste. He once more tried valiantly to put her out of his thoughts. Of course, doing so would have been far easier, were she not currently standing a mere twenty feet away.

The Sherwoods, it would seem, had also been invited to the Strudwicks' ball. It would be incredibly rude of Peter not to at least greet them. And yet, speaking with them would be horribly awkward. Most especially for Miss Sherwood. Perhaps if he slipped away very quietly, giving no indication that he had taken note of them...

But Mr. Sherwood met his gaze in the very next instant, bowing in acknowledgement. Peter could not avoid the meeting now, not without unwittingly dealing the family a cut. He steeled his resolve. One week earlier, Miss Sherwood had found strength enough for what had clearly been a humiliating confession; he could certainly do the same now.

He reached the family in only a few steps and offered the expected bow and greetings. He allowed his gaze to fall on Miss Sherwood for only a moment.

"I would like to apologize for my daughter turning down your offer of a drive," Mrs. Sherwood said. "She too often forgets her manners."

That was near about as odd a comment as Peter might have imagined. She had turned down his offer? And out of a lack of manners? That was not at all the truth. She had allowed him to escape his obligation, out of deference to her family's ill treatment of him. Why would her mother insinuate otherwise?

But then he understood. Miss Sherwood had chosen not to tell her parents that *they* had been the reason for the abrupt change in plans, nor that she had confessed to Peter their half-truths and motivations in asking him to come to the theater. They had placed her and Peter in a nearly impossible situation, and still Miss Sherwood had spared them the knowledge of their own culpability. Had she done so as a kindness to them, though they had forced the situation on her in the first place?

"I was not the least offended," he assured her parents. "Miss Sherwood has ever been a delight and an exemplary young lady."

"So very exemplary that not a one of her dances has been claimed tonight," Mrs. Sherwood muttered.

Peter generally liked people, but he did not particularly care for Mrs. Sherwood. Still, a gentleman did not say as much out loud, nor did he allow his disapproval to show overly much.

He turned his attention, instead, to Miss Sherwood. He had not heard whether or not all was settled between Eleanor and Broadstead. Still, asking her to dance would be acceptable in the eyes of Society, even if she was betrothed. Besides, it was the polite thing for a gentleman to do when informed that a lady was in want of a partner.

"I do hope your next dance is available," he said. "I haven't a partner and cannot think of anyone I would rather stand up with."

Miss Sherwood simply stared, her expression filled with little beyond surprise.

"I promise not to step on your toes," he ventured.

The earliest evidence of a newly forming smile pulled at the corners of her lips. He'd rather enjoyed that smile during their evening at the theater.

"Do stand up with Mr. Havensham," her father said. "Your reputation, not to mention Mr. Broadstead's opinion of you, will benefit from being seen to be at least that much of a social success."

Mr. Sherwood was showing himself to be little better than his wife in his handling of their daughter's feelings. Miss Sherwood deserved some time away from her parents.

Peter turned to her. "The next set does not begin for a few minutes. While we wait, would you care to take a turn about the room?"

She nodded her agreement but remained silent. She'd not spoken since his arrival, which felt out of character for her. He'd not been able to prevent this awkward meeting, but perhaps he should have chosen to keep it brief rather than require her to spend prolonged time in his company.

"I will certainly understand if you would rather not," he offered.

"I would consider it a pleasure to take a turn with you, sir." Miss Sherwood slipped her hand into the crook of his extended arm. "I would particularly appreciate taking a route past the open windows. The air in here has grown quite warm."

"Of course, Miss Sherwood."

He walked with her several paces before speaking. "I hope my presence tonight has not caused you too much discomfort."

She looked up at him, brows pulled. "I assumed *my* presence was uncomfortable for *you.*"

He set his hand atop hers, resting on his other arm. "Why did you tell your parents that you chose to go back on your acceptance of my invitation to drive in the park?"

She shrugged a little. "They would have been angry if they knew I had been as frank with you as I was. Letting them judge me as rude was the pleasanter option."

"But they are upbraiding you for it. And in public."

She raised an eyebrow and gave him a pointed look. "Imagine what they would be doing if I hadn't chosen the less contentious explanation."

"This is not new behavior for them, then?"

Her smile was sad, not unlike the one she'd worn at the end of their conversation in her drawing room. "I have learned to endure their displeasure and to prevent it whenever possible."

"Based on what I know of Mr. Broadstead, I believe he is of a very similar temperament." How Peter hoped all was not settled in that direction. While he was not of a mind to enter into an arranged and unlooked for marriage, he did warm to the idea of Miss Sherwood forever tied to a cad like Broadstead.

"Fortunately for me," she replied, "I have the benefit of experience on my side. I will know how best to withstand the—" For a moment, her gaze wandered, her lips pressing as she pondered. "There is no other word for it. The *misery.* I will know how best to withstand the misery of his company."

"Oh, Eleanor."

He did not know why her Christian name had flown from his lips with such ease, but he didn't regret using it. And she didn't object.

"No announcements have been made and no settlements have been signed," she informed him instead. "I have not yet given up all hope of convincing my parents to change their minds."

"Do you believe they will?"

"I *have to* believe it. What hope have I otherwise?"

They reached the windows at the far side of the ballroom. Peter slowed their progress to a near crawl. The cool breeze ruffled the loose strands of hair framing her face. She brushed them away with a gloved hand.

"Have you attended any musicales since last we met?" she queried.

"Yes, and I am certain Handel is still spinning in his grave."

She laughed lightly. "The performances were that terrible?"

"I don't care to think about it. The pain is still too fresh."

"I took a drive in Hyde Park a few days after we last spoke." The mirth in her tone matched his. "I don't care to think about that."

"With whom did you drive?" He couldn't entirely keep the laugh out of his words.

"A gentleman who enjoys discussing his detailed method of arranging his hair each morning. He also takes great delight in identifying anyone he sees whom he feels does not take enough care with his or her own appearance." Eleanor's eyes darted to Peter before settling once more on the path ahead of them. "Did you know that I could be passably handsome, if I took a bit more care with my morning toilette?"

"This bounder said that to you?"

Far from felled by the insult she had received from the yet-unidentified gentleman, Eleanor grinned up at him. "I told him that he could be passably perceptive, if he made a visit to an optician."

Peter laughed louder than was generally acceptable at a ball. He couldn't help himself. Eleanor Sherwood was a delight. What other young lady would have so neatly put an impertinent gentleman in his place?

"And how did this unnamed companion of yours receive your very valuable advice?"

"He didn't say another word until our ride concluded." Eleanor didn't quite hide her amusement. "I believe that qualified my comment as a rousing success."

"I had no idea a drive with you could be such a potentially dangerous undertaking," he said. "Suppose I had fallen afoul of your sharp wit?"

Her laughing grin turned to what he felt certain was a fond glance. "You would have more than held your own, I am certain of it. And better still, you would have been kind."

Peter stopped their forward movement and gazed more closely at her. "Was his behavior toward you even more reprehensible than you have indicated?"

Her gaze dropped a little, though her posture remained upright and resolute. "His behavior is always at least a little reprehensible."

Always? This, then, had not been a mere acquaintance. Oh, heavens. She was speaking of Broadstead. The insult and belittlement and reprehensible treatment had come from the very gentleman her parents intended she should marry.

She had said she held out hope that they could be persuaded to not pursue the match, and that she meant to do all she could to convince them. If anyone could manage such an impossible task, Miss Sherwood could. Their brief interactions had proven her to be a lady of incredible resolve.

"The breeze through the windows is pleasant," she commented. "It rather reminds me of the cool air of morning, very invigorating and relieving."

"Do you spent many mornings in the out of doors?"

She nodded. "Every morning, in fact. The park nearest our house is very quiet and peaceful, if one can manage to be there before nine o'clock. Beyond that, the nursemaids bring their charges and a number of older ladies gather there to talk and take a bit of air."

"But you arrive before them all?" The ritual fit her. No laziness or half-hearted attempts at success for Eleanor Sherwood.

"I appreciate the peace," was her answer.

Peace. Something she clearly did not enjoy at home.

The musicians struck the opening notes of the next set. Peter, who truth be told was not overly fond of dancing, found himself eager to do precisely that. He would have a few minutes more of Eleanor's company.

"Shall we join the dancers?" Peter asked.

A man's voice, and not Eleanor's, answered his inquiry. "Miss Sherwood would do better to join her parents rather than making a spectacle of herself wandering a room with a gentleman her parents have not chosen for her." Broadstead. His words had been clipped and tight.

"Would I not have made more of a spectacle by refusing to stand up with a gentleman my parents had insisted I stand up with?" Eleanor replied. "How very impolite I would be, and what a dishonorable daughter."

"They gave you permission to dance with Havensham?" Broadstead sounded entirely doubtful.

"They rather insisted on it." Eleanor gave Broadstead an overly sweet smile. "If you will pardon me, sir, I am engaged for this set."

Broadstead's jaw tightened. He took hold of Eleanor's arm and inched her in his direction. Though he lowered his voice, the harsh words spoken to Eleanor were discernible to Peter. "I endured your insolence when we were alone in the carriage, but I will not permit you to speak to me this way in public."

"This is the person I am," Eleanor replied. "If you don't like—"

"Women change when faced with the right motivation."

Broadstead yanked Eleanor's arm with enough force to pull her away from Peter. "Come back to your parents and sit quietly as you ought."

Eleanor, apparently feeling that further antagonizing the man wasn't wise, began making her way back to the other side of the ballroom. Peter hadn't been permitted a single word. He wouldn't have known what to say.

Broadstead was not so tongue-tied. "Do not think I haven't sorted what you're about, Havensham. I know your estate is not as valuable as it once was. The Sherwood girl has a sizable dowry, a quickly advancing age, and a rumored inheritance from a wealthy and childless uncle." He leaned in close, his beady eyes narrowing on Peter. "This is my plum to pick, find your own tree."

Peter held his ground. "Was that a threat?"

"Yes." Broadstead straightened each cuff, then smoothed the front of his jacket. He gave Peter one last look, his lips curled in derision. "Yes, it was."

Robert Carlton, whom Peter had attended this ball in hopes of seeing, stopped beside Peter mere moments after Broadstead disappeared into the crowd.

"Three years away, and you return to Town to spend your nights in company with Broadstead?" Robert never had been one for small talk or unnecessary niceties.

"He has taken to harassing a lady of whom I am growing increasingly fond," Peter informed him. "I am beginning to suspect he intends to make her entirely miserable."

"That, my friend, has become his specialty." Robert's tone was not one of indifference. Indeed, an undeniable dose of personal injury laid in those words.

"What do you know of him?"

Robert lowered his voice. "You care about this young lady?"

"I do."

Robert nodded. "Then there are a few things you ought to know."

93

Chapter Six

WHEN ELEANOR WAS a child she'd fully considered running away from home. Though she'd had no idea where she might have gone or what she would have done to support herself—small children seldom plot with such forethought—the prospect of escaping the unhappiness of home had been terribly tempting. Alas, adulthood had rendered her far too practical to indulge in such fantasies, despite being even more miserable now than in her earlier years.

Once her betrothal to Mr. Broadstead was formal and final she would have no escape.

Eleanor spent nearly every morning in the park adjacent to their London home. For those brief thirty minutes, she could imagine herself far away from her parents, her cares, and her horrible future husband. She could wander amongst the trees and pretend she was deep in a hidden forest where no one could find her.

She stopped this morning beneath a clump of maples, leaning her back against a thick trunk. Though the morning was a cool one, she felt warm beneath her bonnet. Warm. Closed in. Suffocating. She untied the ribbons and lifted the offending article from her head. Sticklers would object, but she was alone, her face shaded by the trees. Surely she could be permitted this small freedom. She had been permitted so little else.

Eleanor let her bonnet hang from her hands by its ribbons. Her thoughts wandered far afield as she stood in her protective copse of trees. As was too often the case of late, those thoughts settled upon Peter. She ought to think of him as Mr. Havensham, but ever since the previous evening at the Strudwicks' ball when he had broken with decorum and uttered her Christian name in his gentle and tender way, she'd been unable to think of him in formal, impersonal terms.

His company had been a salve to her bruised and battered soul. He'd returned a smile to her face. He'd once more given her reason to laugh. She'd confided in him without meaning to, not because she'd been tricked but because she'd trusted him. She, who had learned through hard experience to be wary of absolutely everyone, trusted him. She enjoyed his company. She liked him. Liked him quite a lot, in fact.

That path is strewn with pitfalls, Eleanor. Do not so much as glance down it.

She would not dwell on the loss of another chance to be in his company once her engagement was etched in stone. Neither would she think on the dance they hadn't enjoyed, nor how much different her life might soon become if someone like him rather than Mr. Broadstead had been chosen for her.

She would not regret having refused to press Peter to rescue her. Not only did she object quite strongly to the idea of needing to be rescued, she would not, no matter the direness of her circumstances, abandon her convictions. Right was right. Desperation did not change that.

"Is this a private grove, or are you receiving callers?"

Eleanor turned her head in the direction of the unexpected voice.

"Peter." She pressed her lips closed—a moment too late to have stopped herself from uttering his name. "Forgive me. *Mr. Havensham.*"

He leaned his shoulder against a tree near hers. "I believe anytime a lady holds her at-home in a clump of trees, Christian names are considered acceptable."

"The trees make the difference?"

"Trees make *all* the difference, Eleanor."

His sense of humor was precisely what she'd needed in

that moment. Her heart was so heavy of late and her mind so burdened.

"I did not see you again last evening after Broadstead sent you to speak with your parents," he said. "You disappeared. Fortunately for me, you happened to mention that you walk in this particular park each morning."

"And fortunately for me, you remembered."

His gaze grew more pointed and concerned. "How soon do you anticipate your marriage arrangements being formalized?"

She dropped her gaze to her bonnet where it hung low in front of her. "Within the week, I would imagine."

"Is there no hope of escape?"

To her great surprise, a smile formed naturally on her lips. "I have spent this very morning formulating a plan to run away from home." She caught a whisper of amusement on his features. Encouraged, she continued her rather ridiculous tangent. "I have not yet decided where to go, or how I will support myself, though I am contemplating becoming a notorious highwayman."

He readily followed her down this odd nostalgic path. "The one time my brother and I decided to leave home and seek a new life free of the tyranny of our nursemaid's many lessons and insistence that we wash behind our ears, we chose the profession of stable hands." The memory was clearly a happy one. "We trekked all the way to the stables at a neighboring estate and were promptly assigned the duty of mucking the stalls, which cured us rather quickly of our feelings of being ill-used at home. We returned in time for tea."

"I certainly hope highwaymen are not expected to muck stalls." She appreciated the moment of levity. She clung to it.

Peter pushed away from his tree and moved closer. "There is a question I have kept only just at bay for fear it would be uncomfortable for you, but I am growing increasingly more anxious to have an answer."

That was an abrupt change of topic.

She could not begin to imagine what he intended to ask. With any other gentleman—any other *person*, really—she would have felt almost unbearably nervous to hear an inquiry prefaced that way.

"What is your question?" she ventured.

He turned and rested his back against a tree, facing her. "You realize how horrible Broadstead is and how unhappy he would make you. I see panic more clearly in your face every time we are in company. You admit there is little to no chance of your parents changing their minds, yet they did at one point offer you an alternative."

That alternative had been *him*. He did not pause for even a moment in acknowledgement of that point but continued on.

"I can appreciate your reluctance to suggest such a thing on our first meeting or the next afternoon." Shadows covered enough of his face to make his expression unclear, though his tone spoke of hesitancy and confusion. "We have only encountered each other once more since then, twice if we include this morning. I realize that is not time enough to truly know each other's character or views or preferences, but knowing the misery that awaits you with Broadstead and your parents' willingness to accept me instead, why have— Why do you not—?"

She knew the question he couldn't bring himself to ask. "Why have I not asked you to take his place?"

"It sounds unforgivably arrogant, I know. I've simply found myself wondering if you think me no better than he."

He believed she refused to plead with him because she thought poorly of him?

How could he possibly conclude such a thing?

"I have not posed the request, Peter, because I realize you would likely agree to it out of a sense of honor or gentlemanly duty, and I know perfectly well where that would lead. I would live the rest of my life knowing that you didn't choose me because you wished for the match, but rather because your own sense of honor required it of you. I would always worry that you regretted your actions. It would weigh on me and tear at me. And though I haven't the slightest worry that you would mistreat me, I know that you would, in time, come to resent me for having taken away this all-important choice from you. That is an anguish I am not prepared to face. Life with Mr. Broadstead will be horrible, but it is a horror I know how to endure. Seeing my presence bring misery to you, someone I admire and care for, would eat away at me. That I could not bear."

"You would sacrifice your own happiness for mine?"

She leaned her head against the tree trunk. "Do not make me out to be a saint or a martyr. As I said, a marriage between us that rendered you dismal would certainly not secure my own happiness."

"Do you think, Eleanor, that you could delay your parents in making their final arrangements with Broadstead?"

She eyed him, intrigued. "I cannot say with certainty; my father is determined to move forward."

He stood straight once more, stepping away from the tree. "Will you take a turn about the park with me?"

She nodded and slipped her bonnet on her head once more.

"I have been thinking all night and all morning about your situation, Eleanor." They walked side by side out of the copse of trees and down the narrow path. "More to the point, I have been learning all I can about Broadstead."

She did not at all like the look on his face. "What have you discovered?"

"He attempted to court the sister of my good friend. For her sake, I will not identify her, but sufficeth to say, what my friend learned of Broadstead convinced him to put an end to all contact with his sister." Peter clasped his hands behind his back as they continued their circuit. "Broadstead is heavily in debt, having far too keen a taste for gambling, as well as very expensive taste in... everything."

"In debt?" *Oh, good heavens.* "I have wondered why he has pursued this match. I am far from a social success, and while I don't consider myself homely—"

"Homely?" Peter laughed out the word. "You are certainly not homely, Eleanor."

Warmth filled her face at the compliment. She was not a stunning beauty, but she had never thought of herself as ugly. Hearing that he felt the same was a welcome bit of reassurance.

"I have had two Seasons and was not truly a success during either," she continued. "Mr. Broadstead places so much emphasis on appearances and being the envy of all. I could not make heads nor tails of his determination to move forward with this match. Very little about me fits what he clearly finds important in a wife. Knowing that he needs money puts those pieces very neatly in place."

They turned a corner in the garden, making their way through a bower of roses.

"Broadstead's situation grows more dire each day, as he spends and loses evermore money," Peter said. "His habits would dry up even the most lucrative of wells."

Her heart turned to lead inside her. "My dowry is modest at best, and the inheritance I will receive from my uncle hardly qualifies as a fortune. It will certainly not sustain a spendthrift for long."

"Rendering him all the more unendurable, no doubt." Peter guided her around a puddle in the path.

"I don't know that my parents would change course even with this information," she said. "They are quite resolved. Our family is nowhere near the uppermost rung of Society, and they are determined to climb that ladder in any way possible. Mr. Broadstead resides a touch higher than we do."

"They value his connections," Peter surmised.

"They do. And, though I risk making myself look all the more awful by admitting as much, that is likely why my father invited you to the theater last week. Your family is better connected than ours as well."

Peter pulled her arm through his, settling his hand gently atop hers. "My dear Eleanor, I do not consider you the least bit complicit in your parents' schemes, so please rid your mind of that worry. I am here, not to condemn you, but to do all I can to see to it you are not destroyed by your family's ambitions."

She looked up at him, both touched by his concern and confused by it. "Why would you do so much to help me, a veritable stranger?"

He leaned a touch closer as they walked on. "Because I wanted very much to dance with you last evening, but the opportunity was snatched from me."

She knew he was teasing, but she was ever so grateful for it. "I would have liked to have danced with you as well."

"Be hopeful," he said. "We'll yet have our chance. In the meantime, you do your utmost to delay the finalization of your engagement, whilst I see if I can't plant a few seeds of doubt in your parents' minds."

"How do you mean to do that?"

"I am not entirely certain yet, but I have the inklings of an idea." He stepped away, allowing their arms to slide free. He offered a very proper bow, but with a twinkle in his eye. "Until we meet again, Miss Sherwood."

He straightened his hat and stepped quickly through the park gate, then disappeared down the road. Eleanor remained behind, her mind spinning.

Do your utmost to delay the finalization of your engagement.

Though Eleanor had been rather hopeless to stop the relentless march toward unwanted matrimony, her determination now rose to the occasion.

Delay.

She could, she felt certain, find a means of accomplishing that, though not indefinitely. If the fates held her in any regard whatsoever, Peter would manage to achieve what had proved impossible thus far: changing her stubborn parents' minds.

Chapter Seven

PETER AND ROBERT wove through the gathered gentlemen at their club the next night, a plan firmly in place. When Peter had first asked his friend for assistance in freeing an innocent young lady from the clutches of the deplorable Broadstead, Robert had not hesitated in the least. Indeed, he had taken up the task with determination.

Robert was the first to speak as they searched the crowd for their quarry. "You are going to great lengths to assist this Miss Sherwood. She must be a rather incredible young lady."

"No young lady, incredible or otherwise, should be doomed to the likes of Broadstead." Peter continued his perusal of the gentlemen present. "Miss Sherwood strikes me as quite remarkable. I would very much like the opportunity to discover if I am right on that score."

He spotted Mr. Sherwood not far off, seated in a corner. Broadstead occupied the chair nearest his, with a small end table between them. Peter firmly suspected they intended tonight to work out details of the marriage settlement. Nothing would be signed tonight, what with solicitors not being present, making this a prime opportunity for Peter to perform a bit of not-so-subtle intervention.

Robert met his eye. Peter gave him a quick nod.

They moved in nearly opposite directions, Peter to a nearby window and Robert directly to the table where Sherwood and Broadstead sat. Robert could claim connections to the aristocracy, though his immediate relations had no titles. His standing exceeded Peter's, and far outpaced the Sherwoods'. Broadstead's certainly could not compete.

Robert offered Mr. Sherwood the smallest inclination of his head and a few pleasantries. He made as if startled to realize Broadstead sat nearby.

"Ah." A bit of distaste colored his single syllable. "I did not see you there." He looked back at Mr. Sherwood. "I did not realize you were… friends with Broadstead, here."

"I— uh—" Mr. Sherwood's face twisted in confusion.

"A good evening to you, Mr. Sherwood." Robert repeated his earlier small bow of the head before stepping away. It wasn't a cut to Broadstead, but it came very close to being one.

Sherwood watched Robert as he walked away, still wearing an expression of uncertainty. This was precisely what Peter hoped for. If Eleanor's parents could be led to question the benefit they would receive in Society for being connected with Broadstead, the one true advantage they seemed to hope for, they would be far more likely to reconsider.

Peter stepped away from the window just as Robert passed him. He greeted his friend and received a warm acknowledgement in return. Out of the corner of his eye, he saw Mr. Sherwood take note of the exchange. Robert had shown himself far more receptive to Peter than he had to the gentleman with whom Mr. Sherwood currently shared a corner.

"The fates must be smiling on you, Peter," Robert whispered. "I spy Lord Permouth just come inside. He's a distant cousin and a friend. He's also a sport and would join us in this effort, I'm certain of it."

"An earl." Peter nodded appreciatively. "That'd be quite a pebble in my pocket, wouldn't it?"

"You wander closer to Sherwood and Broadstead," Robert said. "Permouth and I'll make a fine show of it."

Not two minutes later Robert made good on his word. He and the earl ambled over, looking as chummy as school boys.

"Well met, Havensham," Permouth said, as though he and Peter were on quite friendly terms. "It's a fine thing to have you in London again." He even slapped a hand on Peter's shoulder.

Catching Mr. Sherwood's intrigued glance, Peter jumped on a grand idea.

"Permouth, have you met Mr. Sherwood?" Peter adjusted his position enough to more easily make the introduction. "He was an acquaintance of my father's, and I spent the most enjoyable evening last week with his family in their box at the theater."

Permouth sketched a brief bow. Sherwood jumped to his feet and returned the gesture with a bow of his own, one much deeper and more filled with awe.

"A pleasure to meet you," Sherwood blurted, his eyes wide.

The earl played his part well. In a tone ringing with pleasure, he said, "Any friend of the Havensham family will always be a welcome acquaintance of mine."

Before Sherwood could recover from the growing shock of this conversation, Robert spoke again. "Permouth, I'm certain you are familiar with Broadstead."

The earl, unwaveringly friendly thus far, raised an icy brow and skewered Broadstead. "I am excruciatingly familiar with him. He owes me money."

"I will make good on my vowels," Broadstead said. "I swear to it. I'm only a bit short on the blunt just now."

"A gentleman may default on any number of debts," Permouth said slowly, pointedly, almost threateningly. "But he does not fleece a fellow gentleman."

"*Fleece?* My lord, that is not the case at all. I swear to it."

"Walk with me." Permouth's words were anything but a request. "There are a number of gentlemen here just now who I am certain would appreciate the opportunity to discuss your definition of the term 'fleece.'"

Broadstead stood on unsteady legs. He stared at Permouth, fear filling his face.

The earl, apparently unmoved, turned a more friendly gaze on Mr. Sherwood. "Does he owe you money, as well? Would you care to join the five or six of us who mean to give him an education in being a gentleman?"

Sherwood shook his head mutely.

"Well, then, no doubt you will be glad to be rid of his company, regardless of his financial connections to you." Permouth quickly dipped his head before snatching Broadstead by the collar. "Ingram. Redmond. Look at the wriggly fish I've caught."

He dragged Broadstead away toward a waiting group of gentlemen. None looked the least pleased to see him.

Debts of honor eventually caught up to any gentleman who refused to pay them.

"That was a scene," Robert said. "That is what comes, though, of being in proximity with a cheat. Broadstead is not the sort to attract good company."

"He isn't?" Mr. Sherwood eyed them both.

Would the man's brows ever return to their normal position?

"He has never been a gentleman of conviction," Robert explained. "Lately, however, his behavior has put him beyond the endurance of many in the *ton*. I fear as the years progress, and a short few years at that, he will lose much of his claim to good Society."

Peter assumed what he hoped came across as a puzzled expression, speaking directly to Eleanor's father. "There are rumors going about that your daughter is somehow connected with that bounder. Were I in your shoes, I'd put a stop to those whispers forthwith."

"Lud, yes," Robert added. "What a disaster that could be for your entire family."

They left on that declaration. The remainder of their time at the club was spent talking with acquaintances and friends, generally making themselves agreeable, and, Peter hoped, adding some strength to their words by showing how much more acceptable Peter was in the eyes of his fellow gentlemen than Broadstead could ever claim to be.

It would not, he knew, be enough to necessarily put a permanent end to the Sherwoods' plans for Eleanor, but it might be enough to slow them down.

Eleanor had never been more grateful for gossipy matrons.

She and her mother had made morning calls for hours. At every house they had heard whispers of Mr. Broadstead and his questionable standing amongst the influential of the *ton*. The Earl of Permouth and several gentlemen of his set, if rumors were to be believed, had made their displeasure with Mr. Broadstead known in a very public way. The rest of Society were beside themselves attempting to decide how drastic their own displeasure with him ought to be.

Mother did not stop in the entryway of their home long enough for a single piece of her outer clothing to be handed over to the waiting maid. She instead made her way directly up the stairs and, if Eleanor's guess proved correct, down the corridor toward Father's book room.

Do not allow your hopes to soar. The doubts she had seen in her parents these past two days were encouraging. Mr. Broadstead hadn't called even once. Father's solicitor, who was supposed to have arrived that morning, no longer seemed expected.

Though Eleanor had not heard any specifics about the events at her father's club, she suspected Peter had played a part in whatever had happened. He had been as good as his word. Better, even. He had helped undermine Mr. Broadstead's position in her parents' estimation. She would keep her part of the bargain as well, doing her utmost to delay her parents' final decision.

She could hear Mother's and Father's voices as she approached the book room.

"This is very disconcerting," Mother said.

"Perhaps it will be but a five-minutes' scandal," Father replied.

They were, indeed, questioning how to proceed. This was Eleanor's opportunity. She slipped inside the room.

"Forgive the interruption," she said. "I have a question I need to ask."

"We are having a discussion," Mother said sharply.

"The question is a brief one." Eleanor knew she must seize this moment. "When Mrs. Aimesbury said this afternoon that she meant to leave Mr. Broadbent off of her guest list for her ball in a fortnight's time, do you think that meant she intends to leave us off as well? Our names are so often connected with his these past weeks, I wasn't certain. The Aimesburys' ball is a very important event each Season. If we are excluded—"

"We won't be," Mother insisted. "I will call on Mrs. Aimesbury. We will not be excluded."

Eleanor let her uncertainty remain. "I hope not."

She slipped from the room once more, but hesitated just beyond the doorway.

"What if we are excluded from the Aimesburys' ball?" Father asked. "Others will follow suit. We will fall out of favor with Society."

"I will call on Mrs. Aimesbury. We will sort it. In the meantime, we would do well to spend a little less time with Mr. Broadstead. The whispers will soon enough be replaced by something new grasping the attention of the *ton*."

Less time with Mr. Broadstead was precisely the goal Eleanor had been aiming for. Finalizing plans for the engagement would now most certainly be delayed.

"She is twenty years old, Jane," Father said. "This Season was her last chance, and now the only gentleman who has ever shown a willingness to pursue her has disappeared from

Society. She will be firmly on the shelf, and we will never be rid of her."

It was not exactly parental tenderness, but Eleanor didn't truly mind. Their indifference was not new to her. The feeling of near freedom that came with knowing she was not to be immediately tied to Mr. Broadstead was, however, entirely unfamiliar.

She was so near to deliverance, she could taste it.

Chapter Eight

"YOU MUST BE on your very best behavior, Eleanor." Mother had made the same declaration four times in the ten minutes since they'd arrived at the theater. "We are safely on the Aimesburys' guest list for their ball. Mrs. Harley told me this morning that she will extend an invitation to her musicale in two days' time. We have very nearly weathered the storm of Mr. Broadstead's fall from grace."

Mr. Broadstead had, in fact, disappeared from Town. Rumors were rampant about his whereabouts, with most placing him on a boat for the former colonies. More likely than not, he was holed up at his country house hoping his many creditors would not seek him there. To Eleanor's great relief, her parents only spoke in the vaguest terms about the match they had intended to pursue between the man and Eleanor.

She wished she could tell Peter how well this plan had worked, and that she appreciated his efforts on her behalf. More than anything, she simply wanted to see him again. She told herself to be patient.

He had not cut her acquaintance even after her admission of her family's ill treatment of him. He'd asked her to dance, had taken a turn about a ballroom with her on his arm, and he'd sought her out in the park, offering his reassurance and his company. He had helped her tremendously and had done so out of kindness and caring. He'd even expressed some degree of affection.

She had every hope that he would seek her out again. She simply didn't know when.

"Why, Mr. Havensham," Mother said. "What a pleasure to see you again."

When, as it turned out, was *now*.

Eleanor could think of no reason to hide her delight at his arrival. His gaze was on her parents, though she felt certain he'd seen her there.

"I hope I can be forgiven for arriving unannounced," Peter said. "I had such a delightful time with your family when last I was here. I could not resist returning to bid you a good evening and to ask after your health and well-being."

"We are all quite well, thank you," Mother said.

Father did not allow himself to be excluded from the conversation. "I was very appreciative of Mr. Carlton and Lord Permouth seeing to the difficulty with Broadstead." He spoke as though he had always held a vaguely unfavorable view of the man he'd actively wished to make a part of his family. "Society has spoken of little else this past week."

"I had heard he was making life a bit unpleasant for Miss Sherwood," Peter said. "I hope that was not, or at least is no longer, the case."

Mother waved that off. "We put an end to Mr. Broadstead's ambitions very quickly, I assure you."

Peter kept his amusement well hidden, but Eleanor could see it in his eyes. "I am pleased to hear that. I will not disrupt your evening further."

"Nonsense." Father motioned him over. "We insist you stay."

"I thank you for your most welcome offer." Peter moved directly to where Eleanor stood. "Miss Sherwood. A pleasure." He bowed.

They sat in adjacent seats facing the stage below, just as they had on their very first meeting.

"I feel as if we've done this before," she teased.

"Then you will likely truly feel that way when I ask your

parents if I can take you for a drive tomorrow." He leaned a touch closer. "A few days after which, I mean to seek you out at a ball and ask if you will dance with me, then take a turn about the room with you. And talk. And laugh."

"This does sound *very* familiar indeed."

He slipped his hand around hers. "I mean to start again, Eleanor, this time without Broadstead's interference, and without your parents' expectations."

"We could simply make a new beginning?"

He nodded. "And decide for ourselves what our future will be."

Her heart leapt at the thought, at the possibilities. "I would like that very much."

Peter raised her hand to his lips and pressed a kiss to her fingers. She blushed, but didn't pull away.

In the dimness of the theater box, he inched his chair ever closer to hers, so near in fact that his warmth flowed over her. Now and then he leaned in close and asked her a question. Where did she grow up? Which food was a particular favorite? Had she travelled to any other areas of the kingdom? Precisely the kind of questions one would ask when making a new acquaintance. She asked many of her own.

Though they had met already and knew each other well enough for a deep fondness to be growing between them, they were indeed beginning again. This time without deception, without fear or threats.

This beginning held every promise of a happy ending.

About Sarah M. Eden

Sarah M. Eden is the author of multiple historical romances, including the two-time Whitney Award Winner *Longing for Home* and Whitney Award finalists *Seeking Persephone*
and *Courting Miss Lancaster*. Combining her obsession with history and affinity for tender love stories, Sarah loves crafting witty characters and heartfelt romances. She has twice served as the Master of Ceremonies for the LDStorymakers Writers Conference and acted as the Writer in Residence at the Northwest Writers Retreat. Sarah is represented by Pam Victorio at D4EO Literary Agency.

Visit Sarah on-line:
Twitter: @SarahMEden
Facebook: Author Sarah M. Eden
Website: SarahMEden.com

A Second Chance

BY HEATHER B. MOORE

Chapter One

VIRGINIA BRANSON STEPPED into the front parlor of her home, her nose wrinkling at the smell of pipe smoke. *What on earth?* Her husband never smoked inside. And even if he had, he wasn't expected back from the newspaper office for hours.

Virginia had returned a day earlier than expected from a visit across the city to help her husband's Aunt Beth. Aunt Beth was always complaining of one thing or another. But her latest symptoms had required the promise of a few days' stay by her one and only niece. And although Virginia was technically an in-law, that didn't stop Beth from expecting her attention. From their very first meeting, they'd hit things off. They even resembled each other. Like Virginia, Beth was petite, with a head full of thick black hair. Although Beth's eyes were bright green; Virginia's a pale blue.

"Geoff?" Virginia called out. The smoke scent was stale but lingering, as if the smoker had been present in the parlor within the past couple of hours. Perhaps one of Geoff's advertisers had stopped by? A shuffling along the floorboards above stopped her in her tracks. Someone was upstairs.

Virginia strode out of the parlor and crossed to the set of stairs leading to the second floor of the house. Was Geoff ill? Had he stayed home in bed? She'd started up the steps when a movement on the second-floor landing made her heart nearly stop.

A woman stood there, blinking large brown eyes as if she'd just awakened from a mid-day nap. Virginia realized that the stranger was nearly naked. She wore her underthings—a bra, camisole, and a slip—and was clutching a dark lavender gown to her chest. Her blonde hair fell in tangled waves about her bare shoulders.

Had Geoff hired a maid? They'd talked about needing one after the baby came, but Virginia had so far been healthy enough to keep up with the housework. Truth was, she was happy to do her share. She'd grown up in an orphanage after her parents were killed in a train accident. She quickly learned that being obedient and helpful was the best way to secure her headmistress's good graces. Taking on extra chores had also earned Virginia extra food.

While she had always been a thin, petite girl, her slight size followed her into adulthood. So much so, that the doctor had worried over her ability to carry a baby to full term. At six months pregnant now, Virginia was barely showing and had only recently let out her waist seams in a few of her dresses.

The woman on the staircase landing said, "Geoff?" in a warbly voice that made her sound close to tears.

This was not good, Virginia realized. If this woman were a maid, even an unruly maid, she shouldn't be calling Virginia's husband by his Christian name. Which meant…

Virginia lost the luxury of speculating when Geoff stumbled out of one of the upper rooms, his shirt off, his trousers, well, *undone.*

Virginia's shock was so great that she could only stand there, her mouth falling open, as she stared at the two *lovers.* "Oh…" And then she passed out.

Chapter Two

Six months later

VIRGINIA COULDN'T RIGHTLY claim she believed in miracles. But when she'd walked in on her husband and another woman with whom he was intimately acquainted, then had fainted dead away, the fact that no harm had come to her baby *was* a miracle. She'd dare anyone to say otherwise.

What hadn't been so heaven sent, now that her divorce had been granted, and Virginia was living in Aunt Beth's home and trying to raise a baby by herself, was how she'd become an outcast in proper Boston society. And she could see that the living situation was weighing on Beth more and more, no matter how generous the older woman continued to be. The society ladies no longer came to visit Beth, resorting every few weeks to sending inquiring notes instead.

Beth had terrible headaches, almost daily now—something that Virginia couldn't remember the lady enduring before a squalling babe had joined the household. Although little Timothy was a sweet boy, he definitely had his moments of fussiness. And Beth wasn't strong enough to watch the baby on her own; so Virginia either took Timothy with her wherever she went, or she stayed home.

It was this reality that often put Virginia in a black mood. She loved her baby, but her anger against Geoff was far from abating. And if she were being honest with herself, she was still grieving "what might have been," or more accurately, "what should have been." Her days in the orphanage had taught her to never take family for granted. But Geoff, it seemed, was determined to throw her resolve right back into her face, rejecting both her and her child.

With these dark thoughts running through her mind, Virginia answered Beth's front door one afternoon to find her old friend Milly on the porch step.

"Milly!" Virginia said, astounded to see her childhood friend.

They'd been inseparable in the orphanage. When they'd turned eighteen, they'd found work together in a sewing house, and they'd both met their beaus within a month of each other. They'd married in the same week, acting as maids of honor in the other's wedding. Soon, Milly had moved to Chicago, after which the letters they'd exchanged became less and less frequent.

More recently, Virginia had been too embarrassed to write to Milly of what had happened to her marriage, but she should have known the news would reach her friend eventually. However, that didn't explain the woman's appearance on Beth's front step.

"You're… You're here," Milly said, a wide smile on her face, surprise in her eyes.

Nothing about her had changed in the past year. Her curly red hair was pulled up and pinned, topped by a fashionable yellow hat. She wore a matching, pale yellow dress and dainty white gloves. She stepped forward and embraced Virginia for a long moment.

Pulling away, she added, "I meant to call on you and surprise you at your… home, but it seems that you no longer live there."

"No," Virginia said. "Come in, please." She steered Milly inside and sat her down in the parlor.

Beth was in her bedroom, fussing over a new hat she'd ordered the day before. And Timothy was taking his blessed afternoon nap.

"What happened when you showed up at Geoff's?" Virginia couldn't help but ask.

"I knocked and knocked. No one answered," Milly said, her blue eyes rounded. "I expected at least a maid to answer, one you said you'd be hiring to help when the baby came." She stopped. "Is the baby all right? I haven't heard a thing from you."

"Yes, it's a boy—Timothy," Virginia rushed to say. "He's healthy and strong."

Milly nodded. "I'm very happy about that." Then she took a deep swallow. "When I was leaving your doorstep, your neighbor came over and told me that you moved to Geoff's Aunt Beth's place before the baby was born. She was whispering, as if it was a horrible secret. Like maybe something terrible had happened."

Virginia's eyes burned with tears that she blinked back. "Geoff and I are divorced. I caught him with another woman."

Milly's mouth dropped open.

But Virginia was over the shock of it all, and this was her very best friend. If someone should know the truth, that someone was Milly. "He didn't want to leave her. Said she's been his mistress since before we met."

This time, Milly released a gasp.

"He said he was in love with her." Virginia's chest burned hot as she remembered Geoff's cutting words. "He didn't marry her, because she was a southerner and his father had died in the war for the North. He didn't want to upset his mother."

Shaking her head, Milly wiped at the tears spilling onto her cheeks. "My poor, poor Virginia."

"That's not all," Virginia said in a quiet voice. "He said he only married me because I was best friends with you, and you were marrying Leonard—a man Geoff wanted business connections with, so he could expand his newspaper and sell more advertising. Oh, and he thought I was pretty enough to share a bed with."

Milly's face heated red. "Why ever did you not write to me? I could have—I could have shot his kneecaps for you, or something!"

"That's just the thing," Virginia said, wishing she could smile at her friend's defense. "No one can really do anything for me. I'm ruined. A divorced woman is like a Biblical plague in any high society neighborhood. Aunt Beth is being shunned by even her dearest friends, and it's all due to her support of me."

"Oh, pish posh," Milly said. "You'll come to Chicago to live with Leonard and me. He'll finish his business here in two or three days, and then you can take the train home with us."

"Chicago?" Virginia said with a laugh—a bit of a hysterical laugh. "You think I can pack up my baby and move, just like that? On a train?"

Milly's brown eyes gleamed. "We'll have so much fun, Vi. Just think of it, raising our babies together—"

"Babies?" Virginia cut in. "Are you...?"

Milly grinned.

Virginia squealed.

Three days later, Virginia found herself on a train heading west.

Chapter Three

Chicago

"YOU'VE GOT TO come tonight," Milly implored Virginia. "Leonard's cousin will make it an odd number, and you know how fastidious Mrs. Peterson is about numbers. You'd think we were living in England."

For the eighth, or ninth, or tenth time, Virginia shook her head as she continued to work on her stitching sampler. She sat in the suite of rooms that were all hers. One-year old Timothy played nearby on the floor. Milly's home sprawled on a ranch just outside of Chicago, and Virginia had been given an entire wing for her own use. Milly had even hired a nursemaid, Mrs. Blanche Nelson, to help with the babies. Milly's daughter was six months now.

Virginia could hardly believe she'd lived in Chicago for nearly a year. But moving here had turned out to be the best decision of her life. She and Milly were more than best friends now: they were like sisters. And that's exactly why Virginia made a point of staying home when Milly and Leonard went out on the town. Virginia was determined that the couple should have space from her, and time alone together as well.

Someday, somehow, she'd repay her friend for her hospitality. She'd already found a job taking in embroidery for a dress shop, something she could work on at home while watching after Timothy. She glanced over at her son, who was playing contentedly with a wooden truck. His green eyes were like his father's. Whenever Virginia allowed herself to dwell on their similarity, she felt a new pang in her heart. Geoff had signed away all rights to custody, claiming he'd never wanted the child in the first place.

Milly placed a hand over Virginia's stitching work. "Vi, please. I know you're trying to let me and Leonard have our time together, but tonight is different. If Leonard's cousin arrives without a date, Mrs. Peterson will foist her daughter, Julie, upon him. He's in town looking for a home to buy. And if we don't claim him as one of us, someone else will. Someone like Julie Peterson."

Virginia wrinkled her nose at that. Julie Peterson talked a mile a minute and was too tall for her own good. She practically towered over every male in Chicago. She was also an heiress to her father's road construction business. And with his recent death, it was said that Julie was on the prowl for a husband to take over running things, so that she wouldn't have to sell.

Julie's mother had been hosting multiple parties every month, inviting eligible bachelors and making no secret of her efforts to find a suitable match for her daughter.

"Well, we can't have Mrs. Peterson plotting out the rest of someone's life," Virginia said, gazing into Milly's pleading features. "What's Leonard's cousin's name again?"

"Maxwell Pickering," Milly said. "And you'd need to be his official date, or Mrs. Peterson will think he's available."

"An *official* date?" Virginia said. "Whatever does that mean?"

"It's a date; a blind date, I guess. But you'd need to act as if it's *more*. That way Mrs. Peterson will think the two of you are *involved*."

"Involved?" Virginia raised both brows. She hadn't been on a date or any kind of outing with a man since her divorce. "I already have a questionable reputation as a divorced woman. Do I really need more gossip following me? I mean, this Maxwell Pickering will be returning home to wherever he's from—"

"New York," Milly supplied.

"—And then I'll be alone again, and everyone will know that we weren't really involved, and they'll think I'm a loose woman. Loose *and* divorced." Virginia once more took up her stitching. "I've changed my mind. I'll be staying home tonight."

"Too late," Milly said. "They're already on their way."

Virginia stared at her friend. "What do you mean? Who's on their way?"

"Leonard and Maxwell," Milly said, worrying her hands together. "They should be here any moment, too. You need to freshen up and change into that fine gown I loaned you for the Jensen's wedding party. They're bringing the car here to pick us up."

Milly and Leonard had a new, fancy car. Riding in it for the first time had made Virginia's stomach nearly flip over. Now, the thought of taking it on a date, a blind date, when she wasn't ready to spend an entire evening with a man, made her forget her stitching and stand.

"Tell him I've a headache," she insisted, "or I've taken ill, or *Timothy* has taken ill. Yes, tell them that."

Milly grasped Virginia's arm. "What's wrong, Vi? What's really the matter?"

"I—" She closed her eyes. "Geoff broke my trust so thoroughly, and I still feel betrayed. But it's not just my heart I have to consider now. I'm responsible for Timothy's happiness as well." She took a shuddering breath, not wanting to cry in front of her son.

"Oh, Vi," Milly said, hugging her.

Virginia found herself clinging to her friend.

"It's only a dinner party," Milly continued. "If you don't go, think of how miserable Leonard's cousin will be. If he has a horrible time tonight, I wouldn't be surprised if he changed his mind about moving someplace close to us. Can't you help a poor man in need?"

The sound of the car making its way up the long drive to Milly's home was unmistakable. Then there was a sudden ruckus downstairs, as one of the maids opened the door. A man's voice shouted so loudly Virginia and Milly could hear it upstairs, followed by a high-pitched scream.

"What in the world?" Milly said, running to the bedroom door and flinging it open.

Virginia followed close behind. They looked over the landing to see a tall man wearing an open-collared shirt, sleeves rolled up to the elbows. He was trying to control the largest dog Virginia had ever seen, or perhaps to wrestle it back out the front door.

"Maxwell?" Milly called down from the landing. "Is that you?"

The man looked up, his brown hair flopping over the side of his face. His jaw was square, his dark eyes deep beneath darker eyebrows. He grinned up at Milly, his gaze sliding to Virginia, then back to Milly.

"Hello, Milly, sorry about this. Jack's a bit excited. I'll get him into the barn. Do you have a barn on this property?"

"Yes, we do," Milly said with a laugh. "Welcome. Where's Leonard?"

"Uh, he's chasing Jill."

"Jill?"

"The better half of Jack," the man said with a wink. His gaze slid again to Virginia, and this time Milly noticed.

"Maxwell, this is Virginia. My best friend in all the world."

With one hand still holding the collar of the excited dog, Maxwell gave an elaborate bow. "Nice to meet you, Miss Virginia," he said.

Virginia couldn't help but let a smile escape. The man was bigger than life, comical even, and the dog was about to get loose.

"Oh!" Milly said, as the dog did just that. The great beast started to bark as he headed straight for the stairs.

Virginia could only think of her son Timothy on the floor of her bedroom. If the dog burst in there, who knew what might happen? Virginia flew down the stairs and planted herself in the dog's path.

"Stop!" she shouted.

The dog stopped and stared at her.

"Stay," she said in an equally stern voice. "Good boy," she continued, and moved down two more steps.

The dog eyed her, panting.

"Hello, Jack," she said in a friendly but firm voice. She maintained eye contact with the animal as she reached him. "You're not allowed to go upstairs. We have babies up there who will put up a fuss." She held her hand out and gave him a chance to sniff her scent. "If you'll be a good boy and come with me, I'm sure we can find you a treat."

The dog's ears perked forward, and Virginia nodded as if she'd expected his obedience all along.

"Come on, Jack," she said, walking past the dog, down the last few steps, and toward the door.

She felt Maxwell's gaze on her as she continued outside, the dog at her heels. She'd been quite comfortable around canines since the orphanage, where she'd been the designated girl to shoo the dogs that came begging away from kitchen.

Jack trotted at her side, and despite his size she found she wasn't intimidated. They crossed the wide porch, walked down the three steps, and continued across the yard toward the barn. When they arrived, Virginia swung the door open.

"Let's get you some water and maybe something to eat." She led the dog over to the horse trough, and he began to drink eagerly.

She turned from the dog and set off to find Jill—his female counterpart, presumably. She stopped short when a man appeared in the barn entrance.

"I thought your name was Virginia," Maxwell said.

Virginia had to look up to meet his gaze. She'd known he

was tall, but not this tall. Perhaps he *would* be a good match for Julie Peterson.

"It is," she said, wondering what he was about.

"Seems that it should be the Pied Piper, or maybe the Pied Piperess."

Virginia laughed, surprised at how easily the sound rolled out of her. She couldn't remember the last time she'd felt so spontaneously delighted.

Maxwell leaned against the doorframe, folding those muscular arms she was trying not to notice across his chest.

"I'm Leonard's cousin," he said with a wink. "It seems we have a date tonight."

Virginia's stomach felt light and feathery. "It seems we do."

Chapter Four

THE WOMAN IS *delicate, absolutely delicate,* Max thought.

It was hard to reconcile her appearance with everything he'd heard she'd been through. Whoever her ex-husband was, the man was an idiot. Of that, Max was absolutely certain.

Virginia wasn't what he'd expected. She was now petting Jill, who, given how her tongue was out and her tail was wagging, was in heaven. Virginia scratched the dog behind her ears, and Jill gave a happy yelp.

Virginia looked up at Max and laughed. "She likes the attention, doesn't she?"

"You're spoiling her," Max said, grinning back.

He'd been around plenty of women in his bachelorhood, and it took him only moments to discover which to avoid. There were those who were coddled by their mothers and wanted a man to take care of them for the rest of their lives, while they spent money like water. Other women were critical and demanding, not happy with their life's lot, and looking for someone to blame. Then there were those women who were fast, and probably would like to marry eventually, but enjoyed their roles of using men to their advantage.

His mother had almost divorced his father before she died, something that not even Leonard knew. Max's father hadn't been around much, and when he was, he'd carried with him the lingering smell of another woman's perfume. When Max's mother filed for divorce, it became the town scandal. She never recovered from it. And when she contracted pneumonia, she just seemed to give up. She died before the divorce could be finalized, and at her request no one in their extended family was told of Max's parents' marital problems.

Nevertheless, he'd never spoken to his father again. After giving his mother's things away, save for her jewelry, he'd left his hometown and struck out on his own. It had taken him years of working in a lumber yard in upstate New York before he'd garnered the experience and know-how to start his own lumber company. And now he was on the verge of signing a contract with a Chicago company that would grow his business even larger.

This trip to Leonard's was supposed to have been all business, until Max's cousin had mentioned that he and his wife were attending a neighbor's dinner party tonight, and that Milly's best friend would be accompanying them. As Max's date, it would seem. Leonard had then told Max that Virginia was divorced and had a young boy to care for. It seemed the ex-husband was completely out of the picture, having turned out Virginia so he could be with another woman.

Hmm. Max thought of his own mother's melancholy before her death.

Yet this young mother, who was laughing over his dogs' antics, was a vibrant, energetic woman. One who was gracefully calm, but also commanding. At least with animals.

Max smiled at his thoughts. "I might not be able to drag my beasts away, after you're done spoiling them."

Virginia straightened from petting Jill. Almost immediately, Jack bounded over from where he'd been drinking from the barn's trough.

"Oh, you can't stand being left out, can you?" Virginia crooned down to him.

Max chuckled. "I take it you're an animal person?"

Virginia arched her elegant dark brows at him. "I have nothing against animals," she said softly. "In fact, most animals are kinder than humans."

She didn't seem to be expecting pity. Max sensed she was simply stating a fact. One he could agree with.

"You're right." He crossed to where Jill was now drinking her fill of water. "Why do you think that is? I mean, their intelligence only goes so far."

"I don't think it has to do with intelligence," Virginia glanced his way, her expression coy.

That's when he noticed the light blue of her eyes, so light they reminded him of colored glass—the color of the morning sky just after the sun rose.

"Dogs are lovers, that's all there is to it," she said, her cheeks tinting pink. "They love unconditionally, and they aren't afraid to love more than one person."

This woman is remarkable, and beautiful, Max decided. *And not only because she's some sort of animal charmer.* "I like that sentiment—unconditionally."

"Did you raise them from pups?" Virginia asked, giving Jack's ear a vigorous scratching.

"Found them at my lumber yard when they were only hours old," Max said. "Never did discover what happened to their mother."

"Well, they're lucky to have you," Virginia said, turning her attention back to Jack. "Milly and I were friends at an orphanage you know, and I know exactly what it's like to not have a mother."

Max found himself noticing her scent, roses or something. Then he became caught up in staring into the vivid depths of her eyes. "It's remarkable that you and Milly found each other, and that you're still friends."

Virginia gave a slow nod. "Every day, I thank the Lord for her. Now more than ever."

Max assumed she was referring to her divorced state, but he didn't comment on it.

"Well, Mr. Pickering, we've got places to go," Virginia said, giving both dogs a final pat.

He followed her outside, shutting the barn doors behind them. The dogs instantly began whimpering.

"Take a nap or something," Max called out to them.

"Do you think they'll obey you?" Virginia asked with a smile.

"Only if they stop hearing things going on out here, that they think are more exciting than whatever they're doing in there."

"How was the drive down?" Virginia asked as they walked back toward the house.

"About drove Leonard crazy," Max said, grinning. "He told me the two dogs were worse than traveling with a baby."

Virginia laughed. "I can only imagine. Those two are quite full of energy."

He nodded. A slight breeze kicked up, and there it was again—the scent of roses. "I have a feeling they're going to love this place."

A few strands of Virginia's hair escaped her loose bun. He had the strangest compulsion to reach over and smooth them away from her face. He shoved his hands into his pants pockets instead.

"What about you?" he asked. "Do you like it here?"

"It's beautiful, open," Virginia said. "Milly and I grew up in Boston, and that's where I lived until… Well, I love this fresh air and waking up to the sound of birdsong."

"There you two are," Milly said, coming out onto the front porch. "Don't you know that when you go on a blind date, you aren't supposed to get to know one another in advance?"

Max flashed a smile at Virginia, who answered with a smirk.

"Accept our apologies," he told Milly. "We'll endeavor at the dinner party to act convincingly blind-datish."

"Actually," Milly said with a secret smile of her own. "Getting to know each other in advance might turn out to be an even better plan."

Chapter Five

"YOU AGREED TO be my date this evening, because you felt sorry for me?" Maxwell said, giving Virginia an incredulous look as they rode beside each other in the backseat of Leonard's car.

"Well," Virginia started, feeling her face flush. She might as well admit it and be honest from the very start. Something she wished Geoff had been from the beginning of their relationship. "Yes."

Maxwell threw his head back and laughed—a deep, joyful laugh. One that became contagious, and soon everyone inside the car was joining in.

"Well, my darlin'," Maxwell drawled, grasping Virginia's hand and bringing it to his lips. "If we're to deter Miss Julie Peterson's attentions, then I think you'd better call me Max."

Virginia inhaled as he pressed a soft kiss against her fingers. She knew Max was teasing, but the fluttering that had started in her stomach in the barn showed no signs of dissipating. "All right, then I suppose you should call me Vi."

"Vi," Max murmured, and Virginia had to suppress the warm shiver that traveled up her arm from his touch.

He was still holding her hand, looking into her eyes. How did she politely tell him to let go? Even if Milly thought she was being rude, it would be the only way for Virginia to get rid of her blush.

"So, what's our story?" Max asked.

Virginia pointedly looked down at their linked hands.

Max tightened his grip. "We need to make it believable, right?"

"How about the two of you were courting before Geoff," Milly offered from the front seat, "but Geoff proposed first?"

Virginia emphatically shook her head, feeling her face heat up even more. She didn't want Geoff to be part of any conversations.

Max seemed to read her embarrassment. "No, we were childhood friends."

"In the orphanage?" Milly blurted out.

Max blinked. "Yes, I... Well, what if I delivered bread to the orphanage?"

"Your father is a baker?" Virginia asked.

"He is," Max said.

"Truly?" She had no idea what was real, and what wasn't.

Max's smile broadened. "Truly."

"All right," Virginia agreed. Did he know that his brown eyes changed colors in the late afternoon light? A golden-orange glow streamed through the car windows, mixing green with his brown. "How did we reunite?"

Everyone went silent in the car, and then Leonard called from the driver's seat, "You're already looking for a place here, right? Why not combine that with your desire to court Vi, after all your years apart?"

Virginia laughed, and Max just smiled at her.

"All right," she relented. "I don't think we'll attract too much attention."

Max released her hand and settled back in his seat, a contented smile on his face.

Virginia had a feeling that this evening was going to be very interesting.

When they arrived at the Peterson home, her stomach turned fluttery again. It was one thing to plot and plan on the way over, but an entirely different matter to playact in front of acquaintances.

A butler answered the door, and he led them into the main hallway where Mrs. Peterson practically swooped them up.

Virginia at first found herself wondering if the woman was bird or human, with all those feathers dressed in her hair and sewn into her evening gown. Virginia immediately felt self-conscious. This was turning out to be more formal than she'd expected. She felt entirely plain next to the Peterson women, but she greeted their hostess, and then Miss Julie Peterson with enthusiasm.

"Oh, and who's this handsome young man?" Mrs. Peterson sang, grasping Max's hand with both of hers, and it didn't look as if she'd be letting go any time soon.

Leonard made the introductions, and Virginia didn't miss for a moment the way Mrs. Peterson studied Max as if he were a piece of meat hanging in a butcher shop window.

"And how do you know Virginia here?" Mrs. Peterson asked.

Virginia stifled a groan. Mrs. Peterson wasn't even waiting until they were offered a drink or some place to sit down—the interrogation was starting up now.

Their concocted story tumbled out of Max's mouth, and Virginia was grateful to have him doing the talking. He certainly spun a good story, adding a few extra embellishments that Virginia desperately hoped she'd remember.

She felt a pair of eyes on her, and when she glanced toward Julie Peterson, Virginia nearly flinched. Julie's eyes were narrowed, as if she didn't believe for one moment Max's explanation for why he and Virginia had started courting.

"How's the baby?" Julie said, cutting into her mother's questions and Max's answers, her gaze intent on Virginia.

Please don't blush. "He's growing up way too fast."

Julie arched one fair eyebrow and glanced toward Max. She was a striking woman in her own way. Her brows were nearly invisible, they were so light. But her blonde hair was thick and curly, and her blue eyes a deeper, more vibrant blue than Virginia's own. In fact, Julie's appearance resembled Geoff's lover's quite a bit.

"Must be strange, being on an outing while your child's

at home," Julie said in a pointed tone, one that grated on Virginia's nerves.

Max moved closer and linked his arm through hers, startling her, but making her grateful at the same time.

"He's a swell lad," Max said. "Have you met Timothy?"

He remembered my son's name.

But Julie wasn't about to be put off. "Yes, of course I've met the darling." She drew out the word darling, making Virginia inwardly cringe.

"Oh, I'm being rude," Mrs. Peterson blurted. "Come in and have a seat. We're just waiting on the Tolivers, and then we'll go into the dining room."

Max and Virginia followed the others toward the drawing room, his touch steering the way. While they walked, he leaned in and whispered, "How old is your son?"

"He just turned one," she said.

"Perfect," he said.

"What do you mean?" she asked, genuinely curious.

"He won't be able to tattle on me."

Virginia found herself unexpectedly laughing. Julie turned her head, casting a dark glare at them, making Virginia glad she hadn't abandoned Max to attend this gathering without a date.

When Julie was distracted by a question from her mother, Max said, "It looks like you pretty much saved my life tonight. I owe you."

Virginia smiled up at him. "I'll accept those terms, although it might take me a while to formulate suitable repayment."

He smiled in return, and she quickly looked forward again. She was a mother, and a divorced woman; she had no business engaging in a genuine flirtation with a practical stranger.

When they entered the drawing room, several other guests were seated, still more standing in small groups, engaged in various discussions. More introductions were laboriously made. Max stayed by her side, placing himself in every conversation that involved her. She found herself slowly relaxing as discussion moved away from how they'd met to other, more benign topics, such as an upcoming boat race.

The Tolivers arrived at last, and Mrs. Peterson made a great show of ushering everyone to the dining room. She asked the "couples" to sit across from each other, so diners could become better acquainted with the companions on either side of them.

This seating arrangement offered Virginia an easy view of Max. Thankfully, he wasn't sitting directly beside Julie, but between two other women whom Virginia didn't know well. She found herself watching him more than she was paying attention to the conversation swirling around her.

A couple of times, Max caught her eye and smiled. He had a faint dimple on the right side of his mouth, and his dark brown eyes seemed to brighten when he looked at her. She glanced away quickly, but not without her face heating. She was behaving like a schoolgirl—definitely not like a woman who'd been married before and had a child waiting at home for her.

And then as the dinner guests around the table relaxed more, the food and wine taking its toll, Virginia caught Max watching her. The next time she met his gaze, neither of them looked away. She'd experienced a man looking at her the way Max was: his eyes full of interest, amusement, appreciation… and thoughtfulness. Virginia realized she was staring back. She couldn't stop herself, even though her cheeks were warming.

Finally, someone spoke to Max, and he dragged his attention away. Virginia did as well, but she felt his contemplation on her again, more than once as dinner continued.

The evening progressed, and when the company moved back to the drawing room, Mrs. Peterson announced that her daughter would be regaling them with a musical number. Mrs. Peterson sat at the piano bench and began the prelude. Julie established herself near the piano, and within moments she began to sing.

Virginia was stunned by the women's angelic voice. Who would have guessed? Sweet notes filled the room, and Virginia felt rather than saw the attention that everyone suddenly gave Julie. Her talent was mesmerizing and astonishing. Then heat crept up Virginia's neck.

Because Max most of all was staring at Julie, absolutely entranced.

Chapter Six

JULIE PETERSON SOUNDED like Max's mother, when he'd been a boy and listened to her sing. The similarity was quite remarkable, and he found that he couldn't comprehend it. No matter how hard he stared at Julie and told himself that despite her voice, this woman wasn't his mother reincarnated. For one thing, the two of them looked nothing alike. Julie was fair, and Max's mother, though she'd been tall as well, had been dark haired and dark eyed.

As the evening had worn on, he must have allowed himself to become too obsessed with watching Julie. By the time he and Leonard left with Milly and Vi to walk to the car, Max realized he'd been negligent. But then Vi had climbed into the backseat with Milly—for girl talk, or something, they'd said—leaving Max to share the front with Leonard.

Max found himself and his cousin in a conversation about the contracts he was trying to secure, so he could make the move from New York to Chicago. But the entire time, his mind was on Vi in the seat behind him. She was much more quiet than their ride up. Nearly silent, compared to their easy and flirtatious conversation in the barn. What had changed? He'd been mooning over Julie, the very woman that Vi had inconvenienced herself to save him from. That's what.

At least, Max assumed Vi thought he'd been mooning over Julie.

When in fact, he felt as if he'd just walked over his mother's grave.

Chapter Seven

THE RIDE HOME in Leonard's car was far less jovial than their earlier journey. After Julie's performance, there had been a noticeable change in atmosphere at the Peterson home. From then on, as Julie visited with people, she was openly admired. By Max as well.

Virginia didn't know why that was exactly, but she'd witnessed Max go from joking around about Julie to outright admiring the other woman. He'd spoken to her for several moments after her performance, talking to her about music and composers, of all things. It seemed he was quite a music lover. At least that's what Virginia had told herself. Her stomach knotted at the prospect of Max being a flirt and a ladies' man. A man like her husband.

Picking at a loose thread on her dress, she was only half-listening to the conversation in the car. Max and Leonard were discussing his lumber yard—it seemed it was quite a large one—and the contracts he'd just secured with a building company in Chicago. How he'd be in town for a couple more days, meeting with Leonard's contacts and looking for a house to buy.

Virginia knew she was pouting, and that upset her more than all the rest. She barely knew Max, and they had no agreement or relationship. Theirs had been a blind date, for heaven's sake. Timothy was her world now, and his well-being her only concern. She had no business trespassing in the world of single men and women and their talents and flirtations.

But every time she heard Max laugh at something

Leonard said, her heart twinged. Earlier in the evening, at least for a short time, that laugh had been for her.

"Here we are, ladies," Leonard said, turning to glance back at the women.

"What a wonderful evening," Milly commented as Leonard opened his door. He opened Milly's next, and Max opened Virginia's.

"Thank you," she told Max as she climbed out. He reached for her hand, but she didn't see it until it was too late and she was already standing.

He dropped his hand. "Thank you for being my date tonight. I'm glad you were able to come." His voice was as kind as ever, but Virginia felt something missing now. The connection that had been there before was gone.

Leonard and Milly were already walking ahead of them. Virginia set out toward the house as well, Max keeping pace beside her.

"Do you think your dogs missed you?" she asked him, trying to start some sort of conversation, when in fact she wanted to have a good cry.

"Only if they're hungry again," Max said with a laugh.

Virginia smiled at him, although she was wishing this night had turned out differently. Leonard and Milly reached the porch first. Max slowed his step.

"I enjoyed tonight," he said. "It was nice to get to know you, and I appreciate your willingness to come."

So formal, so polite. Virginia ignored the burning in her eyes. "I'm glad I went as well."

He nodded, then seemed to hesitated before saying, "I wanted to ask you a question, and I hope it's not too personal—"

"Max," Leonard called out, stepping back onto the porch, when he'd only just disappeared into the house. He rushed down the stairs. "There's a phone call for you, and the caller says it's urgent."

"Oh," Max said, glancing from Leonard to Virginia.

"Go ahead," Virginia said, though she didn't really need to give him permission.

He hurried up the few steps to the porch. He was tall, broad-shouldered and seemed to be a man who was very capable. He was also kind, and witty, and… What had he been about to ask her?

Leonard held the door open as she ascended the porch steps. She walked into the entryway to where the phone was kept on a table against the wall. From the moment she saw Max leaning against the wall, his head bent forward, one hand rubbing his forehead as he listened to the speaker on the phone, she knew something was wrong.

Leonard stopped next to her, and even though they were eavesdropping, neither of them moved as Max spoke into the phone.

"Thank you for calling," he said in a strained voice, as if he were holding back much heavier emotion. Anger? Sadness?

He replaced the receiver, but didn't look up, didn't even acknowledge that there were others in the hallway. Virginia wasn't sure where Milly had gone off to, but Virginia couldn't very well pass by Max to find out. Whatever had happened at dinner, she felt a great desire to help this man.

When he did lift his head, he was a changed Max. Gone was the twinkle in his eye, the amused turn of his lips. His dark brown eyes were like black pools of grief, and Virginia literally felt her stomach drop.

"Max?" she whispered.

He didn't move, didn't acknowledge her, and she wondered if he'd even heard her speak.

"Max, what's happened?" Leonard spoke now as he crossed to the table with the telephone.

Max blinked a couple of times, then looked at his friend.

"There's been a fire," he said, his voice hoarse and unbelieving. "Everything's gone. The entire yard went up in flames, and the surrounding property is destroyed, too. Remember that my yard borders the Wilson's place?"

"I remember," Leonard said, grasping Max's arm. "You have insurance though, right?"

Max nodded, but his words weren't promising. "I have insurance, but with the fire also destroying much of the Wilson's property, my business will fold at a loss."

Virginia listened with growing horror.

"I'll have to start over," Max said, looking into Leonard's eyes. "Completely over. The insurance assessment will take months, and even if there's anything to be paid out, it will probably go to the Wilsons. I have some savings, but that won't be much of a cushion if my reputation is ruined."

"You'll stay here until you find a new job," Leonard said, his voice firm, although his eyes were rimmed in red with emotion. "You're healthy, young, and have a good head for business."

Max rubbed his face, his hand shaking.

Virginia's eyes filled with tears, and she blinked them away.

"Come on," Leonard said. "Let's go sit in my office and put together a list of options and contacts. A man with a plan is a man with hope."

Max nodded and turned with Leonard. The two men crossed the hallway, and Leonard opened his office door.

Virginia watched them disappear inside. They had forgotten she'd been standing there, listening to everything.

She brushed at the tears spilling onto her cheeks.

The look on Max's face during that phone call reminded her of her own pain and shock when she'd discovered Geoff's betrayal.

Chapter Eight

VIRGINIA DIDN'T SEE Max for over a week. He'd left early the next morning to travel to his destroyed lumber yard. Leonard had driven him, then returned later that evening. When Leonard had walked in the door, his expression said it all. Max's business was finished. During the week that Max was gone, the Peterson women had visited twice, clucking over Max's misfortune.

"Simply bad luck," Mrs. Peterson had stated more than once, Julie sitting by her side. "He's a fine man, though, and none of this was his fault."

Julie had remained quiet for the most part, but that hadn't meant her mind was idle, Virginia had decided. In fact, she'd had a rather pleased look about her, one that wasn't befitting the tragic circumstances being discussed.

At the breakfast table on the following Monday, more than a week after Max's sudden departure, Leonard announced that he'd be driving out again that day to fetch Max.

"Oh wonderful," Milly said right away. "Will he be staying here then?"

"For a couple of weeks at least," Leonard said. "He already has written to several city business owners, and has a couple of interviews lined up. He'll probably have to take a position beneath him for a while, until his insurance claim is settled and his credit reestablished."

Timothy chose that moment to squeal from his high chair and point out the window. "Burr!" he said.

Virginia gazed out the window. "Oh, yes, there's a pretty bird. It's blue. Can you say blue?"

"Boo," Timothy said, then started to cry when the bird startled and flew away.

Virginia tried to soothe him with another spoonful of cereal, but his crying only intensified. She scooped Timothy up and carried him out of the dining room.

"Ows! Ows!" Timothy said, his word for *outside.*

"All right, give your mother a chance to get her hat." The morning sun was deceptive and would quickly grow hot. As she walked past the dining room toward the stairs, she heard Milly say something about a dinner party scheduled for that night.

Virginia slowed her step, but then Timothy started to fuss again. She hurried upstairs and fetched her hat. By the time she came back down, Milly was saying goodbye to Leonard in the hallway. Virginia hung back as Leonard gave Milly a tender farewell kiss.

It was a blissful domestic scene, one that tugged at the deepest part of Virginia, one that she'd never had with Geoff.

"Oh, Vi," Milly said after her husband left. "We're having the Tolivers over for dinner tonight. And now it looks like Max will be joining us."

Virginia suddenly felt nervous. She'd be seeing Max tonight. A different Max. One who was no longer on top of the world.

"What can I do to help?" she asked.

"Just make yourself pretty," Milly said with a laugh. "I'm sure you'll be a sight for sore eyes for Max."

Virginia smiled. Milly wasn't bothering to hide her latest matchmaking attempt. But she hadn't seemed to notice how much attention Max had paid Julie after she'd sung at her mother's dinner party.

At least Virginia wouldn't have to worry about Julie tonight. Though Virginia didn't plan to bother Max after he'd suffered so badly. She just wanted him to know that she understood what it meant to lose a dream.

Virginia spent the morning outside with Timothy, which

included playing with the dogs Max had left at the ranch. After lunch, while Timothy took his nap, she worked on her commissioned embroidery. Even if she worked all day, every day sewing, she could never afford her own home. The only places that rented cheap rooms were places in which she wouldn't want Timothy to grow up.

The afternoon passed by both too slowly and too quickly. Before she knew it, evening had arrived, and Blanche had taken over the nursery, watching both Timothy and Milly's baby. The only thing left to do was to prepare for the party and change into another of Milly's older gowns. She slipped on the light tan dress then pulled her hair back. She pinned it into a twist ending at the nape of her neck. Her earrings were small pearls, also borrowed from Milly.

When she heard voices downstairs, she froze. They were female voices—ones that sounded suspiciously like Mrs. Peterson and her daughter. Dread building inside of her, Virginia stepped out of her room and peered down from the second floor landing to see who was in the entrance.

"We didn't realize you were expecting company," Mrs. Peterson was saying. "We wanted to bring over this pie and give our best to Mr. Pickering. We heard he was returning today."

"He should be here within the hour," Milly said. "Why don't you stay for dinner, and we can have this pie for dessert?"

Virginia felt her body deflate, but there was nothing for it. Milly was the consummate hostess, and Virginia knew if she had been in her friend's position, she would have made the same offer.

"Oh, are you sure?" Mrs. Peterson asked, her voice making it clear that she'd expected to be invited.

In fact, Virginia wouldn't be surprised if the Petersons had known about the dinner party and come over anyway.

Julie was smiling at Milly, her blue eyes bright as usual.

Virginia released a sigh and started down the stairs. About halfway down, the Petersons noticed her arrival.

"You look wonderful, Vi," Milly said.

"Did you wear that last year to the Geddes' wedding?" Julie asked Milly, eyeing Virginia's dress.

"I did," Milly admitted. "But Vi looks much better in it. Tan doesn't complement a redhead."

Julie laughed. "I'm glad you ladies are the same size. It must be nice sharing everything like sisters."

Julie's tone was pleasant enough, but it grated on Virginia's nerves. She smiled and joined them in the hallway.

"Would you mind taking the pie into the kitchen?" Mrs. Peterson said, handing the pie carrier to Virginia. "And let the cook know two more guests are attending."

"Of course," Virginia said, actually grateful for the chance to escape to the kitchen and collect her thoughts. She left the hallway and made her way to where the cook, Mrs. Hayes, was basting a large roast.

"It smells divine," Virginia said, setting the pie on the sideboard. "The Petersons brought pie, and they'll be staying for dinner as well."

"All right," Mrs. Hayes said, her eyes flitting over to Virginia.

The gray-haired and stern-faced woman never seemed to get out-of-sorts over anything. Virginia admired her for that. "Do you need some help?" she asked.

That earned Virginia a softer expression. "You are kind for asking, but you're a guest tonight."

Virginia shrugged and settled onto a kitchen chair. "Growing up in an orphanage, I found I'd often rather be working and staying busy than visiting with others."

Mrs. Hayes nodded at that. "You're a good woman, ma'am. You don't put on airs like others do."

Virginia knew she wasn't referring to Milly or her husband, but to some of their acquaintances. But gossip wouldn't do anyone any good, so she said, "The dogs will love the leftovers once dinner is finished."

Mrs. Hayes cracked a smile. "Don't think I haven't already heard them whining from the barn." She nodded toward the open kitchen window. "Even the flies have started to gather."

Virginia rose and walked to the kitchen window. Sure enough, flies buzzed angrily, or maybe happily, outside, looking forward to sampling the delicious smells.

"Oh, there the men are now," Mrs. Hayes said, joining Virginia at the window.

At the end of the long drive, Leonard's car had just turned in. Virginia watched as it approached the house, and just as it stopped, she heard the front door open and shut. Milly appeared on the porch to greet her husband. And right behind Milly was Julie Peterson.

Virginia's throat tightened as she tried to take in a normal breath of air. As soon as the men were out of the car, Julie greeted Max with a bright smile. Virginia watched him closely. He looked tired, but resilient. She would have expected nothing less. He smiled at Julie, and maybe it was just in politeness. But it still wrenched Virginia's heart just a little more.

Chapter Nine

A GREETING FROM Julie Peterson as soon as he'd returned to Leonard's homestead had been unexpected, and all Max could wonder about was Virginia.

Despite the heartache that had faced him when he'd arrived at his burned down lumber yard, and the grueling paperwork and questioning he'd endured since, he had been thinking of Virginia almost non-stop. The quiet woman with a ready-smile. The woman who had no idea how beautiful she was. The woman who'd been cast away by an oaf of a husband and had lived through much sorrow... Max felt connected to her on a deeper level than he could have ever expected. And he intended on exploring that connection.

But she didn't seem to be part of the greeting crew. Maybe everything he'd thought had transpired between them during his last visit had been in his head alone, and he was reading too much into each interaction he and Virginia had shared. Yet the memories of being in her company had buoyed his spirits and given him something to look forward to, instead of allowing himself to dwell on his newly destitute state. He'd started at the bottom before, and he could climb right back up again. Only each time he'd told himself this, the question that had continued to come to mind had been, with whom might he make that climb?

Milly was all questions, which he answered as politely as possible. That was, until Mrs. Peterson's questions began, at which point he found himself becoming rapidly annoyed.

"You know that my late husband ran a road construction

company?" she asked, linking her arm through his as they walked toward the dining room.

He barely had time to answer, before she continued.

"Our manager, Mr. Larson, is running it now, but it's not ideal, you see." She glanced at her daughter, who was acting as if she wasn't listening in. "If Julie marries any time soon, then it would make much more sense for her husband to take over as manager." She gave Max a broad smile.

Max was looking toward Leonard, silently begging for help, when Virginia appeared, exiting the kitchen. She was just as beautiful as Max remembered. Her hair was pulled into a simple twist; her dress was elegant but quite plain. Yet, the combination made her look classically beautiful.

"What a coincidence that would be," Mrs. Peterson said, loud enough for everyone to hear, "if you found yourself running my husband's company." She sighed. "This world is quite small."

Max hoped that Vi realized the other woman was speaking nonsense. "Hello Virginia," he found himself saying, quite out of turn.

Her gaze connected with his, flitted to Mrs. Peterson, then back to him. "Welcome back. I hope everything went well for you."

Max's heart sank. Her tone was on the cool side. "I'm doing as well as can be expected," he said, painfully aware of the Peterson ladies listening to the exchange. There was so much more underlying his statement than he could explain to Virginia until the dinner party was over.

The doorbell rang, and Milly said something about the Tolivers arriving. It was then that Max realized Mrs. Peterson was literally tugging him toward the table, as if she were going to find his seat for him. He could only guess whom she'd plant next to him.

Sure enough, Julie settled on his other side before Milly could instruct otherwise, caught up as she was in welcoming the Tolivers.

As dinner began, Virginia sat across the table from him. But things weren't as they'd been at the Petersons. She wasn't making eye contact, nor was she sending him occasional smiles.

Although that didn't really stop him from watching her and hoping she'd somehow know that he wasn't sitting by Julie Peterson by choice. Neither was he really supporting the idea to which Mrs. Peterson was hinting broadly... where all of Max's business problems would be solved, if he'd only resolve himself to marrying Julie. After which he'd take over a successful company. Which Mrs. Peterson pointed out by saying, "You won't have to worry about a road burning down, now would you?"

She laughed, but only Julie joined in. The Tolivers offered polite smiles, whereas Virginia's complexion turned quite pale. If she was feeling anything close to the same as Max at that moment, then she was likely plotting ways to escape the dinner party.

Somehow, some way, Max made it through the meal without crawling under the table or saying something he might regret. After dessert was complete, everyone moved to the parlor, and Mrs. Peterson began playing the piano.

Max discovered that Virginia was nowhere to be found, and instead of asking after her, he went exploring himself. He slipped out of the drawing room while everyone's attention was captured by the music.

Voices coming from upstairs gave away Virginia's location, and Max climbed the stairs, only to arrive at the doorway of a nursery. An older woman sat on a rocking chair within, holding a sleeping baby in her arms. The child must be Milly's, Max decided, because there sat Virginia on the floor, playing blocks with a young boy who looked to be around a year old.

Timothy had his mother's coloring: dark hair, although his eyes were a deeper green. Virginia hadn't seen Max yet, allowing him the chance to watch her play with her son as she made him clap and smile. Max grinned. The two of them clearly adored each other.

Max felt as if he were intruding on a private moment, even though the other woman was also in the room. He was about to slip away when Timothy looked over.

"Up!" the child said when he spotted Max. Timothy lifted his arms and said again, "Up!"

Virginia's attention flashed to Max. "Oh, I didn't know you were there."

"Up!" Timothy demanded more loudly.

Virginia shook her head at the boy. "You know better than that. You can walk now. You don't need to be carried all the time." But as she spoke, she pulled him into her arms and kissed the top of his head.

Max laughed. "I see the way it is. Deliver the bad news with a little sugar."

Virginia's smile was slight, but it was there.

At the sound of Max's voice, the boy reached out and once again said, "Up! Up!"

"I don't mind," Max offered, "if it's all right with you."

"Are you sure?" Virginia asked.

Max crossed to the pair and picked up Timothy. The boy laughed and grabbed onto Max's shirt collar, then turned to look down at his mother.

Max held out a hand and helped her to her feet.

"It that better, Timothy?" Virginia asked, grasping the child's dimpled hand.

Standing this close to Virginia, Max caught her scent of roses, mixed with the clean linen smell of the child.

"Well, we should probably return to the party," Virginia said. "Don't want to miss all the music."

Her tone was light enough, but something was off. And he wanted to know what it was. He hadn't built a lumber company from the ground up because he lacked determination. If there was one quality he'd forever own up to, it was perseverance.

A Second Chance

"Virginia," he said, capturing her attention fully. "Would you like to go on a walk tonight after the guests have left?"

Her mouth opened in an O, but then she closed it and said, "Aren't you tired?"

"Not that tired," he said, giving her a hopeful smile.

"All right," she said, although it wasn't a very flattering agreement.

He would take what he could get.

Chapter Ten

VIRGINIA DECIDED THAT Max had been nothing but gracious and solicitous to everyone all night. He hadn't seemed overjoyed when Mrs. Peterson had ever-so-subtly suggested that marrying her daughter would be advantageous to Max in more ways than one.

But now that everyone was in the drawing room, listening to Julie sing yet another song, Virginia wondered why he'd invited her on a walk. It wasn't as if they really knew each other. They'd been on one date. She realized they'd probably be seeing quite a bit of each other if he were living at the ranch until he could secure another job. But the longer the evening stretched, the more nervous she became at the thought of them speaking alone.

She'd delayed her returning downstairs by getting Timothy into his night clothes and fixing his bottle herself. When she stepped into the parlor, Julie appeared to be halfway through singing some ballad, and the only open seat was next to Milly.

Milly patted her hand, but turned her attention back to the singing. Virginia stole a glance at Max. He was gazing in Julie's direction, but didn't seem entirely focused on her. What was he thinking about? His job prospects? That perhaps allying himself with the Peterson family was a viable solution?

Then Max turned his head and caught her gazing at him. She glanced down quickly, but not quickly enough to escape the heat blooming on her face. If Max were still looking at her, surely he'd see her blush.

As the evening finally drew to a close, Virginia wasn't certain if she was relieved or nervous to see the guests depart. She felt Max's attention focus on her as Leonard and Milly walked the guests out to the porch.

"Are you still up for a walk?" Max asked.

"You're not too tired?" Virginia said, looking up at him. His eyes looked exhausted. But he was still handsome, in a tousled sort of way. She really couldn't fault Julie for her interest.

"Come on," he said. "Let's go out the back door, so we won't have to answer a lot of questions."

"Subterfuge, then?" Virginia said.

Max held out his hand.

She arched a brow but allowed him to help her from her chair. When he didn't release her, she felt a shot of warmth spread through her body. He led her into the hallway, and they could hear Milly and Leonard's voices coming from the front porch. Max walked toward the kitchen and opened the back door.

The night air was cool, but Virginia felt as if she were in a cocoon of warmth that began at the point of their interlinked hands. Max still hadn't let go. They walked slowly away from the house, toward the garden. The moonlight made the path easy to follow, and when they reached the low fence separating the yard and garden, Max turned toward her.

"How have you been?"

No question could have startled her more. She stared up at him, only to find him studying her closely. "I imagine I'm much better than you are. You've been through quite a bit in the past week."

He gave a slight nod. "Life's latest twist has certainly been unexpected, but I'm hoping things will only improve in the future."

She nodded back. "It seems you have a lot of opportunities."

He released a sigh. "If you're referring to the Petersons'

suggestions tonight, know that I'm not interested in either of their offers."

Hope buzzed through Virginia, but she reminded herself that she still had no claim on this man. Even if he was still holding her hand, and his thumb was now caressing her wrist, causing her heart to beat double-time.

"Was there more than one offer?" she asked, curious to know if he was saying what she thought he was saying.

"I'm sure you couldn't help but overhear Mrs. Peterson's solution to all of my problems: marry her daughter and take over her dead husband's company at the same time."

"Hmm," Virginia mused. "That does sound like more than one offer, even if the second is dependent upon the first."

Max smiled. "Do you think I should take her up on it then?"

Virginia's mouth went dry. She couldn't tell if he was being serious or teasing. "I think you should do what makes you the most happy."

He brought her hand up and, still smiling, kissed the top of her knuckles. "I was hoping you'd say that."

"I'm happy to oblige," she said, not sure how to reconcile the conflict between his words and his actions.

"Vi," he said in a soft voice. "I'm not going to marry Julie Peterson, and I'm not going to go work for their company. Julie has many talents, but when I was away this past week, there was only one woman I found myself thinking of."

Virginia stared at him and had to ask the question. "Who?"

Max released a soft laugh. "You." He brushed his fingers along her cheek.

Tingles burst across her skin. "And what were you thinking of? In regards to me, that is?" She shook her head at her own rambling. "I mean, if you don't mind me asking."

"I was thinking about how you're an amazing woman who's been through a lot of hard things," Max said, taking a step closer. "And I was thinking about how serene you are, and how you make the best of things, and how you have no idea how beautiful you are."

He was close enough now that she could feel his warm breath on her skin.

"Are you a flirt?" she couldn't help but ask. "I mean I've seen the way you watch Julie when she's singing."

He looked surprised at that, then he started to chuckle. "I'm about to tell you the strangest thing ever. My mother always sang, in the church choir, around the house, and while she was working in the garden. And Julie's voice is so similar to my mother's that I guess I was stunned. I wondered if my mother had come back from the grave to tell me something."

"Like you're supposed to marry Julie and take over her father's company?"

He sobered. "No, it's just a strange coincidence. If anything, that night drew me to look more closely at you." His thumb was stroking her wrist again. "Did you know that my mother filed for divorce from my father? It was unheard of in our town. She died before it was finalized, and she made me promise not to tell anyone. She didn't want her reputation to follow me."

Again, Virginia was stunned. Nothing she'd been thinking, or assuming, was correct. "Why did she file for divorce?"

Max lowered his head and hesitated. "My father was a cheat and a drunk, but mostly a cheat. She couldn't live with that any longer, and I was proud she took a stand against the way he disrespected her. It was difficult for her to think of raising a child on her own, but it was better than keeping my louse of a father around."

Virginia nodded, her own memories of her failed marriage returning with full force. "Is that why you've been thinking of me, comparing me to your mother?"

"Maybe a little bit," Max said. "But I'm only telling you about her so you'll know that I admire you. I think you're an amazing woman for doing what you did."

Tears pricked Virginia's eyes. She didn't want to cry in

front of him. She didn't want to relive the pain of Geoff. But what Max had said was possibly the kindest thing she'd ever experienced a man saying to her.

"You're flirting with me again," she whispered in a choked voice.

His smile returned, gentler this time. "No, I'm being completely honest."

Virginia studied him for a long moment. "Thank you," she said at last, and then she did something that shocked even her. She wrapped her arms around his neck and hugged him.

Max pulled her tightly against him, his arms holding her close. They stood like that for several moments, their pulses thudding in tandem.

Virginia closed her eyes and breathed him in. She didn't know what any of this meant, but she wasn't going to analyze it right now. She wanted to stand in his arms until her tears dried.

"Vi," he whispered. "You're standing on my foot."

"Oh!" She released him and drew away, moving her offending foot.

He laughed and tugged her closer, his hands firm on her waist. "Stay here."

She was in his arms again. But this time, he lowered his head and pressed his lips against her neck. Her skin felt as if she might burst into flames, and she didn't dare move.

"Max," she breathed. She just had to say his name.

"Hmm," he murmured, lifting his head.

Gazing up at the look in his eyes, she suspected that he wasn't finished kissing her.

And, as it turned out, she was right.

Chapter Eleven

MAX REALIZED HE was being forward, especially considering that he hadn't known Virginia for very long. But he'd never felt this deeply connected to any woman. And seeing her with her son earlier had only endeared her to him more. Then he'd witnessed the flash of jealously in her eyes as they'd spoken of Julie. And Max had wanted to pull Virginia into his arms right then and kiss her until he ran out of oxygen.

Now it was as if he couldn't continue existing unless he kept kissing her. She was melting against him. Not drawing away, but not exactly returning the kiss, either. If he'd had the ability to think through what he was doing, he might be more intimidated. She had, after all, been married before. But he wasn't one to give up easily, particularly not after confronting a decade's worth of his work literally going up on smoke.

He raised one of his hands and touched her cheek, watching her eyes drift closed. A puff of air escaped her lips. And he kissed her again, softly, slowly, gauging her reaction.

This time she responded. She wrapped her arms about his neck, her fingers tangling in his hair as she kissed him back. She was warm and soft in all the right places, and he was desperate to get closer. But for now at least, that was impossible.

Her skin smelled of roses. Intoxicated, he felt himself falling—everything he had, absorbing everything she was. Her body nestled into his, and the night breeze stirred around them. Max deepened his kiss until she was breathless. When she broke away and drew in air, he found himself breathing hard as well.

He leaned his forehead against hers, his skin warm next to hers.

"Did I tell you I can't stop thinking about you?" he whispered.

"You did," she whispered back. "Maybe kissing me some more will clear your thoughts?"

"No," he said, brushing his lips on hers; moving to her jawline.

She tilted her head back, exposing the elegant column of her neck. When she released a small groan, he trembled.

"Now I won't be able to sleep," he said.

Her laugh was soft and lovely. She straightened, running her hand along his chin. "You're an interesting man, Max."

"Is that a good thing, or a bad thing?"

She didn't speak for a moment, gazing at him beneath the moonlight. He wanted to kiss her again, but he wanted her answer more.

"For starters," she said, "you're the opposite of my ex-husband in every way."

He didn't know how to respond, so he waited for her to continue.

"And you don't waste much time when you're going after what you want," she continued, tilting her head. "Sort of like Julie Peterson, to tell the truth."

"Ouch," he said. "You're comparing me to Julie?"

"Only to point out that opposites attract, and you and Julie are both remarkably persistent."

"Hmm," Max said. "I find you pretty stubborn yourself."

"If I need to be," she said, smiling.

He ran his hands up her arms. And as he did, he felt her skin break out into goose pimples.

"Virginia, may I officially court you?"

"I think that would be best," she said with a soft smile. "Either that, or Leonard will have to break out his shotgun."

"That wouldn't do at all," Max whispered, pulling her

close once more. "Especially since I've always been the better shot."

She pressed her lips against his. He closed his eyes, memorizing the way she tasted, and the way she fit into his arms as if she'd always belonged there.

"Max," she said, drawing away from his embrace. "All of this kissing has quite turned my head."

He linked their hands. He was pleased to see her cheeks flush.

"Do you not care for it?" he teased.

"Of course it's enjoyable," she said, dropping her gaze. "And that's just the thing. I like you, I really do. But I'm also a mother, and I have to consider Timothy and not let my head stay in the clouds."

He squeezed her hands. "Timothy will always be part of the equation."

She flashed a smile, but her eyes were serious. "I've been married before, and I just… want to take things slow."

Slow, Max could do. It was her *no* that he'd been afraid of. "So, only kissing once a day?"

She gave a light laugh. "That might be too much even, at least for a while."

"All right," Max said, lifting only one of her hands and pressing a kiss to her knuckles. "Every other day?"

"I'll let you know."

She was smiling, but Max wasn't oblivious to the soberness of her request. His first impression had been that Virginia was delicate. And now he knew for certain that her heart was fragile. He intended to treat it with the greatest of care.

"Well, then," he said. "I'll be here, whenever you need me."

At that, she released a full laugh.

"Thank you." She raised up on her toes and kissed his cheek. "You're a wonderful man, Max. Any woman would be lucky to be courted by you."

"I think you have it wrong," he said, his voice unexpectedly husky. "I'm the lucky one here." The light was back in her eyes. And he realized suddenly that her happiness, rather than her kisses, was what he wanted most.

He released one of her hands and tucked her arm beneath his. "We should get back to the house. I think I heard the Petersons' and Tolivers' cars drive away, and I'm sure Milly is wondering what happened to us."

As they slowly walked back to the house, Max took comfort in how Virginia leaned against him. He felt like he was soaring. After losing his business, thoughts of her had kept his head up and his determination strong. She had already become his beacon.

Now, he had the chance to earn the right to become hers.

Chapter Twelve

VIRGINIA WOKE TO the sound of Milly cracking open her bedroom door.

"Are you awake?" her friend asked.

"I am now," Virginia said, stifling a yawn. She scooted up to a sitting position. "It's still early. Is everything all right?"

Milly stepped into the room and shut the door, then folded her arms, saying nothing, just studying Virginia.

Virginia was sure that she looked a fright. She hadn't slept much, her thoughts consumed with Max and her pulse still stirred by the memory of his touch.

"Tell me what's going on," she said to Milly. "It's much too early to guess."

"He kissed you," Milly blurted out, her face growing pink. "Vi, do you know what you're doing? You hardly know the man."

Virginia smoothed her hair back, then climbed out of bed and grabbed her robe. Pulling it on and tying it in front, she was finally ready to face her best friend's interrogation. "*You* set us up on a blind date, *and* he's your husband's cousin. I'd think if anyone endorsed him, it would be *you.*"

"Endorse him?" Milly said. "He's a great man, a good man, but..." She looked away for a moment, and when she again looked back at Virginia, there were tears in her eyes. "I can't bear to see you hurt again. You've been through so much."

Virginia's defenses melted, but then worry set in. Milly

was voicing all of Virginia's own deepest fears. "Do you think he'll hurt me?"

"No," Milly started. "I mean, I don't think so, but I just… I guess what I'm saying is that I care for you both. And if things with Max go wrong, you and I would be affected, since he and my husband are close." She crossed to Virginia and grabbed her hand. "But most of all, I don't want you to be hurt by anyone. I couldn't bear it."

Virginia hugged Milly, then drew back. "I would tell you not to worry, but in truth, I'm worried myself. Not because I don't like Max, because I really do like him. And because my heart is still cracked."

"Exactly," Milly said in a quiet voice.

"I told him I wanted to take it slow. But, we did kiss. A few times." She shrugged and let a smile escape.

"I presume it was enjoyable?" Milly asked.

At that, Virginia felt her face heat. "If it wasn't enjoyable, I wouldn't have made plans with him today."

"Oh, really?" Milly said in a careful tone. "Like what?"

"After his interviews, we're going to go for a drive," Virginia said. "Nothing earth-shattering. Just two people getting to know each other better."

"You *are* smitten," Milly declared. "If you could see your face right now." Her tone had softened with affection.

Virginia brought her hands to her cheeks. "He's… Oh, I don't know how to explain it." She met Milly's gaze. "He's not Geoff, *that* I can promise you. We have a lot in common. Actually, more than I expected. And he looks at me as if I'm something precious." She broke her gaze from Milly's then and released a sigh. "I'm not sure Geoff *ever* looked at me that way. My ex-husband's gazes were full of desire, more than anything else. I guess I should have seen that as a warning. That, and he apparently thought I was the easiest means in which to establish a business connection with your husband."

Milly shook her head. "You couldn't have known; none

of us knew. Geoff hid his true self from all of us." She smiled. A genuine smile this time. "I'm happy for you, Vi. And seeing your reaction this morning has convinced me to back off a little." She laughed, then sobered. "But take things slow. If Max is the man for you and the right father for Timothy, then things will work out that way."

Virginia wiped at her suddenly teary eyes. "That's what I've told myself." She took a deep breath. "You should have seen Timothy's reaction to Max last night when he came into the nursery. It was as if he trusted Max right away. He asked Max to pick him up."

"And what was Max's reaction?" Milly asked, watching Virginia closely.

"Oh, he obliged, and he didn't seem bothered in the least. Maybe that's why I let him kiss me."

She'd meant it as a joke, but her words rang true. Her life was no longer simply her own. Everything she did and every decision she made must have her son's best interest in mind.

Milly grasped her hand and kissed her on the cheek. "I have faith in you. And Max *is* a good man." She squeezed Virginia's fingers before letting go. "I just didn't expect things in your life to change so quickly. I mean, this has been your first date since... Well, there's no use dwelling on the past."

Virginia nodded, swallowing against the sudden lump in her throat.

After Milly left the bedroom, Virginia stood for several moments by the window overlooking the ranch, her arms wrapped about her torso. In the light of the day, she wondered if last night had happened as she'd remembered it. Or perhaps it had been the moon and the stars that had created more romance than had truly been there.

When she saw Max again, would she be thinking more logically and know for certain whether or not there was a potential relationship between them?

As it turned out, when Max returned to the ranch in the late afternoon and entered the drawing room where Virginia and Milly sat with their stitching during their babies' naps, Virginia felt the breath leave her chest. So much for logic.

He'd removed his hat, and he had his dark jacket slung over his shoulder. "Good afternoon, ladies," he said, his gaze moving from Milly to Virginia. Then he smiled.

Virginia's heart melted at the soft light in his eyes.

"You've had a good day, I see," Milly said.

"He had an excellent day," Leonard said, coming into the room behind Max. "Secured himself an excellent position as the head manager at Long's Boat Company."

"Oh?" Milly said, looking at Max. "I didn't know you were a boating man."

"He's not running boats," Leonard answered for Max. "But managing the office and all the accounts."

It seemed Milly and Leonard were doing all the talking, while Max and Virginia just looked at each other.

He lifted his brows slightly, as if to ask if she was still interested in their afternoon ride. She gave him the smallest of nods, and his smile grew wider.

"Well, it seems I have a date," Max cut into the discussion. He held out his hand. "Virginia?"

She was on her feet in an instant, then she paused and turned to Milly. "You won't mind that I leave Timothy here sleeping? We won't be too long."

"Of course not," Milly said. "Have a nice time."

"Thank you," Virginia said, and turned toward Max again.

His gaze was still intent on hers, his hand still outstretched. She placed her hand in his, even though they had an audience. Max's eyes seemed to soak her in before he guided her to the hall. Without replacing his hat, he led her outside and opened the passenger door of Leonard's car, carefully seating her.

When he climbed in the other side, he started the engine, and only then looked over at her. "Ready?"

"For a drive?" she asked.

"To see the house that I just bought."

She gaped at his grin. "What are you talking about?"

He gave her a wink and put the car into gear, steering them down the long driveway. "Well, I did a lot of thinking last night… after, you know, after you said you'd be agreeable to me courting you."

Virginia nodded her head, not sure where his reasoning was going. She just knew that her heart had started to pound like mad. "You bought a house, because I said you could court me?"

"Not entirely," he said, although he was still grinning. "I told myself that if I could secure a decent job today, I'd house hunt on the way back to the ranch, and wouldn't you know it… Leonard told me about a property just a few miles from here that's going up for auction next week."

"Oh, the Jones' house?" Virginia asked, her mind racing. Old man Jones had died, and his grown children didn't want the place. So they were selling it off. "You're going to bid on it?"

"I already did," Max said. "Leonard took me to meet with the eldest son, the executor of the estate, and we signed papers."

Virginia released a puff of air. "Just like that?"

"Just like that," Max echoed. "I did have some savings, and I decided I'd rather put it down on my future and let the insurance issues work itself out." He shifted the car into higher gear. "I want you to be the first to see it and to give your opinion."

"What will my opinion matter?" she asked, giving him a sideways glance. "You've already purchased the place."

Max laughed. "True. But I still want to know what you think." His tone sobered. "It will mean a lot to me, if you'd give me your honest impression."

By the time they pulled off the main road and started driving up the lane leading to the Jones' place, Virginia's stomach was aflutter. She'd been too distracted to pay close attention to the other homesteads along the way. But she did recognize the tree-lined lane that led to the house, and the elegant two-story structure that was painted a glimmering white.

The house came into view, and it was as Virginia remembered it... although now Max owned it. He pulled the car to a stop and turned off the engine.

In the sudden quiet, he said, "What do you think?"

She popped open her door and eased out of the car. Then she walked toward the house, a tingling coming over her. She couldn't believe Max owned this house and that he...

His footsteps echoed as he followed her. When she reached the base of the steps leading to the wraparound porch, she turned. He stopped, close enough to touch her. Although, he shoved his hands in his pockets and smiled.

"You're going to follow me?" she asked.

"I am," he said.

She lifted a shoulder and turned, then started up the steps. The front door was locked, but Max produced a key, of course. Stepping inside, she found the front parlor empty, but there was evidence of where pictures had recently hung on the walls, and indents in the carpet of where the furniture had sat. It was still clear that this house had once been a home.

The place was a good size. Not as grand as Milly's and Leonard's, but Virginia would never complain. She walked into the kitchen and stopped in the middle of the room. What was she thinking? That she might live here? That she might be...

"Virginia," Max said in a soft voice. "Do you think it can be salvaged? With a bit of clean up and paint?"

Everything seemed to be in fine shape. The Jones' had taken good care of the house, and paint would make it look brand new. "I think you made a wise investment."

Max slipped his hand in hers. "I think so, too," he said, lifting her hand and pressing his lips against her skin.

The closed-up kitchen had been warm before, but now it was getting hot.

"Do you like it?" he asked.

"What's not to like?" Virginia said, knowing she was being coy. But perspiration had broken out on her neck, and her pulse was hammering. His brown eyes searched hers, their warmth and depth reeling her in.

"What about Timothy?" he said in a low voice, stepping closer until there was only a breath of air separating them. "Do you think he'd like this house?"

"Max," Virginia said, placing her hand on his chest.

But instead of pushing him away, her fingers curled into his shirt. He lowered his head, and she found herself leaning into him. He kissed her softly, slow and sweet. Sunlight streamed through the dirty kitchen windows, rays of happiness dancing around them as Max drew her more firmly into his arms and deepened his kiss.

She felt herself spinning, falling, and not wanting to stop the rush of sensation from Max's touch. This man had somehow captured her heart and her mind so completely, that she barely remembered her life before he came into it.

"Vi," he whispered against her lips. "I bought this house for you and Timothy. We'll take things as slow as you want, but I want you to know that I've already made up my mind, and you already have my heart. Will you share it with me?"

Tears sprung to her eyes, and she wanted to laugh at the same time. She'd never known anyone like Max, and she had a feeling that she never would. There was only one Max in the world, and he was here, holding her in his arms.

She tilted her head back and looked into his eyes. "This is moving really fast."

"I know," he said, cradling her face with his hands. "If you want me to leave you alone, I will. Just say the word."

She closed her eyes as he brushed the lightest kiss on her lips. Then he released her and took her hand. She opened her eyes to find herself trapped by his gaze.

"I'm falling in love with you," he said. "You know what I want, and now you know how I feel. But if you think I'm a madman for doing all of this, I'll take you back to Milly's right now, Vi. You can tell me to get lost, and I'll honor your wishes." He looked down at their linked fingers. "Or we can check out the rest of the house and start making plans for our future."

He gazed at her expectantly, as if he were waiting for her to make his dreams come true—or to shatter his heart.

Virginia took a deep breath and steadied the trembling that had started in her hands. Then she placed her other hand over his and squeezed. "Let's look at the rest of the house, shall we?"

He grinned. "I'd love to."

ABOUT HEATHER B. MOORE

Heather B. Moore is a *USA Today* bestselling author. She writes historical thrillers under the pen name H.B. Moore; her latest are *Lost King* and *Slave Queen*. Under the name Heather B. Moore, she writes romance and women's fiction. She's one of the coauthors of The Newport Ladies Book Club series. Other works include *Heart of the Ocean, The Fortune Café, The Boardwalk Antiques Shop,* the Aliso Creek series, and the Amazon bestselling series A Timeless Romance Anthology.

For book updates, sign up for Heather's email list: hbmoore.com/contact
Website: HBMoore.com
Facebook: Fans of H. B. Moore

Braelynn's Blind Date

VICTORINE LIESKE

Chapter One

BRAELYNN SAT AT a table for two, trying to look interested in the book she held. Her stomach tightened as she glanced at the clock. Five minutes to six. Five minutes until her blind date showed up. Five minutes, and she could get her best friend off her back.

A pang of guilt shot through her. She shouldn't assume Kari's cousin would be a loser. It was just that she'd been set up so many times. She had little hope of finding Mr. Right by going on yet another blind date.

A man walked into the diner, setting off the bell over the door. He was good looking. *Very* good looking. Braelynn's heart pounded. Must not be her date. She'd never be that lucky.

He looked over at her and smiled, and her chest constricted. Was it him? Could it be? She tentatively smiled back. Good heavens, he was more than handsome. He had dimples, and his jaw line would surely land him on the pages of *GQ*.

He started toward her, and she put her book down. He was smiling at her. Walking toward her. Dang, he was hot. When he got close, she stood and extended her hand. "Hi. I'm Braelynn."

His eyes widened for a split second, like he hadn't expected her to introduce herself, but he quickly recovered and took her hand. "Hi."

Tingles shot over her skin at the warmth of his hand, and her mouth opened in surprise. "You must be Tyler. Please, have a seat." She motioned to the chair, which was dumb, because there was nowhere else he could sit. But her brain didn't seem to be functioning very well.

Tyler hesitated, and then he pulled out the chair and sat. He wasn't saying anything, and Braelynn's nerves took over. "I, uh, wasn't quite expecting you to be so... um... I mean, for a blind date, you're quite..."

Where was she going with this? Why was her mouth spewing out nonsense? She was an intelligent woman. She had a respectable job in the ad department of Fizzy Swig, a national soda company. She'd worked hard to get her job, and she was up for a promotion. Why couldn't she form an intelligent sentence?

His lips twitched, and he shifted in his chair. "Not used to blind dates, are you?"

"Oh, I've had my share. In fact, I think I've been on more blind dates than regular ones since my last boyfriend." She winced. In the blind date manual, it clearly stated not to bring up ex-boyfriends. *Way to kill the mood, Braelynn.*

He nodded, a thoughtful look coming over his face. "I understand. Since my breakup, all my friends have been trying to set me up as well." He leaned forward and lowered his voice. "It gets kind of annoying."

"Exactly!" Elation filled her at the thought that he felt the same way. They had a connection. She shoved her paperback into her purse. It was kind of a silly thing she did, but she always told her blind dates she'd be the one with her nose stuck in a book. It was a subtle way to let them know she was more than just a pretty face.

The door dinged and a man entered. Tyler glanced over. "Hey," he said, scratching his neck. "Do you want to get out of here? Go somewhere a little less... busy?"

He wanted to be alone with her? For a split second she wondered if it was a good idea. But he was Kari's cousin. It wasn't like he was a total stranger. And he didn't look like someone to be nervous about. He was well groomed, wore an expensive watch, and she had her cell with her, so it wasn't as if she couldn't call Kari if he started acting weird. Braelynn picked up her purse and stood. "Sure."

Nathan was in trouble. Why hadn't he told this lovely woman he wasn't her blind date? It would have been easy.

As soon as she said, "You must be Tyler," he could have said, "No, but I wish I was." Something cute and a little flirty.

Instead, he had plastered on a smile and said nothing. And now, instead of coming clean, he was suggesting they ditch the joint, in case the handsome chump who just walked in was this Tyler guy she was waiting for. Not a great idea. And why was he suddenly insanely jealous of a stranger?

Braelynn tossed him a smile and walked to the door, her perfect hips swaying.

Man, he was dumb. What was he doing? He followed after her, unable to think clearly.

"Where do you want to go?" She looked at him expectantly after they got outside.

"Why don't you pick a place?" He led her to his car and pushed the key fob.

Her eyes widened at his Ferrari. "*That's* your car?"

He shrugged and opened the door for her. He hadn't expected to meet a woman. If he had, he might have left his Ferrari at home. He'd rather not flaunt his money.

After he slid in behind the wheel, Braelynn turned to him. "We should go to La Carreta, on 84th and South. Do you like Mexican?"

"Love it."

"They have the best homemade chips and salsa."

"My mouth is watering already. I've been unpacking boxes all day, and I'm famished."

She squinted at him. "Unpacking?"

"Yep. Just moved in."

"Really? Where did you move from?"

"New York."

"I didn't realize you were new to town. Kari made it sound like you'd grown up here."

Tugging on his collar, he gripped the steering wheel and checked his rear view mirror. "I did grow up here. I've just been away for several years." It wasn't a lie. He'd grown up in Crimson Ridge.

"Oh. Huh. Okay. Kari's been trying to get me to go out with you for a while now. She must have been anticipating you moving back to town."

He smiled at her, hoping to change the subject. "So, Braelynn, where did you get your name? It's pretty, but unusual."

She blushed. "My father's name was Braydon, and my mother was Lynn. They wanted to name me after both of them, so Braelynn was the result."

"That's sweet." He glanced at her out of the corner of his eye. "You speak of them in the past tense."

"They were killed in a car accident when I was twenty."

The sadness that filled her eyes made his heart squeeze. "I'm sorry."

"It's okay." She lowered her lashes. "They lived full lives. No regrets. If they wanted to do something, they did it."

"Sounds like a good philosophy."

She crossed her legs, and he couldn't help but notice how nice they looked with her skirt flaring out. "I agree. Something I wish I was better at."

He raised an eyebrow. "You're not happy with your life?"

Braelynn fiddled with her purse. "It's not that. I'm happy. I love my job. Sounds lame, I know, but I've worked hard to get where I am. I'm actually up for a promotion, and I'll find out Monday if I've got it. I'm so nervous, I could spit."

She laughed, and he joined in. He'd never known a woman who talked like that. Most of the women he'd dated liked to act sophisticated. She was refreshing. "What kind of promotion?"

She bit her lip. "I'm superstitious, and I don't want to talk about it too much, or I just know I'll jinx it."

He chuckled. "Okay, then. We'll stay off the topic of work. But if you ask me, they'd be idiots not to give you the promotion."

She smiled and looked down at her lap. "Thanks."

He pulled into the restaurant's parking lot and found an empty space. He should tell her. Now, before they went in.

She turned to him. "I'm so glad Kari set us up. You're nothing like she described. I was worried I'd have to sit and listen to you drone on about algorithms and such." Her hand flew to her mouth. "Not that computer work is boring. I didn't mean to diss your job. Kari says you're amazingly smart."

Nice. Tyler is a tall, dark, handsome computer genius. How could Nathan compete with that? He swallowed and got out of the car. Maybe he would wait to tell her. The problem was, the more time they spent together, the more awkward things became.

How was he going to come clean?

Braelynn couldn't believe she'd played the blind date lottery and won. Tyler was courteous, intelligent, thoughtful, and successful—and he smelled like a slice of heaven. The whole time they'd been eating, he'd been witty and kind. Their conversation hadn't once bored her.

Things had gone so well, they'd decided to take an evening stroll in the park next to Valley River. Could she dare to hope he had no horrible skeletons hiding in his closet? Was it too much to think he was sincerely interested in her?

As they walked, Tyler reached out and captured her hand in his. A warm feeling overcame her, and butterflies started dancing in her stomach. She had just met the guy, but she felt like he was something special. Was she falling for him on the first date?

"What would you say is your number one life goal?" Tyler gazed down at her, his face serious.

She gave the question some thought. A huge part of her life had been climbing her way up Fizzy Swig's corporate ladder, but she knew work wasn't the most important thing to her. She thought of her relationship with Scott. She'd always hoped they'd get married and start a family. Good thing that didn't happen. "I guess having a family has always been my number one goal."

A warm smile spread across Nathan's face. "Mine, too." He squeezed her hand.

Oh, yes, she could fall for a guy on the first date, because she was falling—and falling fast. How could a guy be so perfect? He had to have some flaw, right?

They watched the sun set over the river, and her pulse quickened. How could she ever thank Kari? Her parents had always said they'd fallen in love the first day they met, and Braelynn had thought it was just an expression. But now, she understood. You could have an instant connection with someone.

Tyler took her back to her car they'd left in front of the diner. He walked her to her Toyota, then stopped and rubbed the back of his neck. "Before we end the date, I have to tell you something."

She looked up at him. "Okay. But first, I want to thank you."

He raised an eyebrow. "For what?"

"For redeeming the male population."

His features softened. "Was it a rough breakup?"

Scott's face popped into her head. "All breakups probably are. But it was better than staying with a liar."

"He cheated on you?"

"Cheated, hid things from me, and lied about everything except his name. I found out I didn't even know his real occupation. It was devastating." She blinked away the moisture making her vision shimmer. "I think honesty is the most important part of a relationship. And Scott… he was so good at lying. I think he did it sometimes just for the heck of it."

Tyler's face paled. He looked down at the sidewalk.

"I can't tell you how much it means to me," she said, "to know there are honest guys like you out there."

Tyler didn't say anything, so she continued. "I'm glad Kari pushed me to meet you."

He didn't meet her gaze, and she fiddled with her fingers. Was she was coming across too forward? "I'm sorry. I didn't mean to make you uncomfortable. Here I am, running off my mouth and you're probably wondering what kind of a crazy lady I am."

He smiled and reached up to touch her face. "Not at all."

She looked into his deep blue eyes, and the bottom dropped out of her stomach.

He leaned closer. "I think you're amazing," he whispered.

His baritone voice took her breath away, and a crazy impulse overtook her. She closed the distance and brushed her lips against his. Why she thought kissing him was a good idea when two seconds earlier she'd been afraid of scaring him off, she didn't know. Maybe she'd been lonely too long.

He seemed surprised by her bold move, but soon his arms encircled her. He pulled her to him. He took command of the kiss, his lips sending sparks of electricity through her.

She'd been kissed before, but kissing Tyler was like nothing she'd ever experienced. His strong arms and masculine scent combined with his soft lips caressing hers made her heart pound out of her chest. She grew dizzy.

When he finally pulled away, she was left breathless and weak. An odd look came over his face, and he backed away from her. "Thank you for an unforgettable evening."

She fished out her phone. "Can I have your number?"

He took two more steps back. "I'll have Kari give it to you."

Kari? Why would he have Kari tell her? That didn't make any sense. "Just tell me, and I can program it in my phone right now."

He swallowed and looked like he'd been caught stealing a cookie. Braelynn's heart sank. She knew that look. She'd seen it too many times on Scott when she'd cornered him, and he'd had to come clean. Nathan was lying about something.

But instead of giving her a lame excuse, he rattled off a number, and she punched it into her phone. Maybe she had been mistaken or read him wrong.

"Bye, Braelynn." He looked so apologetic, she knew she wasn't imagining it.

Something wasn't right.

He rushed to his car and was gone before she realized she was holding her breath.

She was left staring after a trail of exhaust, wondering what had happened and feeling a heaviness in her chest. Her big win had just turned into a bust, and she had no idea why.

Chapter Two

BRAELYNN'S PHONE VIBRATED while she searched through her purse for her keys, alerting her to some unread texts. She stared at the screen.

6:35pm Kari: You stood up Tyler? How could you? You promised you'd meet him.

7:29pm Kari: Call me. Where are you?

8:12pm Kari: Are you okay? You're worrying me. Call me. Now.

Braelynn scowled at the phone and turned off the silent mode. How did Kari get so mixed up? She punched her friend's name and waited for her to answer.

"Brae? You okay? Why weren't you answering your phone?"

"I'm fine. I've been out." She opened her car door and plopped down.

"Tyler's crushed you blew him off."

Braelynn squinted in her rear view mirror, pulling out onto the street. "I didn't blow him off. He's the one who started acting funny."

"What are you talking about? Tyler showed up to the diner right at six, but you weren't there."

Braelynn's mouth fell open. "That liar! We went out on a date. He just dropped me off."

"Honey, Tyler's been sitting right here for the past hour."

Braelynn slammed on her brakes, her heart hammering. "What? Tyler's there?" And then comprehension slowly dawned. She pulled off the road. "Just a sec. I have to call you back."

She stabbed the phone and called up the number Tyler…
or not Tyler… had given her. She got a recording. The number
wasn't in service.

Anger surged through her, and she gripped her phone.
That… that man had pretended to be Tyler. He'd coaxed her
out of the diner. She'd gotten in his car! Fear crept up her
neck. Who was this guy? Her palms grew sweaty as she dialed
Kari back.

"Kari, I need to talk to you. I'm coming over."

"What happened?" Kari's voice sounded concerned.

"I'll tell you when I get to your apartment."

Braelynn's hands shook as she related the story to Kari.
The real Tyler sat staring at her as if she had two heads.

Kari interrupted, holding up her well-manicured hand.
"Wait, did he introduce himself as Tyler?"

Braelynn hesitated. "No, I guess not. I just assumed."

"So he used the misunderstanding to his advantage. Did
he try anything?" She put her hand on Braelynn's arm. "He
didn't hurt you, did he?"

"No," Braelynn said, thinking back over the date. "He
was a perfect gentleman."

Tyler scoffed at her. "Really?"

"Yes."

"He didn't ask you for money, or try to get you to go
home with him?" Kari asked.

She shook her head. "No, it wasn't like that. He was—
nice."

Kari made a face.

Tyler snorted. "Nice? He lied to you."

Braelynn bristled. Why was Tyler being such a jerk? "All
he did was talk. And he held my hand when we walked
through the park."

Kari's eyes grew wide. "You went to the park alone with

190

this man? Oh, honey, I'm so glad he didn't drag you in the bushes and slit your throat."

Braelynn had to admit, she felt betrayed by what the man had done. But she'd felt perfectly safe with him, even though she was angry he'd lied. "I don't think he was trying to do anything shady."

"If he's not shady, why did he give you a fake number?" Kari folded her arms across her chest.

Her anger surged. Kari was right. He should have told her the truth. There was no reason to lie to her. Even if it had been her fault for assuming he was Tyler, he should have come clean.

But instead, he'd lied about it. Just like her ex.

She clenched her hands into fists. Were there any honest men out there?

Nathan cursed his stupidity. He should have told Braelynn who he was right away. He'd spent the entire time wondering what kind of a jerk her ex was to give up such a wonderful woman. Smart, full of life, beautiful... she was perfect. How could someone have let her slip away? He realized, too late, that he'd been doing the same thing her boyfriend had. Lying to her. Deceiving her. Hurting her.

Stupid.

And in the end, he'd been too much of a coward to tell her the truth. So, instead, he'd ducked out. Tucked his tail between his legs and disappeared on her. Given her a fake number, for heaven's sake. Who does that?

Guilt bubbled up in him. He'd been horrible. But there was nothing he could do about it now. He didn't even know her last name.

He took a deep breath and let it out slowly. Monday he started his new job, working directly under his father. He'd bury himself in his work and forget all about the spunky woman who took his breath away.

Chapter Three

MONDAY MORNING BRAELYNN thrummed her fingers on her desk. In ten minutes, Mr. Davidson would announce the new department head. She was a shoe-in. In fact, he'd mentioned her determination and drive several times over the last month. He knew she wanted this more than anyone.

She tried not to think about the man she'd taken to calling Mr. Ferrari. She had no idea what his end game had been, but he was gone, and there was nothing she could do about it. Which didn't stop her from fantasizing about bumping into him on the street and slapping him in the face. The mental image gave her a little satisfaction.

The intercom clicked and Mr. Davidson's voice came on. "Would everyone meet me in the conference room? I'd like to introduce you all to our new head of advertising."

This was it. Braelynn grabbed her folder, both to look busy, and also because she'd jotted down a few notes in the corner in case he asked her to make a speech.

The conference room was large, but it was incredibly crowded by the time she got there. Many people were standing, but she felt conspicuous. She sank into one of the last conference chairs near the back. She didn't want to look too eager, or worse, as if she were assuming she had the job.

A movement at the front of the room caught her eye, and she leaned to the side to see who was up there with Mr. Davidson. She couldn't tell. Some guy with a short haircut.

Mr. Davidson cleared his throat. "Thank you for gathering here this morning. I have an exciting announcement."

The guy with the haircut moved, and Braelynn leaned over even further. She could almost see his face. Who was he? Did he get her job? Was it Fred in sales? He didn't even want the position, and he was hardly qualified.

"After ten years out on his own, my son's finally agreed to come back to the family business—to take over our ad department. Please welcome Nathan Davidson."

Everyone applauded. Everyone except Braelynn. She was too stunned to move. She'd lost the promotion, and to family no less. How could she compete with that?

The room quieted down, and another man started speaking. "I'm honored to join this fine team."

That voice. She knew it. A prickle worked its way down her spine. She leaned over one more inch, and his face came into view.

Mr. Ferrari.

She sucked in a breath just as the chair shot out from under her, and she landed on the floor in a loud clatter. Everyone turned to look at her.

Heat assaulted her face as she slipped back onto the chair and tugged on her skirt. "Sorry," she said, ducking her head and hoping beyond hope that Nathan didn't see her.

"Are you okay, Miss?" Nathan peered through the crowd and their gaze connected. His mouth dropped open, and for a fraction of a second Braelynn thought he was going to say something. But he regained his composure and shifted his weight, waiting for an answer.

"I'm fine," she mumbled, clutching her folder to her chest. Fine if she didn't count her utter humiliation.

The meeting didn't last too much longer. Nathan thanked everyone, Mr. Davidson said how wonderful it would be to be working alongside his son again and that there was cake in the break room, and then he dismissed everyone.

Braelynn shot out of her chair and made sure she was first out the door and down the hall. She thought she heard someone call her name, but she ignored it as she fast-walked to her cubicle. Unfortunately, she had no office door to shut, so she plopped down in her chair and pulled up her current project on her computer. Anger and embarrassment made her hands shake. Maybe he would ignore her. Pretend the whole thing never happened.

After a few minutes of undisturbed working, she started to relax. That is, until Mr. Davidson showed up. She swiveled in her chair to face him.

"Braelynn, I wanted to thank you for all you've done for Fizzy Swig."

Wait, what? He was firing her? Panic climbed its way up her throat. "I love working for Fizzy Swig. Please don't let me go."

"Let you go?" He drew his eyebrows together in confusion. "I'm not firing you. I'm promoting you."

"What?" The room swirled.

"I'm promoting you to Assistant Head. I know you wanted the Head of Sales position, but I don't think you're quite ready for it yet. But as Assistant Head, you'll get to work closely with Nathan. The position comes with a ten percent raise, and you'll get your own office, next to my son's."

She stared at Mr. Davidson, his words sinking in. She was getting a promotion. But she would have to work with Mr. Ferrari.

Super.

"Um…" She forced a smile and shook his hand. "Thank you."

"You can gather your things and move today. Oh, and my son says he wants to speak with you right away in his office. I'm sure he just wants to introduce himself and congratulate you."

Sure, that was what he wanted. Braelynn nodded and mumbled another thank you. After Mr. Davidson left, she buried her face in her hands.

Tanya peeked over her cubicle, her curly red hair bouncing. "You did it! You got a promotion!"

Braelynn tried to act enthusiastic. "Yes."

"It wasn't the big one, but you're one step closer. You deserve it."

She smiled up at Tanya. "You're right. I should think positive."

Tanya gave her a big smile and a thumbs up, then ducked back down into her space. Tanya was always bubbly. Fitting, that she worked at Fizzy Swig.

Braelynn's stomach churned as she walked down the hallway to Nathan's office. His door was slightly ajar, and she hesitated for a moment before walking in.

Nathan looked up from his desk, those mesmerizing blue eyes of his penetrating her. He motioned to her. "Please, would you come in and close the door?"

Her nerves quickly melted into anger as she entered and stood before the man who had lied to her face the whole time he was with her. She left the door open, folding her arms across her chest. "What, are you afraid I'm going to yell at you, and the whole company will find out what you did?" The petty side of her hoped her voice would carry, and someone walking by would hear.

His face blanched and he swallowed, guilt consuming his expression. "I wanted to apologize."

"Oh, this should be good. Go ahead, then. Apologize." She glared at him.

He glanced at the open door, stood, and crossed the room. She stepped out of his way as he closed the door and turned to her. Even though she was livid, his cologne made her stomach flutter. "I'm sorry," he said. "I tried to tell you, but you started going on about honesty—"

"Wait." She held up a hand, silencing him. "*That's* your apology? It's *my* fault you lied?"

"No." His cheeks flushed. "That's not what I meant."

"Scott used to blame me, too. It was always my fault he couldn't tell me the truth, because of how I'd react."

"That's not what I'm saying."

He seemed flustered, so she stayed quiet and let him speak.

"When you mistook me for Tyler, at first I was too surprised to say anything. But then you started talking, and I wanted to get to know you. I found myself… mesmerized by you. I never meant to let you believe I was Tyler all the way through the date, but as time passed, it became harder and harder to tell you."

"How uncomfortable for you," she snapped. "So much more awkward than it was for me when Kari told me I'd stood up Tyler. That I had, in fact, not been on a date with her cousin. That I'd gotten in a car with a total stranger!" She shoved Nathan's chest, partly because she wanted to emphasize her words, and partly because he was getting too close and she needed the space.

"I'm sorry—"

"No. I'm not done. I want you to think about how I felt when I called your number and got a recording. How I felt when I realized I didn't even know your *real name*. And, just for fun, imagine how I felt when I came to work today to find out the jerk who did all of that is taking *my promotion!*"

He opened his mouth, but no words came out. He closed his mouth and took a step back, shaking his head. "You're right. I am a jerk."

"Ya think?" she shouted. Instantly, she regretted it and clapped her hand over her mouth. Boy, she was losing it. What was it about this man that made her do crazy things?

Nathan shoved his hands into his pockets and took another step back. "Can we put this behind us? My father's counting on us to work together on an important rebranding."

Nathan had her there. Unless she wanted to walk off the job—which was tempting but unrealistic in this economy— they had work to do together. She'd have to suck it up and pretend their fake date hadn't happened. Ignore the fire that burned inside her every time she thought about how he'd lied.

She clenched her jaw. "Fine. But understand that I will never forget what you did."

She shoved her way past him and out the door.

Tuesday morning, Nathan buzzed Braelynn and asked her to come into his office. He couldn't put off talking with her anymore. Yesterday, he'd watched Braelynn storm out, guilt eating away at him. She was right, about all of it. He hadn't had the guts to do the right thing, and he'd hurt her, thinking she'd get over it if they never saw each other again. Really bad plan.

He'd watched as she walked back and forth past his window, moving her things into her new office, but he didn't bother her for the rest of the day.

The temperature in the room dropped fifty degrees as Braelynn entered. She took a seat in the chair next to his desk and crossed her legs, a tablet on her lap.

"Thanks for coming in." When she didn't respond, he forged ahead. "What Fizzy Swig needs is new branding. Our current logo was created fifteen years ago. We need to update. Along with this new look, we need a new advertising concept."

She jotted down a note. "I've been saying that for the past year," she mumbled under her breath.

"Good. Then we're on the same page."

She looked up at him, straightening her back. "Okay. Are we done?"

He frowned. She wasn't going to make this easy, was she? "No. We'll need to work on this together."

She slumped back in her chair. "Okay."

As they dove into the work, Braelynn seemed to relax a bit. Neither one brought up the awkwardness between them, and it slowly settled into the background. At one-thirty, Braelynn's stomach made a loud gurgling noise, and Nathan chuckled. "Sorry, I didn't realize it had gotten so late. We should break for lunch. Want to go together?"

She bristled. "I usually eat a sandwich at my desk."

Ouch. Okay, so she didn't want to eat lunch with him. Fine. He smiled politely. "Okay. I'll order something in. Come back when you're done eating."

"Sounds good." She was out the door before he could blink.

Chapter Four

BRAELYNN HAD TO work closely with Nathan for the next three weeks as they tried to come up with a whole new look for Fizzy Swig. They had been working with the team for ideas, but nothing was coming together. As the deadline drew closer, they knew they needed to bang out something to present to Mr. Davidson on Monday.

Braelynn sighed. She was having a devil of a time concentrating. Each time she inhaled, the smell of the insanely handsome jerk behind the desk took her thoughts in a direction she didn't want them to go. He was not the nice guy he pretended to be. He was a man without integrity, and she needed to stay far away from someone like that. The connection they'd had wasn't real. At least, that's what she kept telling herself. But working with him these past few weeks had been hard on her.

Why did he have to have heart-stopping dimples? It wasn't fair. Each time he laughed, the sound washed over her, making her insides turn to mush. Not to mention that her skin betrayed her with excited little shivers every time their fingers accidently brushed. She couldn't wait until they were done with this project, and she could breathe normally again.

Nathan scrubbed his hand over his face. A collection of logos and sketched ideas lay on his desk. "If we go in this direction, we'll appeal more to the kids." He lifted one card with a cartoon-looking logo. "But demographics show it's the adults who are buying our soda."

"Who wants to buy a serious looking bottle of Fizzy Swig? Our branding's never gone in that direction." She pointed to the other logo mockup. "We might as well be peddling Pepsi."

"Which is a multi-billion dollar company."

"Yes, but they don't sell a…" She fished around the cards until she found the one she wanted and lifted it. "Cotton Candy flavored soft drink."

He nodded. "You're right. This is not a serious soda company. We have to stay on brand, whatever we decide for the new look."

She looked outside at the setting sun. "It's getting late. I'd better go eat something or I'll regret it."

"Why don't I order something to be delivered? We're up against the deadline. We need to make a decision."

She reluctantly nodded her head. She didn't want to make a habit out of it, but if they didn't eat together it would just mean staying even later. "Fine."

"What are you in the mood for?"

"There's a sub shop up the street."

"Do you want to just run over there together?" He said it nonchalantly, but an underlying tension made her think he was holding his breath, waiting for her answer.

It was silly to keep pushing him away. They were stuck together, for the meantime at least. Might as well make the best of it. "Sure."

He smiled and stood, pulling on his jacket. "Great. I could use the exercise."

She stopped by her office and grabbed her purse, and then they started down the hallway. The cubicles they passed were empty. The central lights were off since everyone else had gone home, but it wasn't completely dark until they turned a corner and headed toward the elevator.

Braelynn focused on the exit lighting. Apparently, she was too fixated, because her foot hit something, sending her reeling.

Nathan reacted instantly. His strong arms wrapped around her, keeping her from kissing carpet. She stared up at him in the dim hallway, her heart pounding. Her throat closed as her body melted into his.

"Sorry," she croaked out, determined not to sound breathless.

"You okay?"

"Yeah." She pulled away from him and looked down. "I think I just tripped over my own feet."

"Well, at least you didn't fall off your chair. That would have been embarrassing."

She slugged his arm. "Funny."

He chuckled and warmth pooled in her stomach. Why did he have to be so charming? Gah. She needed to get outside and breathe some fresh air. They stepped into the elevator, and she pressed the button, willing the doors to close.

"My father is hoping I'll groom you for my job," he said.

She jerked her head to look at him. "What?"

"He likes you. Thinks you're a capable woman. He wants you to learn from me, then take over when I leave."

"You're leaving?"

"Don't sound so happy. I might take it as an insult."

His tone was teasing, and she smiled.

"But," he said. "I didn't mean leaving the company. Just transitioning away from head of advertising. My father wants me to take over so he can retire."

Something about the way Nathan said it made her brow wrinkle in confusion. "You don't want to?"

He hooked his thumbs into his pockets. "It's not that, really." The elevator dinged and they exited. "I just have no passion for the business. I mean… it's soda."

He held the door open for her, and they stepped out onto the street.

She'd probably regret asking, but it came out anyway. "What are you passionate about?"

He just stared ahead. She waited him out, and he finally smiled down at her. "Not soda."

Well, that was ambiguous.

Maybe his passion is lying about who he is. The thought had popped into her head without warning, and she mentally scolded herself. He was trying to be nice. The least she could do was give him a break.

They walked the two blocks to the sandwich shop and stood in line, waiting their turn.

"You must have experience in advertising," she said. "Otherwise, your father wouldn't have put you in charge of it."

"I majored in business and minored in marketing. Mostly to please my dad. It wasn't difficult for me, since I'd grown up working for him."

She nodded. "You have good instincts."

His dimples came out in full force. "Did you just pay me a compliment?"

"It slipped."

His laugh filled the sub shop.

⁓⁓⁓

Relief washed over Nathan as he and Braelynn ate. Suddenly, she was the woman he'd first met a few weeks ago. Playful and funny, and not giving him death glares. Maybe she wouldn't hate him forever after all.

"Where did you go to school?" he asked, because up to now she'd refused to share any details about her life.

Her cheeks colored. "I started out at Boston University, but had to quit college when my parents died. Your father gave me a job when no one else would. I started at the bottom. Worked my way up."

"How far at the bottom did you start?"

"Cleaning toilets." She laughed. "Not very glamorous, but I told Mr. Davidson that I was a hard worker, and he told me to prove it. I scrubbed bathrooms for two years. He promoted me to a clerk job after that."

"I'm impressed you worked your way up into the advertising department. I mean, it's not usually something you can learn on the job."

"I took online classes when I could. And I kept giving your father ad campaign ideas." Her gaze met his. "I think he got tired of me bothering him."

"He never told me any of this. He must have liked your ideas."

"I appreciate that he gave me a chance."

"He's a good man." Nathan took a long swig from his bottled water.

Braelynn nodded, tucking her hair behind her ear. "And that's why you don't want to disappoint him."

Nathan didn't deny it. Instead, he changed the subject. "It's why we need to get this re-brand right."

Chapter Five

BRAELYNN WAS GAPING at Nathan. "You've never tried Fizzy Swig's signature soda? French vanilla? Our most popular flavor?"

They'd been at the office for hours. The sun had long since set, and they were no closer than before to their re-branding proposal. It was looking more and more as if they'd be spending their weekend working on it.

He sat back in his chair and toyed with the logo sketch in his hand, offering her a sheepish grin. "I've never been much of a soft drink guy."

"I know, but didn't you grow up helping your dad build this business?"

"Yes. But on the management side of things."

"Surely you've tried some of your own product."

"Some. I'm just not that into soda."

She tugged on his arm. "Then we need to do some market research, pronto. Come on."

He acted like he didn't want to stand, but his lips twitched and belied his amusement. "All right."

She dragged him to the break room and flipped on the light. Mr. Davidson kept a refrigerator stocked full of company product, free for employees. "We're trying eight flavors. You pick four, and I'll pick four."

She grabbed a French vanilla first, then a mango peach. She picked out a pomegranate, and last, a roasted marshmallow. Nathan wasn't as decisive. He finally settled on a sugar cookie, a cinnamon bun, a red hot tamale, and a salted watermelon. Braelynn pocketed a bottle opener.

They carried their stash back to his office and set them down on the desk. Braelynn grabbed two small cups from the water cooler stand. She handed him one. "Which do you want to try first?"

"Signature flavor?" He reached for the French vanilla.

She popped the top off, and he poured some for her, then himself.

She lifted her cup and pretended to clink it against his. "Bottoms up."

They both drank the soda. Braelynn eyed him as he finished.

He cocked his head to the side. "It's sweet, but not too sweet. It's smoother than I would have thought. And definitely tastes like Fanilla."

"You like it?"

He considered her question. "Yes. As far as soda goes, this isn't bad." His long eyelashes gave him almost a boyish look.

She ignored the way her stomach flip-flopped. "Good. Now pick another one."

He selected the salted watermelon, and she opened the bottle. Nathan winced this time, his eyes squinting, his mouth twisting.

Braelynn laughed at his obvious disgust. "No good?"

He choked, trying to swallow. Then he opened and closed his mouth, apparently trying to get the taste off his tongue.

She giggled. "Take another drink of the French vanilla."

He downed a swig straight from the bottle. "That helped. A little. Are we done yet? Please tell me we're done."

"Nope. Six more to go." She shouldn't be deriving as much pleasure as she was at his pained expression. She picked up the mango peach. "This has mass appeal, whereas the salted watermelon is an acquired taste."

Braelynn's Blind Date

They each tasted, and Nathan nodded. "I actually like this one a lot."

They continued to sample their selections, with only one other choking incident—this time, the red hot tamale.

"Spicier than I expected," he croaked.

Which left them both cracking up.

Nathan finally set aside his cup and turned to her. "You've shown me something."

"What?"

"Fizzy Swig isn't just for kids. I mean, the kids drink it, but I see the appeal now for the adults. It's fun. It brings a little bit of... nostalgia."

"Yes!"

"It reminds me of when I was a kid, and I'd get a bag of Jelly Belly's, and we'd try each one, guessing what flavor it was, and making disgusting faces at the ones we didn't like."

Braelynn smiled to herself. He'd hit the nail on the head. The Fizzy Swig "adult" customer was nostalgic for some harmless fun, trying out different flavors like their kids tried new trends in candy. For the adult, a Fizzy Swig purchase wasn't the same as buying a Coke or a Pepsi. It was an adventure, like her and Nathan's tasting party just now.

"My idea is that Fizzy Swig for adults would sell best as a sampler set. A small taste of each soda we sell, packaged in various combinations."

Nathan's eyes lit up. "Brilliant idea!" He shoved some papers aside and pulled out a pen. "With a more stylized logo. Something reminiscent of the good old days."

"Maybe a fifties style font?"

"More eighties. Something techie."

While he rough sketched, she jotted down slogans in her notebook. Energy surged in the room as they worked. They compared notes and ideas, and by two o'clock in the morning, they had a finalized idea.

Nathan held up his drawing. "Fizzy Swig. Just plain awesome."

209

The slogan and the logo were perfect, and Braelynn clapped her hands. "Love it."

He rubbed his eyes. "Good, because I'm so tired, I could fall asleep right here."

"Me, too."

Nathan pushed his chair back. "Come on, I'll walk you to your car."

The suggestion was innocent enough. Braelynn knew that. But she cringed, flashing back to their date. Still, she didn't want to walk through the parking garage by herself. She nodded, and he led the way.

In the elevator, he turned to her. "Thanks for staying late and working on this with me."

"Sure."

Suddenly lost in his blue eyes and the memory of their one amazing kiss she couldn't take in enough air. She fought not to glance toward his lips.

Why was she still hung up on this guy? Especially right now, when they were alone, in the elevator? She didn't want to think of that kiss, or the way she'd felt with him on their fake date. He couldn't be trusted on a personal level, and she couldn't ever forget that.

The elevator doors opened, and she practically ran out into the parking garage. Nathan kept up with her, following her to her car. She beeped the doors unlocked and tossed a quick smile at him.

"Thanks." She hopped in and slammed the door, her heart pounding.

Good grief! She was like a school kid with a crush. She was doomed if she couldn't even be around him without going all wobbly kneed. She'd been ignoring her body's responses to him over the past few weeks, but it was getting worse.

She needed to get her head on straight! Maybe some sleep would help?

Nathan waved as he walked toward his car, his dimples making her mouth water. She groaned.

Yes.
Sleep.
That would fix everything.

Chapter Six

MONDAY MORNING, BRAELYNN rushed into the office building, five minutes late. Everything had gone wrong that morning. She hadn't been able to find her left shoe, she'd burned her hand on the toaster, and her car hadn't started. Thank goodness a kind woman had given her a jump, but now she needed to take the heap to the shop.

She hoped Nathan had waited for her before presenting their ideas. As she rounded the corner, she saw his office was empty. She tried the door, but it was locked, which meant he wasn't in yet. Good. At least she wasn't holding up their presentation.

After plopping down in her office chair, she took a deep breath. Centering herself for a moment, she looked outside at the gathering storm clouds. It would be raining in another hour.

Mr. Davidson popped his head into her door. "Nathan tells me you guys came up with a great idea." He smiled. "Come to my office whenever you're ready."

"Okay. He's not in yet, but we'll come down as soon as he gets here."

"Sure thing." Mr. Davidson pointed at her and did his mouth clicking thing. He probably thought he looked cool doing that. He didn't.

Stifling a laugh, she opened up the file folder for the campaign she and Nathan had worked on into the early hours of Saturday morning. His drawings weren't in there. She shuffled through the stack of papers, not finding them. She couldn't have lost them! Nathan must have taken them with him. She picked up her phone and dialed his cell.

The line rang four times before he answered. "Hello?" His voice was low and muffled.

"Nathan? Did you just wake up?"

"What? Oh, no. My alarm didn't go off." He groaned. "I'll hop in the shower and be right there."

"Your father's anxious to see the new ideas we came up with. Where are the sketches?"

He hesitated. "They're here. I wanted to see if they still looked as good the next day. I'm sorry. I shouldn't have brought them home."

She sighed. If she were being paranoid, she would be assuming right about now that he was trying to do something underhanded. But with plans for him to take over the company, there wasn't any need. Especially since his heart wasn't in the business. "That's okay."

"Why don't you come get them? You can present them, and if he has any questions I'll be in soon." He rattled off his address. "There's a key under the mat."

"Really? Under the mat? 1960 called. They want their hiding place back."

His deep chuckle made her smile. "The presentation is on my desk. You'll see it when you come in."

She hung up the phone and grabbed her purse. Five minutes later, she pulled into his parking lot. She probably shouldn't have, but she'd stopped to pick up his favorite coffee. A dumb move, but she'd grown closer to him over the weekend, and wanted to do something nice for him.

His apartment complex had a modern, industrial feel. The doorman waved her inside. "Nathan's expecting you."

"Thanks." She pressed the elevator button to Nathan's floor and waited, clutching her folder and his coffee. The doors swished open, and she stepped in.

His apartment was the first one outside the elevator, and she made sure no one was looking before getting the key from under the mat and unlocking the door. When she entered, she drew in a sharp breath. His loft apartment was stunning. The open space and exposed brick combined with the modern fixtures made the space warm and inviting. But what caught her attention the most were the beautiful sculptures artfully placed around the space.

In the entry stood a life-sized wire sculpture of a pregnant woman, looking down at her swollen belly, hands covering it protectively. It sat pushed up against the wall and had some kind of white board erected behind it. Emotion swept through her as she stared at the image. The sculpture was made out of wire, almost like a line drawing but in three dimensions. It was beautiful, although she couldn't figure out why a bachelor like Nathan had such a sculpture in his home.

She took a few more steps into the apartment, and she became aware of the sculpture's full effect. The shape of the woman disappeared as Braelynn walked and her perspective of the sculpture shifted. Fascinated, she kept circling the piece, its lines continuing to move and shift.

Suddenly, another image snapped into place. Now, she was looking at a mother cradling her infant child. Braelynn gasped, and her hand flew to her mouth. The sculpture was pure brilliance. She understood why Nathan had to have this piece. It was remarkable.

She turned and gazed at other installations as she walked further into the apartment. Sculptures made from clay, glass, and metal made the place look like a gallery. Large picture windows filled the far wall, letting in light and giving her a spectacular view of the city. Then she spied the desk sitting in the far corner and strode over to it. Their ad images lay in a neat pile, and she scooped them up and slid them into her folder.

"Good, you found them."

His voice startled her, and she jumped and turned around. But he wasn't there. She glanced up and saw him in the loft area above, leaning on the railing, his hair wet. He was shirtless, and she looked away, terribly embarrassed by the way she'd just checked out his abs. *Really* nice abs. Dang!

She stared down at the Styrofoam cup she held. "I brought your favorite morning beverage."

"Black, one sugar?"

"Do you want me to put it in the kitchen?" She chanced a glance at him.

He'd slipped into a shirt, and was buttoning it. He grinned. "You're a lifesaver. I'm on my way down."

As he started down the steps, she couldn't help but stare at him. He could easily land a modeling gig. She turned away. She didn't need to be thinking of him like that.

When he took the coffee from her, their fingers brushed. "Thanks."

The way he said it—packed with hidden emotion—made her heart pound. "You're welcome."

He took a sip and that heavenly smile graced his face. And suddenly he was close. Too close. She could feel the heat from his skin, as if they were touching. Shouldn't she be getting back to the office? She took a step back and bumped into the desk.

She lifted her folder. "I'd better go. Your father…" She left the rest hanging and squirmed away from him.

"Okay." Nathan nodded, frowning. "I'll finish getting ready and be there shortly."

She gave him a half-hearted wave and started toward the door. The sculpture of the woman with the child stopped her. She pointed at it. "This is amazing."

He shoved his hands in his pockets. "You think so?"

"Yes. You must have spent a fortune on it."

He shrugged.

"I wish I knew how this was done," she said. "The artist is extremely talented."

He cleared his throat. "Thanks."

She stared at him, realization dawning. "You did this?"

"Yeah."

Her heart squeezed inside her chest. "Nathan, this is stunning. You… are amazing." What a beautiful expression of a mother's love. She glanced around. "Did you sculpt all of these?"

"Yes."

"Is your work in a gallery?"

He ran a hand through his wet hair. "No."

"Why not? Doesn't your father approve?"

"It's not that. It's just… I don't want to disappoint him." He took a breath and the rest rushed out. "I know he'd support me, whatever I decide to do with my life. But me going to business school made him happy. Then I left the company to pursue my art. And even though he didn't try to stop me, I could tell he thought it was a mistake. When I agreed to come back, he was so excited and proud. He'd be crushed if I left again."

"Couldn't you do both?"

He lifted his eyebrows at her.

"You're good at the business stuff, even if soda isn't your passion. You could run the company and work on your art on the side."

"I'm sure I could. I just…" He left his sentence hanging, and shook his head. "I should let you go."

She took a step toward the door. "Think it over. This stuff is too good not to be in a gallery."

The smile he gave her was soft. Appreciative. "Thank you." His cell buzzed, and he glanced at it. "That's Dad. I'll let him know you're on your way."

She nodded and left his apartment.

217

Chapter Seven

BRAELYNN CLIMBED INTO her car, parked on the street beside Nathan's apartment building, and tossed the folder on the passenger seat. She couldn't get that sculpture out of her head. Nathan had an amazingly soft side to him, to be capable of crafting something so pure and touching. What did his art say about him? His goals in life? He'd said he wanted a wife and family, but she'd discounted that as one of his lies. Maybe she shouldn't have.

She turned the key. The engine didn't turn over. She whacked the steering wheel with her palms and tried again, praying it would start. A clicking noise sounded, but nothing else. As if on cue, rain began pouring onto the roof.

Now what? She didn't have any roadside assistance. And she really didn't want to go back inside to admit to Nathan that she was stranded. How professional was that? He was Mr. Ferrari. He'd never understand her situation. She called Tanya.

"Hello?" Tanya's voice was chipper, as always.

"I need a jump start."

"Where are you?"

"I'm sitting on the corner of 27th and Cottonwood."

"What are you doing there?"

"It's Nathan's apartment building."

Tanya made a high pitched sound. "Whaaaaat! Did you spend the night with him?"

"What? No! I'm here for work." What would Tanya spread around the office now? "Just come give me a jump, okay?"

"I'll have to ask Mr. Davidson."

"Fine. Whatever. Just get here fast." Braelynn hung up, extremely frustrated. Lightning streaked across the sky as rain pelted her windows. A few seconds later thunder crashed. The temperature had dropped about ten degrees since she'd arrived.

She took out her phone and scrolled through her email messages. Nothing important had come in that morning. She took a minute to file the ones she didn't want to delete and was just about finished when there was a knock on her window, startling her.

Nathan stood in the rain, his suit getting wet. She rolled down her window a crack.

"Dad called. Said you couldn't get your car started. Instead of sending Tanya, he asked if I would help. Why didn't you tell me?"

Great. Just what she didn't want. Here she was, trying to loathe him for lying to her, and he was not only an amazing artist and a good son, but now he was a damsel-in-distress rescuer. She didn't know what to think of him anymore. Heat crept to her cheeks. "I don't know."

He smiled and motioned to the front of her car. "Pop the hood."

How totally embarrassing. She wanted to crawl under her seat, but instead she did as he directed. She then noticed he'd pulled his car around, nose to nose with hers.

After he gave her the signal, she turned the key. Her car sprang to life.

"Thank you," she called out the crack in the window.

He came around, put his arm on the top of her door and peered in, rain dripping from his face. "There's a shop up about five blocks. I'll follow you."

"You don't have to—"

He held up his hand to stop her. "You'll need a ride."

She couldn't argue with him. And she really did need to get her car fixed. She sighed and nodded. He jogged around to unhook the cables. She felt a surge of emotion for his genuine willingness to do whatever it took to help her and make sure she wasn't stranded again.

At the shop, she explained to the mechanic what she thought was going on with her car. As she and Nathan left, he opened his passenger door for her, and she once again slid into his Ferrari. She swallowed the hurtful reminder of the first time she'd been in his car with him. She shouldn't dwell on such things. He was doing his best to redeem himself.

"Thanks," she blurted into the awkward silence that filled the car as he drove. "I mean, it was really nice of you to follow me to the mechanic. I should have arranged for another car when I found out mine wasn't starting." And now she was rambling. Nice.

They'd arrived at Fizzy Swig, and he pulled into his parking spot. "It was nothing."

"You're soaked."

"I'll dry."

He got out and walked around the car. He helped her out, and she couldn't ignore the tingles when they touched. She quickly let go of his hand, and took a step back. She couldn't afford to start thinking of him as her knight in shining armor.

Nathan hated the way Braelynn backed away from him whenever he got close. As if he had the plague or something.

For the thousandth time, he wished he could go back in time and do over their first encounter. If he could, he'd tell her right away who he was. He'd be funny and charming and ask for her phone number, and then he'd leave her to her real date and hope she'd call. Getting to know her the way he had these last three weeks, he was almost certain she would have.

He pressed the elevator button and the doors swished open. He motioned for Braelynn to enter before him, while his heart ached to hold her in his arms the way he had the day they'd met. He wanted back that kiss they'd shared, the one he'd wanted to reclaim less than an hour ago in his apartment. He kept hoping she'd come around, but they were running out of time.

Once they made their presentation to his father, Nathan would lose his business reason to see her every day.

They entered his father's office, and Nathan motioned for her to start. Braelynn showed his father the drawings they'd worked on over the weekend and explained the overall concept. The presentation went well. Braelynn was articulate and very capable. Qualities that just made her more appealing to him.

She wrapped up her presentation, and his father sat looking at the drawings. "You're going with an 80's theme?" He rubbed his chin, frowning at the images.

Braelynn shot Nathan a panicked look.

"Yes." She rushed on. "We feel the 80's image will bring back the nostalgia of our customers. The wording of the slogan and the design will appeal to our audience. Based on the demographics of who is buying Fizzy Swig—"

His father raised a hand. "It's okay. You've sold me." He smiled. "And I like the sampler idea."

Relief poured over her face, and she smiled.

Nathan stood. "I knew you'd like it," he said to his father. "Braelynn's ideas are top notch."

"Well, it wasn't just me. Nathan played a big role in the strategy, and his artwork for the branding is brilliant."

Nathan's father nodded. "I look forward to seeing what you come up with for television and magazine spots."

"We will start working on them right away." Braelynn shook his hand. "Thank you."

She and Nathan left and walked down the hallway. She followed him into his office and, once inside with the door closed behind them, squealed, throwing her arms around his neck. "We did it!"

At first, he didn't know how to react. He carefully put his

arms around her and inhaled the light scent of her shampoo. Vanilla and almond. Quite sexy. She felt so right in his arms. He never wanted to let her go.

She pulled back and grasped his hands, her smile brightening. "I'm so glad he liked our concept!"

"Me, too."

His heart pounded at their close proximity. Electricity seemed to sizzle between them. Did she feel it, too? She sobered as their gazes connected.

Braelynn was amazing. These past few weeks he'd spent with her had shown him she was right for him. She was kind, and supportive. Spunky, and tenacious. She wasn't afraid to work hard for what she wanted.

He longed to show her how he felt. He leaned down a fraction of an inch, wanting her kiss. But as before, he didn't want to rush her. Would she close the distance?

Time slowed as she flowed toward him. Almost as if she couldn't help herself, she closed her eyes and their lips met tenderly, the softness of her touch igniting a fire deep within him.

He cupped her face with his hands and kissed her more passionately. She wrapped her arms around him, pulling him closer. His body came alive. Kissing Braelynn was like sucking energy from the sun. He wanted nothing more than to be in this moment with her, feeling her needing him in return.

She moaned and pulled away, gasping. Her eyes widened as if she'd only just then realized what she'd done. "Sorry, I—"

"Braelynn…" Her name came out broken. He had no idea what else to say. His emotions swirled around in him, and he decided to put everything on the line. "I think I'm falling in love with you."

She blinked at him in shock. Then she slowly backed away, throwing up an emotional wall that turned her expression to stone.

"Please." She shook her head. "Don't."

It was too soon. She wasn't ready. Panic settled deep, but he couldn't take the words back. They were true. And he suddenly wasn't sorry that his growing feelings for her were out in the open.

He grabbed her hands with his. "I would do anything to take back what I did. But I can't. Isn't there any room in your heart for forgiveness?"

She stared at him, and the seconds ticked by. He could see the indecision on her face. He waited, his heart in her hands.

"I… I can't," she whispered, and fled from the room.

Chapter Eight

Two months later, Braelynn sank into her chair and wiggled her mouse, bringing her computer screen to life. She'd been avoiding Nathan, ever since their earth shattering second kiss. The day Nathan had told her he was falling in love with her. Why had she allowed that kiss to happen? He never would have said what he had if she hadn't thrown her arms around him and let him think she was interested in anything but a strictly-business relationship. She'd been foolish. Caught up in the moment.

The only logical next step had been to retreat, and she had. She'd dodged his every attempt to get close again. Of course, they saw each other because they worked together. But she'd made sure work was all there'd been between them. She no longer looked him in the eye. In fact, these days she never looked at him at all if she could avoid it. Lunches were spent alone in her office. She hadn't brought him any more morning coffees. She'd stayed aloof, and that was just how things had to be.

The only problem was convincing her heart. Nathan kept turning out to be everything she wanted in a man... except for the way he'd so easily lied to her. When she was cold to him, he nevertheless greeted her with a warm smile. He politely asked each day if she'd like to go to lunch, and he didn't get upset at her continued rebuffs. When she worked in her office whenever possible on their joint projects, he ignored the obvious snub. When they did work together, he was patient with her and showed her what she would need to know when she took over his position.

He was almost the perfect guy. It was the "almost" part that ate away at her. She'd cried herself to sleep too many times over Scott. She couldn't do that to herself again.

She clicked on the magazine copy that needed her approval. The words refused to sink in. If she thought any more about Nathan, she'd go insane. Maybe she'd take the afternoon off. She needed a breather.

Mr. Davidson knocked on her open door, then walked in. "May I have a word with you?"

She turned toward him and motioned for him to sit. "Of course."

He pulled the leather chair closer to the desk and sat. With his elbows on the arm rests, he steepled his fingers and tapped his chin, which usually wasn't a good sign. Dread wormed its way into her chest.

"Is something wrong?"

"No, I just wanted to tell you that next week I'll be promoting you to head of advertising. Nathan claims you're ready, and I agree. You've shown great work here, Braelynn. I'm quite proud of you."

Elated, she clasped her hands, forcing herself not to squeal with excitement. "Thank you, Mr. Davidson."

"Call me Thad."

"Thank you, Thad." It sounded weird, and felt awkward, but she'd call him Pumpkin Head if that's what he wanted. He'd just given her the job she'd been working toward since forever.

He cleared his throat. "I'll be retiring next week as well." His face fell.

"I'm sure Nathan will do a great job running the company," she assured him.

His eyebrows raised. "He hasn't told you then?"

Confusion set in. "Told me what?"

"He isn't taking over. Some art gallery in New York wants

to represent his sculpture. He's moving. Heading out tomorrow."

Her heart pounded in her chest. Nathan was leaving? Why didn't she know about this? Instant regret filled her, and she pushed it away.

"Oh." She mentally smacked herself for her ignorance. She'd been too busy avoiding him.

"I haven't officially announced it yet, so please don't say anything until I do, but I'm selling the company. Rob Granger will be taking over." His frown deepened in disappointment, and she felt horrible for him.

"I'm sorry."

He smiled. "No, it's okay, really. I need to let go of this image in my head. I just assumed Nathan would succeed me. But it's not in his blood like it is mine, I guess." He shifted in his seat. "He's got his own ambitions, and I'm proud of him for sticking it out here as long as he did. He'll go far in this new world of his."

Remembering his amazing sculptures, she nodded. "Yes, he will."

Mr. Davidson stood. "Well, I'd better go talk to the other department heads. Congratulations on your promotion. You deserve it, Braelynn."

She didn't know if it was appropriate or not, but she came around the desk and gave him a hug. "Thank you. You've always been so good to me."

He squeezed back. "I'm proud of you."

He left as she blinked moisture from her gaze. Why on earth was she so emotional about Mr. Davidson leaving? Or was it not only him that she'd miss? Could it be…?

She wrung her hands and looked at the wall that separated her office from Nathan's. She should go talk to him. Congratulate him. Leaving things as they were wouldn't be right… Right?

Her stomach knotted as she walked through Nathan's door. The shelves were empty. There were a couple of boxes on the floor, with his things piled inside. He was busy typing on his computer and at first didn't notice her. She took a moment to look at him.

He was handsome, there wasn't any doubt about it. So good looking, he made her weak in the knees. But there was more to it than that. She respected him, she realized, surprising herself.

He glanced up and froze. He stared, and then he sighed. "Braelynn."

"You're leaving."

"Don't sound so happy. I might take it as an insult." He smiled, but it didn't reach his eyes.

She tried to force herself to laugh at his joke and failed. A hole opened up in her chest. "I... wanted to wish you luck."

He sobered, and looked back at his computer. "Thank you."

He was retreating from her, like she had so many times from him. Which was to be expected after the way she'd treated him, but it still stung.

She blinked, unable to think of anything else to say. She was getting exactly what she'd thought she'd wanted. She wouldn't have to work with him anymore. No more happy greetings. No more invitations to lunch. She didn't have to worry about him professing his love to her ever again.

And it felt terrible.

She twisted her fingers and stared down at the carpet. She should go. Let him finish up. There was only an hour left on the clock. He probably had things to do. But her feet wouldn't move.

He stopped typing. "Did you need something?"

"I..." What did she think she was going to say? That she was sorry for the way she'd treated him? That she wished she'd given him a second chance? A real chance?

She looked away. "I don't know if I can do this."

He stood and crossed the room, but he stayed at an arm's length. "You excel at whatever you do. Of course you can."

He'd misunderstood and clearly thought she was nervous about taking over the department. When what she was really trying to say, in her own clumsy way, was that she didn't want him to leave. But that was dumb. She needed her life to get back to normal, and the only way that would happen was if he left, so she could stop thinking about him all the time.

"Thanks," she said.

His Adam's apple bobbed as he swallowed. "I'm glad you got your dream job."

She nodded, but the emptiness inside her was expanding. She took two steps back. She had to get out of there. "I'm glad you're fulfilling your dreams, too."

Before he could say another word, she left, the pain of never seeing him again an unbearable reality she'd just have to get used to.

Chapter Nine

TANYA WALTZED INTO Braelynn's office, a grin on her face. "Hey, girlfriend, how're you doing?"

Braelynn smiled and turned away from her computer. Tanya was always a breath of fresh air. Braelynn needed that this morning. It had been weeks since Nathan's move to New York. But the smell of his cologne lingered in his office, and the constant reminder of him was driving her nuts. She had no business sitting around sniffing the air, wondering what he was up to.

"I'm fine," she lied. "What can I do for you?"

Tanya slapped something down on her desk. "Look who's debuting next week in a SOHO gallery."

Braelynn stared at the full-color brochure, featuring the sculpture that had so mesmerized her. It was named, "Woman with Child." Her heart squeezed at the sight of Nathan's photo on the back.

"Mr. Davidson sent a bunch of them. Mr. Granger wanted me to pass them around." She grinned. "He's looking good, right?"

Braelynn sighed and tossed the brochure on the desk. "Yes."

Tanya cocked her head. "You missing him?"

"No, I just have so much to get done."

Tanya's eyes narrowed. "You know lying to me doesn't work."

"I'm not lying. I just…" What was she doing? She was missing him. Terribly. And then it hit her. She *was* lying. She was lying to Tanya, and to herself.

Tanya waited, but Braelynn couldn't finish. She couldn't even breathe. She had pushed Nathan away for lying, even after he'd apologized and explained that he hadn't meant to. And here she sat doing the same thing.

Did that mean she didn't deserve forgiveness, either?

Tanya waved her hand in Braelynn's face. "You zoning out on me?"

"Yes." She blinked, her focus snapping back. "I'm sorry. I just realized something."

Tanya smirked. "You're going to New York, aren't you?"

Was she?

"Do you love him?" Tanya asked.

Braelynn matched her friend's grin and accepted the truth she'd fought for so long.

"Yes," she said timidly. "I suppose I do."

"Ha, that's great!" Tanya bounced on her toes. "Then go get him!"

Braelynn smoothed a hand down the skirt of her cocktail dress and tried not to fidget. What was she going to say to Nathan? Words had been twisting in her mind all day as she waited in the airport and sat on the plane, but none of them seemed adequate. She'd convicted, tried, and sentenced him unfairly. And now she needed to make it right.

She studied the sculpture before her. It was of an arm, reaching up, the hand never quite grasping whatever it was seeking. The fingers were thin and bony with broken fingernails, the arm frail, and Braelynn could feel the desperation. Whatever this person was focused on, it was destroying them.

Then she read the title and sucked in a breath. 'Braelynn.' Nathan had named it after her.

Was that how he felt about her? That she was destroying him? Her vision blurred.

Maybe coming here had been a bad idea. Maybe what

she'd done to him was irreparable. She turned and headed toward the gallery's expansive glass doors.

A man with a tray of hors d'oeuvres veered into her path. To avoid a collision, she took a quick step backwards. And it was at that moment that her heel decided to wobble, and she tripped over her own feet. She landed unceremoniously on her rump, everyone in the room turning to stare.

"Braelynn?" Nathan's voice cut through the gasps that followed, and he appeared as if by magic.

She tried to stand up. Nathan extended his hand, and she grasped it. He unsuccessfully attempted to mask a smile. "What are you doing here?"

She tugged at her dress, making sure everything was covered that should be. "I... uh..."

What was she doing there? All rational thought left her brain when she looked into his eyes.

"I came to see your art," she blurted out.

Surprise briefly brightened his expression before he masked it. "Thank you."

In the throes of a full-body blush, she desperately needed air. "I actually was just leaving. It was nice to see you again." She brushed past him, exiting the building into the cool night air. A steady stream of traffic rushed by.

"Wait," he said, rushing to join her at the curb.

She caught the look of desperation on his face. The same desperation he had captured so well in his sculpture. She swallowed. "I'm sorry. I shouldn't have come here."

He was close enough to touch her, but kept his hands to himself. "Why *did* you come?"

"I..." Her words abandoned her again, but she needed to tell him. She had to get this out, everything, once and for all. "I realized that I've done to you the same thing I've been so upset about you doing to me."

He raised an eyebrow but didn't respond.

"I lied to you." She took a breath and rushed on. "I lied to myself, too. I thought I was protecting myself, but instead,

I was covering up my feelings. And I shouldn't have. When I realized I was lying… I realized how completely unfair I'd been to you."

He took her hand, a sizzling energy spreading between them. "Unfair?"

"I thought… I was so sure that if a man lied, it meant he would always be a liar. But I was wrong. We're all human. We make mistakes." She blinked back tears. "And I've made a big one, hurting you in the process."

He wiped her cheek with the pad of his thumb, then cradled her face in his hand.

She reveled in his touch and the open, honest connection between them that she could finally allow herself to feel.

"I'm sorry," she whispered, closing her eyes and praying that she hadn't waited until it was too late.

He wrapped his arms around her, and she laid her head on his chest. Being there, in his arms, at that moment felt like nothing else. She breathed in his smell, allowing the warmth of his embrace to envelop her.

"I love you, Braelynn," he said in the deep voice that had haunted her dreams.

His words washed over her, emotion making her throat tight. "I love you, too."

He kissed with a hunger that she gave into and returned with her own.

She needed him. All of him, not just the perfect parts. Sure, he had flaws, and she accepted them. Loved them, even.

Someone nearby sounded off a wolf whistle, and Nathan pulled away, laughing. He pressed his forehead to hers. "Come with me. I want to show you something."

He led her back into the art gallery and to the sculpture of the hand. "I named this one after you."

Her chest grew heavy. "I'm so sorry I made you feel this way."

A puzzled look crossed his face. "What?"

"I never meant to hurt you so badly."

He turned her to face him, his gaze piercing. "This isn't me. It represents you. All that you've strived to achieve and accomplished in your life. This is you, succeeding, even through life-altering challenges. You've reached past the pain, and have never stopped pursing your goal." He blinked, and swallowed. "I wanted a visual reminder of how much I admire the way you've worked your way up from the bottom."

She stared at the sculpture, seeing it in a new light. He understood how difficult it had been for her. He was applauding her for her hard work and tenacity—for achieving what she'd always wanted. And he'd done it so beautifully, she ached.

"I... I don't know what to say."

"You don't have to say anything," he assured her. "I have one more I want to show you."

They walked through the gallery, past people crowded around different sculptures, until they came to one against the wall, in the corner. She recognized the style from the Woman with Child. A line drawing, in air. The sculpture depicted a man and a woman, holding hands.

She knew if she walked to the other side, she'd see something different, and she couldn't wait to experience how it transformed as she moved. Nathan led her to the other side, where the man was down on one knee, and the woman had her hands over her mouth.

When she looked back at him, he was down on one knee as well. She gasped.

"Braelynn," he said. "I don't have a ring, because I didn't know you were coming tonight. But you are my inspiration, for more than this sculpture. I didn't know real love, until I met you. You have brought me the greatest joy I've known. Your smile lights up my day, and your laugh leaves me longing to hold you. And now, I don't want to wait another minute before asking you. Will you marry me?"

A crowd of people had gathered around them, as soon as Nathan had dropped to his knee.

Braelynn blushed, but her embarrassment didn't stop her from answering. "Yes, I'll marry you."

A cheer rose up, and Nathan stood. He lifted her off her feet, swinging her in a circle until she laughed, her world spinning out of control. A sensation she once would have feared, but now, in Nathan's arms, nothing could have felt more right.

Epilogue

NATHAN STOOD ON the front porch, taking in the sunset, his arms around his wife. It still felt weird to think of Braelynn that way. They'd only been married a few months.

She gazed up at him. "Do you miss New York?"

He brushed a hair from her face and smiled. "No."

He'd moved back to Crimson Ridge after he proposed. The gallery was willing to work with him long distance, as long as he flew out for events. He'd only moved to New York because it had broken his heart seeing her every day at work and knowing he couldn't have her.

"Good." She snuggled up to him. "Manhattan's no place to raise kids."

"Kids?" His pulse rate sped up. "Are you saying what I think you're saying?"

She giggled. "It's time to create another sculpture. How about calling this one Wife with Child?"

He hugged her close, laughing, too. "Are you sure?"

She nodded, her eyes sparkling.

Overjoyed, he brushed his lips across hers. They were going to be parents. She wrapped her arms around his neck and deepened their kiss. When they broke apart, he traced his finger down her face. "You're the most beautiful person I know."

"You're not so ugly yourself."

He loved the way she looked at life. She was driven, and he loved that about her. "So you're not disappointed I'm not a genius computer programmer?"

VICTORINE LIESKE

She laughed. "I tried to have a conversation with Tyler, after my date with you. He was condescending and rude."

"Maybe because you'd just stood him up?"

She shook her head. "He acted like he was doing me a favor, just talking to me. He and I wouldn't have gotten along."

"I'm glad." He took her hands. "I couldn't stand thinking of you with him."

She lifted an eyebrow. "Is that why you didn't tell me I'd mistaken you for Tyler?"

"One reason. I was talking to a beautiful, interesting woman, and I didn't want to stop. And then a man walked into the diner. Your real date. He was handsome, and I was sure he'd sweep you off your feet."

"Handsome? What did he look like?"

"Tall, black hair. Muscular."

"Are you kidding me? Tyler's blonde. And really skinny. And definitely not handsome."

He blinked. "You mean I lied to you to keep you from meeting a man that wasn't even Tyler?"

She slugged him. "Way to go, Romeo."

He shook his head. "That's what I get for assuming."

She snuggled up against him again, a light breeze carrying with it the smell of the lilac bush growing in their front yard. "I don't care anymore how we met. I'm just glad we did."

He kissed the top of her head. "So am I." He hugged her close and watched the sun slip below the horizon.

ABOUT VICTORINE E. LIESKE

Victorine Lieske self-published her first book, *Not What She Seems*, in April of 2010. In March of 2011, *Not What She Seems* began its 6-week run on the *New York Times* bestselling eBook list. By August 2011, she had sold over 140,000 copies. Victorine's first romantic comedy novel, *Accidentally Married*, hit the *USA Today* bestselling books list in January 2015.

Victorine is the immediate past president of the Nebraska Writers Guild. She is active in many writing groups and forums and has given dozens of interviews for TV, radio and print media and has been a panel member and keynote speaker at several major events, including The Business of Writing International Summit.

Victorine lives in western Nebraska with her husband and kiddos. She loves all things romantic, and hordes craft materials like there's going to be an apocalypse. She's also a graphic designer. She loves reading clean romance novels and spending time with her hubby.

Website: VictorineLieske.com

Facebook: Victorine Lieske

Bianca's Hope

(A Lily's House Novella)

RACHEL BRANTON

Chapter One

Bianca

THE FIFTEEN MINUTES of waiting in the small conference room at the Phoenix law firm Eaton & Eddington made me feel claustrophobic, despite the wall of windows overlooking the wide corridor. I wished Stephen Carey would hurry. It was bad enough needing an attorney in the first place, and waiting had only increased my anxiety. I still didn't know how I was going to pay, but if I didn't act, the past eight years of work and everything I'd created could be ripped from me.

I pulled out the little white card and stared at the silver embossing. I didn't remember who'd given it to me, but it was in my purse with two others I'd gathered in the past month since I'd discovered someone was using my logo on pottery that closely resembled my signature designs. I'd chosen this appointment with Mr. Carey because his name sounded familiar, and because I liked the artsy, interlaced E's on the law firm's logo.

The door opened, surprising me with the suddenness of the motion. I straightened as a man in a dark brown suit entered the room, filling up the small space even more. "Hi," he said with a smile. "You must be Bianca Mendez. I'm Stephen Carey. Sorry to keep you waiting—and sorry to startle you."

"No, it's fine." I stood and shook his extended hand, my eyes having to travel far up to reach his face. At five-foot-three, I had to look up at a lot of people, even in ultra-high heels. Our gazes connected as his fingers closed over my hand. His eyes were blue, the color of the sky on a brilliant summer afternoon, and framed with short brown hair that made them more prominent. For a moment I couldn't find my breath. He was handsome in a way that set my heart skipping beats. I had expected someone a lot more . . . stuffy.

His hand retracted quickly from mine as if touching fire. "Please have a seat." He indicated the conference table.

I tried not to be offended. "Thank you, Mr. Carey."

"Please, call me Stephen." He sat in the chair kitty-corner to mine.

I couldn't help noticing there wasn't a ring on any of his fingers. If we'd met under other conditions, I'd try to find out more about him. A man hadn't made my heart skip like this since my freshman year in college.

No, I warned myself. *Keep it professional.*

He took out a pen and laid it next to the pad of paper he'd set on the table. "Before we begin, I want to clarify that I'm an intern with Mr. Eddington. I'm currently in law school, and while I've been studying law for several years, I am not yet an attorney. What I can do today is discuss your case and let you know your options. If we proceed from here, I'll likely be working on your case. Which is good for you, because my involvement will cut down on attorney fees. But Mr. Eddington would be attorney of record."

"So you're not an attorney?" I'd just assumed he was, since someone had recommended him. "I thought they gave the first consultation here—with an attorney—for free."

"Oh, yes, absolutely. But since we're here, and Mr. Eddington's in court today, why don't we talk a little about your case? Afterwards, if you decide to continue, we'll set up a joint meeting with Mr. Eddington."

Something in his tone made me bristle, as if he didn't expect me to continue past our consult. Was he not taking me seriously? And why not? It wasn't as if I was wearing ratty jeans. And I was almost certain I'd gotten all the clay out of my hair from yesterday's attempt at my pottery wheel. I'd even slipped on fancy high heels before heading into the law firm.

"What do you mean *if* I decide to pursue the case? I don't have any choice."

"Maybe not. So, someone is using your logo?" He leaned forward, tenting his hands on the table. He suddenly felt too close.

I inched back in my chair. "Yes, his name's Kent Fletcher. He runs a pottery shop here in town. I first learned about him using my logo a month ago." Four weeks ago to be exact, while I was still recovering from surgery after the accident caused by the big storm. "Two days ago when I tracked him down, he practically admitted what he's been doing. But when I said I was going to seek legal help, he just laughed and said to have my attorney talk to his."

"Did he say who his attorney was?"

"He gave me a card, but I don't have it with me." It was crumpled on the floor of my truck. "He's also using my designs. But I know copycats are always out there. I just want him to stop using my logo. It's my initials—very distinctive. A large B with an opening and M inside the bottom curve of the B. I've been using it for eight years. Since high school and all the way through college. Here, I'll show you."

From the pocket of my suit coat, I extracted a small, blue-marbled, fluted candy dish I'd made, turning it over to show him my potter's mark. "I carve one into each of my pieces."

He examined the dish before placing it on the table. "It's unique. Did you file a trademark?"

"No." My mouth suddenly went dry. "Is that bad?"

His lips tugged downward into a slight frown. "It makes your claim more of a hurdle, especially if someone else has trademarked it in the meantime."

Frustration flared inside me. "You mean it doesn't matter if I've been using it for eight years? That can't be right! I'm

245

finally starting to be noticed. I have regular orders from retailers, people are beginning to ask for my work—for quality, handmade pieces. But last month when I contacted my clients to set up a time to show them my latest patterns, four of the shops I called had already bought dozens of new pieces from Fletcher. Pots that all had my logo on them."

Those orders represented half my potential quarterly income, and just thinking about the loss made me panicky. Maybe if I hadn't been injured two months ago, I'd have been able to contact the retailers sooner and Fletcher would have had less opportunity to step in. I breathed deeply and waited several heartbeats before adding, "And they weren't even good pieces."

"So, not like your work?"

What was he implying? "No. I mean, yes, they were copies, but bad copies. Uneven formation, ragged edges, poor artwork, improperly glazed." I dug in my purse for a second piece of pottery, a different color, but similar. "See? This dish isn't symmetrical. The glaze is spotty, and the logo is completely lopsided."

"But the owners of the shops felt this man's work was good enough to sell to their customers?"

"His pots are less expensive," I clarified. "I don't know how this Fletcher can afford to live off what he's charging—unless he's paying a bunch of kids next to nothing to make pots for him in his shop."

"Wouldn't be the first time." Stephen made a face. "Unfortunately, it happens."

"I'm not some big-time artist. Why would he target me?"

"I'd have to do some legwork to answer that definitively, but my bet is that you've cut into his market by offering quality pieces, so he's pushing back."

"How can I stop him from using my logo?" Was that desperation coming from me? "Shops are thinking it's my stuff—so are customers. He's going to ruin my name, my livelihood."

Stephen leaned back and folded his arms, his eyes intent on my face. What did he see? A strong, independent woman with a college art degree? Or a part Latina girl who was too stupid to trademark her own logo?

"We can send him a notice to cease and desist," he said, glancing at his watch, "and maybe file an injunction. But without a trademark backing us, and given his reaction when you confronted him, you may have to sue to get him to stop permanently. Even to file the lawsuit, we'd be talking in the range of seven thousand dollars. If he's trademarked the logo in the meantime, it'll be an uphill battle to prove you used the mark first."

Was he kidding? I couldn't breathe again, and this time it had nothing to do with his proximity. "There's no way I've taken that much business from him. Would he spend so much to defend himself?"

"It costs a lot less to respond to a lawsuit, at least in the beginning. His attorney may advise him to let you sue him, hoping you'll give it up because of the expense."

"Then what can I do?" To my utter mortification, tears threatened behind my eyes.

"Well," Stephen said, "you have a case for common trademark and copyright violations, but speaking from experience, the expense of proving it would likely be far more than what you'd want to spend. A lawsuit could cost one hundred to three hundred thousand dollars, depending on how willing this guy is to keep your logo. And damages are almost impossible to obtain without a registered trademark. There are attorneys who will take cases like yours on contingency—receiving money only if they win the case—but that's usually when it's a corporation or wealthy individual who has infringed on a trademark."

"I see." No, I would not give into tears. Not in front of him. He'd barely heard a few details and already he'd made a judgment. He had no idea what this meant to me.

"Miss Mendez, I know this isn't what you want to hear, but perhaps you should consider redesigning your logo and filing a trademark for it instead."

As if that would be so easy. "And what's to stop him from stealing the new one?"

"In that event, you'd have proof, and it would be easier for a judge to order him to stop. You'd also have a better chance of winning statutory damages."

I surged to my feet. "I don't want to design a new logo. This one is mine! And by using it, he's cut my clients by half!" Or more.

Slowly, Stephen rose, too, and I lost my height advantage. "I understand that he's in the wrong. I just want to be clear about expectations before you pursue any legal options." His voice became placating. "Aside from the money, a lawsuit takes a huge emotional toll on people."

"Having my life's work stolen is already emotional." In fact, since returning to work in the past two weeks, I hadn't created a single piece that was worth selling. "You know what, you said it yourself—you're not even a real attorney. I think I'll find someone who is." I turned and strode the four steps to the door.

"Miss Mendez," he called. "If you want to meet with Mr. Eddington…"

I continued out the door and down the corridor without a backward glance. That negative intern was not getting me down. I would find a way to fight this with a *real* attorney at a better law firm who would believe in me and my work. There had to be some justice in the world.

There had better be, or I'd be starving soon.

Chapter Two

Stephen

BIANCA MENDEZ STALKED from the conference room with all the grace and taut energy of an angry tiger. I couldn't help stepping to the door and watching her petite figure until she rounded the turn. I didn't blame her for the emotion; many people were frustrated when they realized how hopeless a case could be. How costly. Three times I tried to call her back, but the words caught in my throat.

I didn't know what I'd expected when the scheduling assistant returned Ms. Mendez's call and set up our appointment, but it hadn't been this firebomb dressed to kill in a form-fitting suit that set off her slender curves and especially those gorgeous legs. From the moment I'd walked into the room, she'd brought out every bit of protective desire inside me. Especially because what she'd told the assistant about her personal situation led me to believe there was no way she could afford to pursue this lawsuit.

That was the reason I hadn't scheduled her to meet with Eddington. He was one of the best attorneys I knew, but he wasn't averse to letting a client pay out whatever life savings she had before urging them to drop the case and go on with their lives. In the past two months, I'd seen too many clients regret filing lawsuits, even though they were clearly in the right.

Eddington also wasn't one to take on pro bono work that didn't boost his career, and Mendez's case had nothing to entice him. Well, except for Mendez herself—but Eddington was happily married.

I looked back at the conference table, replaying the scene in my mind. I should have taken it more slowly and let her talk through her anger. If I had explained her situation more gently, more tactfully, maybe I could have convinced her that she'd only victimize herself further if she pursued the matter. Instead, I'd been distracted by those golden brown eyes and the touch of her hand.

Well, I'd never see her again. Even if I called and asked for another meeting, she would probably ignore me. I just hoped the next attorney she sought out had the guts to tell her the truth like I had instead of immediately taking her money.

Alternatively, I could track down some of the shop owners she sold wholesale to, and find out what they knew. But what was the point?

My phone gave a soft chime, alerting me that it was time to prepare for my meeting with Eddington about my own case—or rather, my uncle's. Then I had to drive three hours to a blind date that would probably end in disaster. Despite that thought, some part of me hoped that this evening would somehow turn out to be exactly what I needed. I'd been too busy these past months to bother with women.

After the date I'd be close enough to my aunt and uncle's place to drop in for an overnight visit. They'd supported my decision to stop managing their exotic wildlife sanctuary, but in the six weeks since I'd come to Phoenix to intern at Eaton & Eddington, things between us had been slightly awkward. The strain in our relationship bothered me. They were the only parents I'd ever known.

My eyes fell on the candy dishes that my almost-client had left on the table. Ms. Mendez would probably return for them. Too bad, because the blue-marble one that she'd made was really quite good, and I would love to use it in my office. Maybe I could buy it from her to assuage the guilt I shouldn't be feeling after speaking honestly with her about her legal standing.

Eddington was right. I'd better grow some backbone, or I was going to be the poorest attorney in the history of the world.

I picked up the candy dishes and took them to my office. The blue dish felt smooth in my hand, still warm from the woman's pocket.

A feeling settled on my shoulder, one that felt a lot like regret.

Maybe during Monday's lunch hour I'd call around to a few pottery shops. It couldn't hurt, even if Bianca Mendez never knew I'd tried.

Chapter Three

Bianca

I HEFTED MY last bag, threw it into the passenger seat of my pickup, and stared up at Lily's House one final time. It was silly, the nostalgia that filled me at once again leaving, because I'd be coming back to visit often. This weathered, sprawling house had been the first real home I'd ever known, and it represented everything Lily, my foster mother, had been to me and so many other girls over the years. Most of my happy memories were tucked into the nooks and crannies of the house, except a few of my early ones with my older sister, Zoey, and our mother before her death.

With all the changes in my life, I felt myself clinging to my memories of Lily's House. I still didn't know what I was going to do about my logo—or winning back my customers.

"You're always welcome to come home whenever you want."

I lowered my gaze to see Lily on the front porch, her creamy white skin, blond hair, and blue eyes a decided contrast to the darker features of the baby in her arms. After dozens of foster girls and two sons, Lily finally had her own daughter, one who looked just like the baby's European daddy.

I went to hug Lily. "Thank you for taking care of me."

"You sure you're ready to leave?"

"I don't mean just after the accident. I mean since I was a kid."

"Aw, sweetie." Lily pulled me tighter into her one-armed embrace. "You're welcome. I've enjoyed every minute."

I knew that couldn't be exactly true. I was ashamed to admit that I'd gone through a period of time when I'd made Lily cry and stay up late worrying—something Zoey still didn't let me forget.

I couldn't resist taking the baby from Lily's arms. Cherie owned a heaping handful of my heart, like she did with all the foster girls. "It's been two months. The cast is off my arm, the scar on my stomach is practically invisible, and that annoying boot is no longer dragging me down." I pounded on the cement with my foot, now comfortably clad in a flat sandal. "Ankle barely twinges, unless I try to put on heels. The doctor says I only have to wear that smaller brace if I'm hiking or swelling too much. So I'm good to go."

"I guess you're excited to get back to your pottery full-time."

I wished that were completely true, that the panic hadn't removed so much of my joy and the desire to create beautiful things. "I do need to concentrate on working. Plus, Zoey needs me in Kingman. It's not good for her to live alone in a strange city." I'd been driving to Zoey's to move in with her on the day of the accident. Today, I'd finally complete that trip.

"Doesn't Zoey have a new boyfriend there? He's probably keeping her busy."

"That's exactly why she needs me. They've only known each other, what, three months? Dating for only two. I know they work together, but she's already hinting at marriage and about changing her whole life. I need to make sure it's the real thing."

"I thought you said she was happy."

"Zoey's happy working with the animals, yes. But suddenly thinking about grad school to become a vet because of them? It's crazy. He might be pushing her."

Lily laughed. "It's crazy to you because you're an artist.

Your sister loves science. Whether or not she marries her boyfriend, she'll make a perfect vet."

"Well, you're right about that." I kissed Cherie's dark hair and reluctantly handed her to Lily. "It will be a few weeks before I can visit—or pick up the rest of my things." The three-hour drive to Kingman wasn't that long, but one I dreaded. "Once I get my pottery wheel set up at Zoey's, I have to concentrate on making up lost time." Or try to.

My eyes strayed to where the wheel sat in the back of my truck with the rest of the equipment Lily and her husband had helped me move from their shed this morning before I'd driven their car to the attorney's office. Once the wheel had been my best friend; now I almost dreaded seeing it. But the move to Zoey's should help.

Lily hugged me again. "Have a safe trip. Promise me you won't take that road."

She meant Hackberry Road, the unpaved one where I'd had the accident—though the cause had been a terrible storm, not the road. "I'll be fine. Isn't that what my new pickup is all about?"

New to me, I meant. The compact Ford had four-wheel drive and a bed big enough to carry a lot of inventory. It would be a lot better for my line of work than my old car had ever been. "Anyway, I'm taking the I-40 right to Kingman. Don't worry. I'll call when I get there."

I didn't add that I still had nightmares about the hours I'd sat huddled in the trees by Hackberry Road, hoping my car didn't wash away in the sudden storm.

No, I didn't plan to go anywhere near Hackberry Road ever again.

What I would do is move to Kingman, somehow resolve the problem with my logo, and create wonderful designs again so I could help Zoey pay our rent.

As I pulled out of Lily's driveway, my thoughts wandered to Mr. Carey from the law firm. I'd been thinking almost continuously about our conversation while I finished getting ready for my trip. Strangely, it wasn't the impossibility of my situation that came to mind so much as the blue color of his eyes.

❦

"You're serious?" I stared agape at my sister, Zoey. "You bought that cabin off Hackberry Road, the abandoned one we broke into the night of the storm? That's where we're going for our double date tonight? To that dump? You've *got* to be kidding."

Zoey pulled a heavy box of tools from my pickup, getting ready to carry it into her garage in Kingman where we were setting up my new studio. "Not me, exactly," she said. "Declan bought it. He's been fixing it up." She stared dreamily into space.

My sister, who had double-majored in biology and chemistry and was now thinking about veterinary school, was acting like any young woman in love. I had only met her new boyfriend briefly when she and Declan had found me after the accident, but I was already impressed at the changes in Zoey. For too long she'd been taking care of everyone—especially me—and any man who could put that expression on my sister's face was probably in our lives to stay.

"Do you love him?" I asked as she put down the box. I was sure it certainly didn't hurt that he was a biologist who worked at the same wildlife sanctuary Zoey did and shared her interests.

She laughed. "Yeah. I do. I never thought I'd find someone like Declan, and now . . . it's just so right. That's why I set up this date tonight. I want you to be as happy as I am."

"About that." I set down my own box, looking away from her. "I've had a pretty rotten day. I don't know that I'll be much company, and blind dates are always so awkward."

Immediately, she was concerned. "What happened?"

There was no use in trying to hide anything; my sister would get it out of me one way or the other. I stopped trying to avoid her gaze.

"Okay, so that's why I didn't come yesterday like we planned. I went to see a guy at a law firm about my logo earlier this afternoon before driving here, and he pretty much told me it was a waste of time. He wasn't exactly tactful about it, either. I'm not sure what I'm going to do now. Probably get a second opinion."

Zoey smiled. "Then tonight's going to be perfect, because my friend can help. I told you all about him when I visited you in Phoenix—he has connections."

"The last time you visited me at Lily's, I was still on narcotics." I touched my stomach where they'd opened me to fix the internal bleeding after the accident.

"There is that. Well, I'll forgive you then for not following through on his business card."

"You gave me his card?" I didn't remember getting one from her.

"Never mind. Anyway, like I told you then, you're going to love this guy. Seriously, I'd be dating him myself if I hadn't already fallen for Declan. Stephen is smart, gorgeous, and super nice."

Before I had time to wonder why the name sounded familiar, her gaze slid past me. "Oh, look, there's Declan now—just in time to help us get your pottery wheel off the pickup. That thing weighs a ton."

"The kiln's even heavier," I muttered. It was a small, second-hand portable machine, nothing like the brick kiln I'd built at Lily's House, but it would do for now with all the work I wasn't getting done.

No response from Zoey, who was already sprinting across her driveway to throw herself into Declan's arms. They made a striking contrast: Declan so fair, curly-haired, and freckled by the sun, while Zoey's even, light-brown skin and straight dark hair linked her to our mother's heritage. I'd always envied Zoey her skin. We had the same parents, but I felt pale beside her.

When Zoey finished kissing Declan with a passion that left me jealous, we moved my pottery wheel and the kiln into the tiny garage of Zoey's rental house.

"Don't you think you'd better change?" Zoey asked suddenly, turning a critical eye over my shorts and T-shirt that was showing wet in the front and under my arms after an hour of unpacking the truck. I didn't know how she did it, but Zoey still looked fresh.

She handed me a suitcase from the passenger seat of my truck. "We'll get the rest. Hurry, he'll be here any minute."

Declan laughed. "There's time."

"I just want it to be perfect." Zoey grinned at me as though she was doing me a huge favor. "If it hadn't been for that stupid accident, they would have already met."

I stifled an internal sigh. Zoey and I had never been attracted to the same kind of men, so this night, even if I hadn't been preoccupied, was already doomed. Unless the guy really could help me with my case—though he probably wouldn't want to, once we inevitably didn't hit it off. I'd never hit it off with a blind date.

Then again, maybe Zoey knew something about me that I didn't know myself. She said he was smart and nice *and* gorgeous. Maybe once he found out I made pottery, he wouldn't immediately suggest that we reenact the sensual scene from the old movie *Ghost.* Not that playing in clay with the right man wouldn't be fun. Yes, the right guy could make a huge difference.

What were the chances? Not high, but somehow I found myself humming with anticipation as I stepped into the shower.

Ten minutes later, I was wearing a hot pink, cotton dress that set off my hair and skin but could still be worn with sandals. I wasn't about to endanger my ankle by putting on heels again today.

In the living room, Zoey was with Declan and another man discussing a tiger at the sanctuary. The stranger's face was turned away, and for an instant I registered an impression of lean strength. Then he turned and I gasped.

"You!" There was no mistaking that square jaw and those sky blue eyes: Stephen Carey. The anger and helplessness I'd felt at his office that afternoon returned in force.

He stared at me, looking every bit as shocked as I felt.

"You're Zoey's sister?" He glanced from me to Zoey. "Well, that explains why you seemed familiar this afternoon. I, uh, you have a different last name."

"I use my mother's maiden name." By the time I'd been born, our father had split so my mother had put Mendez instead of Morgan on my birth certificate.

"Wait." Zoey's forehead furrowed with worry. "You two know each other?"

I tore my gaze away from Stephen. "He's the attorney I saw today—or rather, the *intern* I saw."

"I thought you didn't use the card I gave you," Zoey said.

"Narcotics," I reminded her. No wonder Stephen Carey's name had sounded familiar, both at his office and when I'd arrived at Zoey's today. She'd probably told me all about him.

"Narcotics?" asked Stephen.

Zoey turned on him. "Never mind. So you're the jerk who told my sister she was wasting her time when she came to you for help today? Really?"

"Well, not exactly." He took a step back. "I thought I was—"

"What? What could you have possibly been thinking?" Zoey's eyes flashed, and her color deepened. "I thought when you left the sanctuary to be an attorney that you'd be helping people. Oo! I'm so mad at you right now. I bet you never guessed the person you would end up *not* helping would be the girl you asked me to set you up with."

Stephen winced. "I asked you to set us up?"

Great, just great. This was getting better and better. Zoey

259

had probably twisted his arm to get him to go out with her poor dateless younger sister.

Declan nodded. "You did ask—that night of the storm. I was there. But to be fair, you had a broken leg, and we really haven't seen you much since."

I backed away from the group. "Look, this is clearly not a good idea." Stephen didn't want to go out with me, and I certainly didn't want to go out with him. It wasn't like I was a hermit or anything. I went out plenty—or I did before the accident. "Let's just call it off."

An abrupt silence fell over the small living room as everyone stared at me.

"I didn't say I didn't want to go out," Stephen said. The flush covering his face was almost amusing. "I do. I was, uh . . . just giving you a way out."

Zoey elbowed him. "Lame."

I laughed at that despite all the awkwardness. "Honestly, I have no desire to go back to Hackberry Road. I still have nightmares of that place."

"She's afraid of the dark," Zoey explained to the men.

Later, I'd kill her. "Thanks," I said with a false sweetness I didn't feel. "But I do sleep without the light on."

Well, sometimes. Okay, never, but Stephen and Declan didn't need to know that.

"Let's get going," Declan suggested. "We can talk about it on the way. I was there yesterday, and the road repair is finally complete. I can't wait to show you the cabin."

"I'm game." Stephen flashed me a sudden grin that did crazy things to my stomach.

Probably because I disliked the idea of this date so much. Yeah, that had to be it.

Zoey turned puppy dog eyes on me. "Let's just start over, okay?"

"Okay," I said, caving. I could make it through one lousy evening, and then I'd come home and pound clay in the garage until I released the anger.

Stephen stepped forward and offered his hand. "Hi, Bianca. I'm Stephen Carey, and I'm really pleased to meet you."

When I stared up into his eyes, I could see only sincerity. "You learn to bluff like that in law school?" I asked.

"No, at Safe Haven Exotic Wildlife Sanctuary. My aunt and uncle own the place, and I used to manage it—Declan's job now. Zoey started with us about a month before I took off to Phoenix. Anyway, you learn to stare down the big cats. You know, pretend they don't scare you."

A smile somehow found its way to my lips. At least he was comparing me to a tiger or a lion instead of a cranky tourist. Okay, so maybe this evening wouldn't be pure torture. I stuck out my hand and shook.

His touch sent a current rippling up my arm, and for that instant we might have been alone for all I cared about the others.

Oh, no.

I might be in trouble.

Chapter Four

Stephen

DESPITE HER SMILE, Bianca seemed to pull away from my touch faster than necessary. Nothing I could do about it now. We'd both have to endure this evening for Zoey's sake.

Declan was driving with Zoey riding beside him, which put me with Bianca in the back seat of the car. I wasn't surprised that she hugged the door, but instead of remaining silent, as I expected, she and Zoey began to chat about the baby raccoons at the sanctuary.

"The videos you posted online are so adorable," Bianca said. "If you hadn't told me how terrible being domesticated was for them, I might have tried to buy one for a pet."

Zoey laughed. "Never a good thing with a wild animal."

"I can't wait to see them in person—to see all the animals again." Bianca's smile included me, and an unexpected heat stirred in my belly.

Bianca had come to the sanctuary? Up until two months ago, I'd spent most of my days there. Why hadn't I seen her? But then Zoey and I had only worked together a month, and I was often traveling on sanctuary business. Or Bianca had come on a weekend—when I never worked.

"Looks like they did fix the road." Bianca craned her neck to peer out the front window. Her long hair cascaded over her shoulder, blocking her face. I stifled the urge to feel the silkiness of it between my fingers. "Or at least there aren't any huge ruts."

Her voice was strangled, and I looked at her more intently. Was she actually nervous about being on this road?

Zoey turned in the front seat. "You're going to love what we've done to the cabin." Her abrupt change of conversation suggested she'd also heard the anxiety in her sister's voice.

"Can't wait." Bianca gave her sister a grin that fell flat.

I'd studied body language too much to miss the sign of how very much Bianca didn't want to go to the cabin. Or maybe she just wasn't excited about going there with me.

I leaned over and said quietly, "Look, about this afternoon. Please understand I wasn't trying to be a jerk. I've just seen too many people lose too much in the search for justice. One advantage you have is that you're a creative person, unlike the guy who stole your logo, and you can create something else that's just as amazing."

For a few seconds Bianca studied me without replying, her gaze briefly straying to Zoey and Declan in the front seat. "I guess I'll take that as a compliment."

"It *was* a compliment. I've seen your work—at least a little bit of it." I remembered her candy dish, still on my desk where I'd left it. "In fact, I'd like to see more. Maybe buy a few pieces?"

In the front seat Zoey snorted. "Since when are *you* interested in pottery?"

"You don't have to," Bianca said in a rush.

She thought I was trying to placate her. "Well, I need decorations for my office, and clients love candy."

Bianca nodded, but made no attempt to sell me anything. Either she was a lousy saleswoman, or she didn't want to interact with me after tonight.

"So how'd your boss like the write-ups for your uncle's case?" Zoey asked. "For your summary-whatever thing."

"Motion for summary judgment." I stole a glance at Bianca, and for a moment, something caught in my throat. "He loved them. But apparently our opponent is threatening to file a lawsuit saying Cuddles was outside her pen when he was attacked."

"What?" Declan and Zoey exclaimed together. Zoey whipped around in her seat to stare at me, and Declan's gaze met mine in the rearview mirror.

"As if we'd let a full-grown Bengal tiger walk around, ready to bite any dumb trespasser," Zoey muttered darkly. "Although in the case of this guy, it might be tempting."

"Wait, is this about that guy who used the text and videos from the sanctuary's website to steal donations from people, pretending the money he collected was being used to care for the animals?" Bianca looked at me with one brow arched.

I nodded. "Yeah, he raked in over a million dollars before we discovered why donations plunged so drastically. At some point he snuck into the sanctuary to get a video of himself with one of our Bengals and got himself bitten."

"Just a nibble," Zoey protested. "Cuddles has a right to protect her turf."

"He was lucky it wasn't fasting day," Declan added.

"Yeah, exactly," I agreed. "Unfortunately, the new law-suit would include a motion to put Cuddles down as a danger to society. But the man's attorney came right out and said he won't file if we drop our lawsuit."

"That's crazy—all of it," Bianca said. "If that man is willing to lie and threaten to kill an innocent animal to save himself for being prosecuted for fraud, what else will he do?"

"I wonder the same thing." I met her curious stare, the car suddenly feeling too warm. Maybe because my heart was pounding in my chest. What was it about her that made me feel so self-conscious? "Anyway, this means I'll have to add information to my motion so that the judge rules on our behalf."

"You really love the law, don't you?" Bianca said quietly.

"Yeah, I do." My voice was just as low as hers, and I couldn't tell if the others were still listening. I could only stare at Bianca and wonder if the skin of her cheek felt as soft as it looked.

"I can tell."

Her smile made me break out in a light sweat. Why did it suddenly seem like a good idea to lean over and kiss her?

"It's good to find what you were meant to do," she added.

Did she feel that way about her work? Of course she did. But asking about that now seemed a bit like throwing what happened with her logo in her face. The irony that I was pursuing my uncle's case when I had advised her to cut her losses didn't escape me. It wasn't the same thing, though, and I hoped she'd understand.

"What if the judge doesn't decide for summary judgment?" she asked. "You go to court and battle it out, right?"

"Right. And everyone loses more money—except the attorneys. I'm doing as much as I can to limit my uncle's legal expenses. But the idea that Ross is benefitting so much from this whole thing burns me up."

"Ross?"

"Baxter Ross. The counsel for the defendant." In fact, Baxter had been a major pain in my side for the past fifteen months. The more I learned about the law, the more irresponsible I found him.

Bianca's brow furrowed slightly. "His name sounds familiar."

"He does an annoying commercial," Zoey put in from the front seat.

"I haven't watched commercials in years," Bianca said. "Not since I got Netflix."

Zoey shrugged. "He's the kind that gives all attorneys a bad name. Not like the kind Stephen's going to be."

I knew this wasn't so much a compliment as a little jab at me at how she thought I'd treated Bianca in my office, but I didn't take the bait.

"Well this Ross guy will probably settle as soon as he's

spent all the money his client stole," Bianca said, her laugh smoothing over Zoey's remark.

Bianca might even have moved away from her door a few inches, which I shouldn't care about but did.

"Well, here we are." Declan pulled off the road and started up a short hill.

So we were, and there had barely been an awkward moment the entire thirty-minute drive.

As Bianca hopped from the car, I wished more than anything that our meeting this afternoon had been scheduled for next week. I'd blown it big time, because from what I could see, Bianca was everything Zoey had promised—fun, witty, smart, and talented. I wondered if she could ever see me as anything but the guy who told her to give up years of work without a fight.

Maybe.

Regardless, Zoey was right that I'd gotten into this business to help people, and as hopeless as Bianca's case seemed, I was somehow going to help her.

Chapter Five

Bianca

WALKING ACROSS THE new porch, I stepped into the cabin, whistling in appreciation. "Nice. This doesn't look like the same place we broke into during the storm. New windows, wood floor, paint. Even a cool couch."

"The best thing is that there are no more mice." Declan shivered dramatically.

That made me laugh. "Seriously? A big guy like you, afraid of mice?"

"Only animals I can't stand. Them and rats."

I smirked. "Remind me not to show you my new pets, then. And I hope you don't plan to spend much time at our place. Rats are sensitive creatures."

Only Stephen laughed. He got my humor, or at least pretended to.

"Wait until you see the kitchen," Stephen said. "I helped Declan lay the tile."

I was surprised that a wildlife guy turned law student knew anything about home repairs. "Lead the way."

The new tile turned out to be a marbled tan, adding an unexpected elegance to the rough little cabin. Wasn't the remodel a bit overkill for a place Declan used only on the weekends?

Zoey began setting the kitchen table with dishes from a new-looking cabinet while Declan unpacked a heated container with heavenly-smelling chili and corn muffins.

I examined the old black stove, running a finger along the cool surface. "I seem to remember this was already here?"

Declan laughed. "It's a classic. Heats the entire place—and you can cook on it. But don't worry. I'll put in a microwave for you."

I pivoted on my heel. "For me?"

Zoey set down the last plate and turned in my direction. "Declan's going to move here permanently after I begin school, because it's closer to the sanctuary than his place in Kingman."

I blinked at her. "So you've decided for sure to go to veterinary school?" School meant her leaving Kingman, and I'd only just arrived.

"Yeah, but I can't get into any veterinary school until a year from this fall, so I'll just be doing a few online classes until then." She smiled at me. "Don't worry. You're not getting rid of me that fast."

Relief waved through me.

"Anyway, we've been spending a lot of time here, and now that you're living with me, you probably will be, too." Zoey shrugged and gave Declan a glance full of hidden meaning I couldn't interpret.

I was happy for her, despite having the odd sense of being left out—which was silly. "This place is a little out of the way," I commented.

Zoey laughed. "Bianca likes the city," she explained. "Not sure that even Kingman will have enough people for her."

"Actually, no people is exactly what I need." I hooked my purse over the back edge of a chair. "I've spent too much time streaming movies lately. I need to focus on work."

I'd only worked a few times on my wheel at Lily's since the accident—and that wasn't only because my right arm wasn't strong enough to throw a decent pot without pain. The biggest issue was the shutdown of my creativity.

But I wasn't going to let it take over my life. That was why I'd pushed myself to track down Fletcher and had made the appointment with Stephen—and part of why I'd moved to Zoey's. I needed to regain control.

"Ready to eat?" Declan asked, indicating the pot of chili.

"I am." Habit had me checking my fingernails for clay. To my chagrin, I found a little bit under my thumbnail that must have become lodged there when we'd hauled my stuff into the garage. Not even my vigorous shower had worked it loose. I headed to the sink.

Apparently Stephen had the same idea about washing, and our hands brushed as we collided. At least with the prolonged absence from work, my hands didn't have their normal texture of sandpaper.

I looked up to see Stephen watching me. My heart began doing odd things in my chest, and heat filled my face.

I dove for the water and flipped it on. But there was no bar soap, and in my hurry I put too much dish detergent on my hands. The water didn't seem to want to wash it off.

As Stephen waited his turn, he glanced back at Zoey and Declan, and I followed his gaze. They were wrapped in each other's arms, ignoring us completely, which for some reason made my heart do even more gymnastics.

Forgetting the bit of clay, I abandoned the sink and hurried back to the table. "I'm starving."

For the next half hour, I let the others talk while I busied myself eating. I'd lost weight after the accident and hadn't had much appetite in the past weeks, and now was as good a time as any to start making up those calories. Plus, it meant I didn't have to participate in the conversation.

When everyone did finally look at me during a lull in the discussion, all I said was, "These corn muffins are fabulous."

I used the rest of the muffin to sop up the dregs of my chili, but when I put it into my mouth, my fingers tasted like dish soap.

"Something wrong?" Zoey asked me.

I forced myself to swallow. "No. It's great. Really."

I popped up from the table to rinse again at the sink,

271

knocking my bag off the chair and spilling its contents. I bent to collect everything, and Stephen stood to help. Why hadn't I thought to remove the two oversized Ghirardelli chocolate bars I'd shoved in there before my drive? At least I'd eaten the other two on the way, or I'd really look greedy.

He scarcely glanced at the chocolate. Instead, he stared at the crumpled business card I'd retrieved from the floor of my truck after our meeting this afternoon. "Did you go see this guy?" He thrust the card at me, but when I reached for it, he didn't let go.

"Actually, that's the card Kent Fletcher gave me when I confronted him about stealing my logo." I could still see Fletcher's smirking face, the unruly salt-and-pepper growth on his chin reminding me of the bum who foraged for food in the garbage bins outside my old apartment in Phoenix. "After I called him to ask for a meeting, he must have wasted no time tracking down a sleazy ambulance chaser to represent him."

"It's Baxter Ross."

I looked at him blankly. "And?"

"You mean the attorney defending that jerk who wants to kill Cuddles?" Zoey glared at us, and for an instant it was difficult to remember her emotion was for the "jerk" and not us.

"Oh." Now I understood. "That must be why his name sounded familiar when you were talking about it in the car. I only just read it the once."

Stephen finally relinquished the card, and I shoved it with the chocolate bars back into my purse. "I should have figured Fletcher would have an attorney with the moral fiber of a"—I glanced at Declan—"rat."

Zoey laughed. "Fletcher probably saw his commercials. But don't let them ruin our evening. Anyone want more chili before the chocolate cake?"

"Sure," I said at the same time Stephen muttered, "No, thanks."

Wait, maybe he had the right idea. The faster we ate

dessert, the faster we could finish this mockery of a date. "Actually, cake is a better idea."

"Good. Declan, would you get out the games while I cut the cake?"

Games. Seriously? I opened my mouth to protest, but my sister looked so content that I shut it again. She deserved to be happy, and even if I had to bite my tongue all night and pretend I wasn't annoyed at being here with Stephen Smarty-pants Lawyer-in-training, it was worth it to see her smile like that.

We ended up playing Monopoly of all things, which surprised me because Zoey hated the game. When we lived at Lily's House as teens, I'd always beaten her and any one of the other foster kids who dared play. However, this time I wasn't the only one taking the game seriously. After Zoey and Declan surrendered, Stephen and I battled head-to-head—until he landed twice on my Pennsylvania Avenue Hotel and went bankrupt while I spent a happy three turns hiding out in jail.

I smirked at him.

"Nice game," he offered.

"Are you this agreeable when you lose in court?"

He laughed. "I don't know. We haven't actually lost any of the cases I've worked on. But I'm sure there'll be a first time."

His eyes went to my bag, still hanging off the chair, and his smile vanished. I wished I'd kept my mouth shut. He was actually fun to be around when we both forgot about my logo and the way we'd met.

The game had lasted long enough that Declan and Zoey called it a night. Even though it was Saturday tomorrow, they'd both be going into the sanctuary to make sure feeding time for the big cats went smoothly.

"Bianca," Stephen called as I tried to follow Declan and Zoey to the car.

I turned, gazing at him where he stood on the porch. "Yeah?"

He came down the steps to stand beside me. Moonlight bathed the path in a soft, romantic light, and I was all too aware of his closeness. His hair seemed almost black in the darkness, and his eyes navy. He was taller than me by at least a foot, so I had to look up to see his expression. But there was no indication of his thoughts—until his gaze lowered to my lips.

My mouth watered suddenly. He wasn't going to try to kiss me, was he? That would be ridiculous. Yet I didn't back away. What would I do if he tried? All at once, I very much wanted to find out.

"About your case," he said, redirecting his attention to my eyes.

I arched a brow. "I thought you said I didn't have a case."

"You know what I mean." He paused and then rushed on. "Look, there are a few things I can do. I know this guy Ross, and sometimes with clients like his, sending a cease and desist and showing intention to pursue can make a big difference."

"That's not what you said before. Why the sudden change of heart? You said it probably wouldn't make a difference."

"It might not. But like I said, I'm familiar with Ross, and if he really is representing this Fletcher guy, Ross knows I don't back down easily. I'll just remind him how hard I've pushed in my uncle's case."

"You mean, threaten him?"

He nodded. "If you want to call it that."

"I don't care what you call it. My designs and my logo are mine, and Fletcher deserves a lot more than threats." I swallowed hard, trying to control my emotions. I wanted to scream at the injustice of it all. I wanted to hurt Fletcher for upsetting my life, but most of all I wanted to yell at Stephen for making me feel so hopeless this afternoon and now suddenly changing his mind. I had enough anxiety without this roller coaster ride.

"Then why not take my offer?" He scrubbed a hand

through his short hair, making it stand up in front, which I found oddly appealing. "You seem upset at the suggestion. Why? Legal work can be very expensive; I can cut those costs."

"You're right—I am upset. Because this afternoon you told me to give up, and then tonight when you learn who Fletcher's attorney is, suddenly you're willing to help me. *That's* what bothers me. My case hasn't changed, but apparently you hate this Ross guy so much that you're ready to do anything you can to fight him. It's not my case that's important, is it? It's beating him that you care about."

Stephen's jaw clenched and unclenched, but when he spoke, his voice was still calm. "Look, I admit I dislike Ross, and maybe I do want to push back at him. But you're Zoey's sister, and she asked me to help you. That's what's important."

So on top of everything else, I was a charity case, just as I'd been since my mother died. He didn't want to help me because he was attracted to me, or because I had rights. He would help because Zoey forced him and because he hated Fletcher's attorney.

"I appreciate the offer," I told him, "but I think it's best if you forget the whole thing. We made it through tonight for my sister. Let's leave it at that, okay?"

Turning on my heel, I hurried after my sister, but a pebble caught in my sandal, and I had to stop and finger it out. When I glanced back at Stephen, he was still standing where I'd left him, a sorrowful expression on his face.

A tiny bit of guilt crept into my mind, but I pushed it away. I didn't need Stephen's help. I'd find another way. Maybe going public with my story on social media would open some avenues.

The drive home was subdued, but somehow Stephen and I made it without exchanging more words. Zoey and Declan were so caught up in each other, they didn't appear to notice.

When Declan and Stephen walked us to the door, Stephen pushed a card into my hand. "If you change your mind, call me."

I wouldn't, but I nodded and watched from the window as he climbed into his own car. I wondered if he was driving all the way back to Phoenix tonight, or if he was crashing at Declan's. I told myself I didn't care, but as he drove away, my determination to carry on my fight alone faded. He knew the legal process, and maybe I'd been hasty rejecting his offer. His reasons might not be important. After all, how far was social media really going to take me?

I wouldn't be honest if I didn't admit that I had enjoyed the game part of the evening. Stephen had stolen my breath away more than once, but somehow my pride had gotten in the way. Maybe I'd even been a little rude.

What was I going to do now?

Chapter Six

Stephen

THOUGH IT WAS AFTER eleven when I arrived, my aunt and uncle, Lena and Josh Carey, were waiting up for me in the house they'd built on Safe Haven Exotic Wildlife Sanctuary property. They both hugged me and invited me in for some of my aunt's special sleep potion: warm milk blended with melted chocolate, cream, and vanilla, then topped with whipped cream and chocolate shavings.

Lena poured me a mug. "So how did the date with Zoey's sister go?"

I nodded. "She's nice. Not to mention beautiful."

"I figured as much with a sister like Zoey," Josh said. "Declan spends far too much time at work staring at her."

Lena dug her elbow into his side. "It's good he does that. They're perfect together. And it's not like he doesn't work far more hours than he should." To me she added, "So, you going out with her again?"

Not if Bianca had her way. But I didn't want to kill the hope in Lena's eyes. "Maybe. We'll see. She's an artist."

"That's good," Lena said. "She can keep you from burying yourself too much in all that legal stuff."

I searched for another topic that would catch their attention. "So how's the new tiger adjusting?"

"He's doing great!" Josh launched into a detailed story about his beloved tigers.

My guilt at leaving their dream—the sanctuary—to

pursue my own was a burden I might never fully overcome. They'd been everything to me after my parents died in a car crash when I was three, and I wanted to be as much to them. Or at least everything their estranged biological daughter hadn't been. I would never stop owing them for giving me a happy, contented childhood.

The truth was that if Zoey hadn't pushed, and Declan hadn't been so ready to take over as manager at the sanctuary, I'd still be working there—making my uncle happy, but dying a little bit inside each day. In a big way I owed Zoey and Declan for the direction my life had taken. But the first time Zoey had asked for help, I'd made a mess of it.

Then there was Bianca . . . it was hard to even think about her, standing there so beautiful in the moonlight with disdain in her eyes, accusing me of only caring about beating Ross. I didn't know what made me angrier, the allegation or the fact that maybe there was some truth to her claim.

Whatever my motives, I *had* decided to help her before I'd learned about Ross being Fletcher's attorney. Even before I knew she was Zoey's sister, I'd been thinking about calling the local pottery shops.

Not that Bianca would believe me.

When Josh had finished his story about the new tiger, my aunt gave an exaggerated yawn. "You're probably tired, aren't you? If you're going to the sanctuary with your uncle in the morning, you'd better get to bed. I have your room all ready."

"Thanks." I kissed her cheek, nodded at my uncle, and headed to my room, grabbing my overnight bag where I'd left it in the hallway.

I spent the next few hours researching common law trademark cases on my laptop and drawing up the rough draft of a cease and desist letter that would make even Ross think twice about using Bianca's logo.

If only I had something to up the stakes.

Usually, if someone stole and got caught, it wasn't the

first time. Maybe with a little research, I could find out more about Kent Fletcher and other scams he might be running.

Around two in the morning I found it. "This is it!" Laughing, I began taking screenshots.

Tomorrow after visiting the sanctuary and catching up with the staff and the animals, I was going to see Bianca—whether she liked it or not.

I couldn't help but hope that she'd like it, because no matter the awkwardness between us, I wanted to see her again.

Chapter Seven

Bianca

THE SLANTED LIGHT of the sun through the window danced on my face, waking me. It had to be at least ten. I should have been up hours ago, arranging my equipment in the garage and maybe throwing a simple pot or at least doing something productive, like searching the Internet for a new attorney.

Instead, my hand reached for the remote to the TV sitting on the dresser against the wall.

No! What was wrong with me?

Not so long ago, the idea of spending the entire day making my ideas come to life in clay had been my idea of paradise. Now the thought of going to the garage and putting my hands in clay filled me with panic. My heartbeat pulsed in my ears, and I wanted more than anything to pull the covers over my head, squeeze my pillow to my aching chest, and stay there until Zoey returned from work.

I recognized the anxiety for what it was. After becoming our foster mother, Lily had taken me to a psychologist because of my fear of the dark. It had been years since I'd had to deal with the anxiety, but the symptoms had crept back since the accident—at first so slowly I hadn't recognized it, but increasing after I learned about my logo. I could no longer ignore the problem.

"I can do this," I told myself after several deep breaths.

The first step was the hardest. It always was.

I forced myself from the bed and down the hall to the

only bathroom. A warm shower, clean clothes, and a good breakfast with plenty of protein went a long way toward helping me feel normal.

I washed the dishes by hand, though we had a dishwasher, and started sweeping the floor before I caught a glimpse of my wide eyes in the shiny reflection of Zoey's microwave. What was I doing?

"Stop stalling." Dropping the broom, I headed to the garage. Already, the place smelled familiar, with my tools and bags of clay, half-finished pots, and jars of paint filling up the space. For now, the unpacked boxes could wait.

Using a cutting wire, I sliced off a good chunk of porcelain clay from a new rectangular block, and an equal lump of ball clay. Slowly and methodically, I began wedging the relatively soft masses together, like my grandmother used to knead bread. Not even a twinge from my arm. So far, so good.

The wheel was next, and for that I needed to fill a small bucket with water from the kitchen sink. Finally, I slammed the clay onto the wheel and begin centering it. Yes, this was nice. The clay was much smoother and more malleable than the castoff bits I always kept and reworked. I dipped my hand in the water before working the mass up and down, shaping it first taller and then shorter and wider.

What should I make?

For no reason at all, the memory of Stephen saying he needed a candy dish came to mind. The one I had brought to his office had been a simple bowl-like design, with hand-fluted edges added after throwing. But for a law office, something more dramatic would be in order. A larger, vase-like piece with intricate designs, a fancy lid, and vibrant glaze.

Like coming home after being away far too long, the piece formed under my fingers, the act of creation a breath of magic. The first two pots were halfway decent, but not as good as my usual. I left each on a removable bat as I set them on the worktable before slipping a new bat in place and starting again. More pots formed under my hands. My right arm began to ache where it had been broken.

And there it was—maybe the most perfect dish I'd ever made. Far from finished, of course, because it would have to dry a day before I could trim it and bring out the details, but the bones were there. The lid would be the crowning piece, and my suppliers would be eager to get their hands on similar ones.

Then a week after they showed up on store shelves, Fletcher would probably use my logo on inferior copies.

My breath caught in my throat, and for a long minute, I felt like drowning. My heart pounded and panic blackened my vision. My hand came down on the piece, crushing it.

Tears leaking down my face, I pushed back from my wheel and curled in on myself. Flashes of memories flooded me. Of nights huddled in bed, listening to Zoey cry. I hadn't known then what my uncle was doing to her, but I knew he was hurting her even more than she was hurting herself with the knife she used on her arms to release her pain. There had been nothing I could do, nothing but shiver in the dark and wet my pillow with tears.

"Bianca!" Zoey's voice came from the kitchen doorway. The next minute her arms were around me. "Sweetie, what happened? What's wrong?"

I buried my face in her shoulder and let myself cry.

"Is something wrong? Are you hurt?"

My sister's anguish drove me to my feet. "No! I just have to get rid of these. They're no good!" I reached for one of the five other completed pots, crumpling it and throwing it into the five-gallon bucket I used to store scraps. The lid and another pot followed. I was reaching for a third when Zoey grabbed my hands.

"Stop it! Bianca, tell me what's wrong." Tears shone in her eyes, and the worry in her face made me feel ashamed.

"What's the use? Now that I can finally work again, it's not the same. That man's just going to steal my designs and fool the shop owners. He'll make horrible copies with my name on them. Better that it all end up in the garbage!"

"That's not true! Your work is good, and those shop owners will see the difference."

"He sells his stuff too cheap. I can't compete."

"I know it seems that way now, but that's the panic talking. You know that, right? We're going to make this work out. I promise." She hugged me tightly.

I clenched my eyes against the light, willing myself to be calm. This wasn't Zoey's problem, it was mine. I wasn't a child anymore that she had to take care of. I needed to find control. I could overcome this. *I would.* "I'm sorry," I murmured.

"No, *I'm* sorry." Zoey paused for a moment. When she spoke again, there was a hint of the old pain in her voice. "I didn't realize how this was for you. Not until right now. It's like . . . being violated."

I pulled back from her then and opened my eyes. "No, not like y—"

But she was right. It wasn't exactly like the kind of physical violation my sister had suffered as a child, but it was still an attack. Fletcher's mocking laugh as he'd handed me his attorney's card had made me feel utterly violated.

"It's going to be okay." Zoey put her face close to mine. "You will deal with the panic—you did it before. And you'll regain all the business you've lost."

I nodded because I believed in her, even if I sometimes didn't believe in myself. "Okay. But I'm not sure where to begin."

"First, we're going to get some food in you. It's past three, and I bet you haven't eaten. Then you're going to talk to Stephen Carey."

I stared at her. "What?"

Her eyes narrowed. "Don't play stupid with me. He was at the sanctuary today, and he told me he offered to help you last night. Said you shot him down."

"He only offered after he found out who was representing

Fletcher. He has it out for that attorney, and I don't want my chances of winning to dwindle even more because two attorneys hate each other."

Zoey shook her head. "Nope, think again. Stephen told me he'd decided to help before he learned about the attorney."

I scowled. "Anyway, it's only because I'm your sister."

"So?" Zoey rolled her eyes. "How many wall plates have you made for friends of friends? You wouldn't just do that for everyone because you couldn't make a living. Neither would Stephen."

"Are you forgetting he told me to give up yesterday?"

"Look, I'm not saying you have to date him, but you can't throw out the idea of him helping just because he didn't offer to burn through your life savings when first you went to see him yesterday."

My mind churned at her words. She was right. Obviously, my perception of Stephen had been colored by my emotions—both the panic about my logo and my attraction to him.

"Well?" Zoey said.

"I'll think about it."

"Good. Now let's get something to eat."

Two hours later, Zoey left somewhere with Declan, and I faced the garage and the mess I'd made earlier. The garage was over-heated now, after soaking up the afternoon sun, and I opened the automatic door to ventilate the stuffiness.

First, I moved the three undamaged pots to the wall of shelves Zoey had installed for me along one entire side of the garage. The pots were nearly ready to put plastic over to stop them from drying too quickly. My heart sped up a little as I thought about actually finishing the candy dishes and sending them out into public. I could do this.

I put a cover over the bucket of water, now mixed with

clay scraps after my work this morning. Together it made "slip" and was silky smooth, exactly the way I liked it. Next, I had to deal with the rest of the scraps and the ruined pot still on the wheel. Once I threw them into my scrap bucket with a little water, everything would soon be ready to form into something new.

The sound of a clearing throat startled me into nearly dropping the scraps of clay onto the ground instead. I turned to see Stephen Carey standing just outside the garage, his figure framed by the light of the late-afternoon sun.

The little jump my heart gave wasn't at all related to panic. He looked good in snug jeans and a T-shirt that hinted at the muscle beneath. He might be currently working in an office, but he was obviously accustomed to physical work. His hair was slightly tousled, as though he'd been running his hands through it.

Zoey had given me his number, and I'd promised to call, but I hadn't worked up the courage. I realized I owed him an apology. I hadn't meant to be so awful to him.

"Hi," he said, shuffling one foot like a nervous boy. "Can we talk?"

I opened my mouth and hoped this time the words would come out right.

Chapter Eight

Stephen

I TOOK IT as a good sign when Bianca didn't immediately throw me out.

She wore clay-spattered jeans and an equally messy yellow T-shirt. Her skin glistened with moisture, and her shirt looked partially damp. Pieces of dark hair had escaped her ponytail. Her tongue wet her lips, and my eyes wandered there and stayed, even as I reminded myself that this was a business call.

I stood in the opening of the garage, feeling awkward as I awaited her response. Zoey had texted me that Bianca was going to call me about her case, but I wasn't leaving things to chance. Zoey was an eternal optimist these days.

"Been working?" I surveyed the open boxes of unpacked tools and the three fresh-looking pots on a shelf against the wall. A collapsed pot lay abandoned on her pottery wheel.

"Something like that." She indicated the ruined piece with a delicate snort. "That one's yours." There was a lightness in her voice that hinted she was teasing.

I grinned. "Uh, can I pick another one? That looks too much like my efforts all those years ago back in high school." Though now that I thought about it, if my teacher had resembled Bianca, I might have paid more attention in art class.

"Sorry, only one per customer." She brushed her hands together before wiping them on a rag. Then she folded her left arm across her chest, rubbing the biceps of her right arm, as if it pained her.

"Look," I began. "I know you're upset with me about yesterday, but I've been doing some research, and I think there's something I can do to help you." I hesitated a moment before adding, "I probably should have done some checking before I advised you to give it up. Your case is stronger than I thought."

Her lips parted as if I'd surprised her. "What did you find out?"

"Last night I came across a blog by another local artist. He claims Kent Fletcher stole his logo and designs four years ago. He filed a lawsuit but later had to drop it for lack of funds."

"Really?" Arms unfolding, she took a few steps toward me, and a pleasant, earthy smell reached my nose, probably from the clay on her hands and clothing. "That's great. I mean, sad for the other artist. But to know I'm not the only one…" Her eyes glowed. "I should contact this man."

"I talked to him this afternoon."

Her eyes flew to mine. "You were up late finding him, and you already talked to him? You've been busy."

"I couldn't sleep. Anyway, this artist—name's Chad Peterson—ended up creating a new business logo and filing a trademark for it. He says he's barely returned to the level of business he had before. He lost all his savings in the lawsuit."

She looked down, rubbing a tiny bit of clay between her fingers. "Poor guy. It's not fair that Fletcher could do that to him. It shouldn't cost so much to defend what's already yours."

She took a deep breath, her gaze going to the three new pots on the shelf, and then wandering over her equipment and the unpacked boxes. Her teeth bit down on her lower lip, as if holding something back. Finally, with a little shake of her head, she turned to me.

"I don't want to lose everything I've worked for. I'm creative. I can design something new . . . eventually."

Her voice was strained but determined. I could almost swear her skin had paled significantly. How had I not seen yesterday at my office how much this meant to her? I wanted to wipe that sadness off her face.

"Maybe you won't have to," I said. "You said you've been using the logo for eight years. We'll find people who have your work and get them to testify, if it comes to that. But with the other artist on our side, I think we can resolve this before it gets anywhere near a court. Fletcher lost money, too, when he hired Ross, and he only won the other case because the real artist couldn't afford to continue. If Ross and Fletcher see me backing you, even if I can't get my firm to sign on, both of them will think twice."

"Why? Wouldn't they just think I'd run out of money to pay you?"

"No. Because you'd be a *pro se* litigant—which means representing yourself. Any citizen has a right to act in their own behalf. Usually, it's a terrible idea because too much depends upon knowing how to navigate the system, but with my experience, you'd still have the advantages of legal representation. You can push this all the way. Or make them think you'll push it all the way."

Her gaze held mine, and I had the gentle sensation of drowning in them. "How much will it cost?"

"I won't charge you anything for my time, and if my firm agrees to help, it'd only be the time I take to report to them about it. They might even write that off. There would be incidental fees if we have to go further, but we can discuss that if we get there." I didn't think telling her that I'd cover any fees would convince her to agree. I'd already seen evidence that she was as stubborn as Zoey about taking care of herself.

"Okay." Bianca's arms dropped, and the smile she gave me now was real, as if she'd been faking all the others before. "Thank you. And I'm sorry about being a jerk last night."

"Does that mean I get a new pot?" I nodded at the misshapen piece on her wheel.

She laughed. "Yeah, I think so."

"One of those?" I waved at the others on the shelf.

She scooped up the ruined attempt and tossed it into a large white bucket of scraps. "Maybe. Depends on how they turn out."

I hoped that meant she wanted to give me a good one and not something she'd normally discard.

"Tell you what," I said, looking around the garage once more. There were still numerous boxes scattered over the floor and a second worktable by the opening of the garage that should be moved to wherever she wanted it. "I'm not heading back to Phoenix until tomorrow night, so I have time to help you set up here, if you want a hand. I'm thinking you could move that wheel closer to that little window. With a small air conditioning unit there, you should be able to work here even during the hottest summer days. Might need some insulation along the walls, though. It's easy to install. Declan and I could help."

"First tile and now this. You're full of surprises."

Why did that make me feel ridiculously proud? "I get it from growing up with my uncle. He's the quintessential do-it-yourselfer."

"Zoey mentioned you'd lived with them since very young. How was it practically growing up at the sanctuary?"

"Best life a boy could have."

I wondered if she knew how my parents had died, and I wanted to tell her. Maybe sometime soon. We were both orphans, though from what little I got from Zoey, the sisters had experienced more hardship than I had. Maybe someday Bianca would tell me about her childhood, about why she was afraid of the dark. Her dreams for the future.

Because I wanted to know all of it. There was something here between us, something I'd felt if not from the moment I'd seen her at the office, then for sure at the cabin last night.

It wasn't only the way she looked but had a lot to do with her determination and personality.

And maybe just a little bit because of the way she'd obliterated me at Monopoly.

"That reminds me," I said as Bianca opened a box of unglazed pottery and started arranging the pieces on a shelf. "I demand a replay. You would never have won last night if you hadn't convinced Zoey to sell you Pennsylvania Avenue."

Her eyes glinted. "She had to sell it to me or go bankrupt. I won fair and square."

"Maybe so. I still demand a rematch."

"Okay, you're on."

By the time the garage was completely organized and Bianca's air conditioner and insulation ordered, it was dark.

"I have to admit you know how to get things done," she said. "If you're even half as good at law stuff, my logo will be the only one carved into any pot."

"Can I see that? You carving it?"

Her eyes went wide, and she seemed to hold her breath.

"If that's okay," I added.

She nodded sharply. "Yeah, I just haven't . . . since I found out about Fletcher." She glanced around. "I don't have a leather-hard pot to carve—one that's still wet but dried enough to handle without deformation—but I can show you on a block of fresh clay."

She grabbed a tool from a plastic organizer while I brought up the video feature on my phone. It took less than three minutes for her to make a perfect logo.

"Amazing," I said. "Looks like a stamp."

"I had a stamp made, but I only use it on pieces that are too thin to carve well."

"Do you have a receipt for the stamp?"

That was only one of a million questions I'd asked during

the afternoon and evening, typing her answers into my phone. She was wary around me still, like a wild animal new to the sanctuary. Talking while we worked had made getting information easier.

"I probably have a copy of the receipt online," she said. "I'll email it to you with the names of my high school and college teachers. Come on, let's go wash up." She led me inside to the kitchen sink, where the remains of the pizza we'd shared for dinner still sat in the delivery box.

"Thanks for all your help today," Bianca said.

I leaned back against the counter as I dried my hands. "Actually, I had fun. I haven't taken too much time off lately."

"What do you mean, time off? You were working on my case all day."

I grinned. "And here I thought I'd been discreet with my grilling."

"I'm really grateful."

I tossed her the towel. "Look, just leave Fletcher and Ross to me. You go back to doing what you do best."

"And you'll let me know when I need to worry?" The irony in her voice was unmistakable.

"Something like that." Keeping my eyes on her face, I stepped toward her. My pulse raced. I wanted to kiss her, maybe as much as I'd ever wanted anything.

She held my gaze and didn't move away.

"Bianca." My voice came out hoarse.

"Yeah?"

"I think I'm going to kiss you."

"Well, then do it already."

I closed the space between us, leaning down and pressing my lips against hers, one of my hands behind her neck. So soft, so good, so right. I'd meant it to be a simple kiss, something just to let her know I was interested. But a shudder went through me as she kissed me back. Heat effused my body, and I lost it a little as her arms slid around my neck, bringing us closer. Before I realized what I was doing, I picked her up and placed her on the counter. She tasted so good. My arms went around her, pulling her against me. I might never stop kissing her.

When we did come up for air, Bianca's eyes were huge, and again I felt myself drowning in them. I didn't mind in the least.

"I'm sorry," I said, feeling suddenly embarrassed at my lack of control.

"Don't be," she whispered. "I've been wondering what that would be like since last night."

"Last night? That explains why you were so cranky."

She laughed and started to kiss me again.

"Uh, sorry to interrupt," said a voice.

I jerked my head over to see Zoey standing in the door between the kitchen and the living room.

"Zoey!" Bianca said. "We didn't hear you."

"Obviously." She gave us a wide, knowing smile. "You two must be making headway on the case."

"Really?" Bianca's hands pushed on my chest as she jumped off the counter. "You had to say that?"

"And I have something more to say." Zoey held out her left hand where a ring glinted on her fourth finger. "Look, Declan just proposed! We're getting married!"

"Oh, Zoey!" Bianca launched herself at her sister, and the two hugged and squealed in excitement.

"Congratulations," I said as the women gushed over the ring and began discussing dates. They looked prepared to discuss wedding details all night, and I had a cease and desist to revise and more research to conduct. "Uh, I'm sure you two have a lot to talk about. I'll see you both later."

"I'll walk you out." Bianca grabbed my hand, pulling me through the living room to the front door.

For a moment we stood on the cement porch in the moonlight. "Thanks again," she said.

"Can I see you tomorrow?"

She grinned. "Only if you'll let me beat you at Monopoly."

"Never."

"Okay, then you can come over. I hate it when people let me win."

I kissed her one last time. A simple kiss, the way I should have kissed her before. But the passion still burned beneath, promising much more.

She watched from the porch as I drove away, and I had an overwhelming sense of rightness. I was falling—maybe too fast. And I didn't care.

To think I'd almost missed this, getting to know Bianca, earning her trust, helping her. Even if nothing more ever developed between us, I was glad to be in a position now to do the right thing.

"I won't let you down," I told the absent Bianca. "I promise."

Chapter Nine

Bianca

EARLY SUNDAY AFTERNOON when I'd barely awoken from a brief afternoon nap, Stephen appeared on my doorstep, his eyes bright. My face was probably flushed as I recalled our kiss from the night before. I hoped he attributed it to the heat of the day.

"Here." He handed me a paper, his face bright with anticipation. "Read this."

"What is it?" After Stephen's kiss and Zoey's excitement about her wedding, I hadn't fallen asleep until around five a.m. Then Zoey had awakened me early for church. So despite my nap, I still felt fuzzy.

"A cease and desist letter that I intend to deliver to Fletcher in the morning."

I began scanning the letter: a no-nonsense accusation of copyright and trademark infringement, a request for Fletcher to account for his use of my logo and designs, and a demand to cease all usage. Included were the names of people who could verify my use of the logo and designs.

"This would scare me to death," I said. "But that list of people is only from the beginning of my college years."

"Yep," he said. "I'll call Ross in the morning and tell him we have additional proof for earlier use that we'll use when we ask for a court order. And I'll mention that we know about the other artist. No doubt Ross and Fletcher can find people to say he's been using the logo for years, but if he doesn't know the exact year we're claiming…"

"Then he won't know when to say he began."

"There are ways he can get around that, so we're more posturing than anything for now. But Ross understands that sort of thing. I'm banking on Chad Peterson's involvement to be the determining factor. If not, we can request a court order to stop him temporarily."

"Thank you so much." I couldn't help hugging him. The minute we touched, the tension between us increased. His eyes went to my lips, and then away just as fast. Ah, so he was thinking about last night, too. That seemed a good sign.

"I'll let you know how it goes tomorrow, though we probably won't hear anything for a couple of weeks."

"That long?"

He grimaced. "That fast."

"I see."

"Try to focus on work. Leave the rest to me. Try not to worry."

I found it impossible not to believe him. "Okay, I'll try."

"Now how about that game of Monopoly you promised me?"

"Zoey and Declan should be here any minute. They had an appointment this afternoon to talk to the pastor about their wedding plans. We might be able to twist their arms to get them to play."

"This time, I'm going to win."

"No way."

Turned out he did win, but only because Declan sold him Park Avenue.

That night before Stephen left, he placed a soft kiss on my mouth. "I like you, Bianca Mendez. I like you a lot."

I liked him, too.

The next week slipped by as I divided my time between working and helping plan Zoey's September wedding. Three months suddenly seemed like nothing when we were talking the rest of her life.

"How's it going with you and Stephen?" she asked, looking up from the eggs we'd made for Friday morning breakfast. "He's been calling every night."

I forked up a piece of egg. "We only talk about the case."

Her eyes took on a mocking glint. "No, you don't. I'm not deaf, you know. I hear you laughing and flirting in your room. You really like him."

"Maybe a little."

I'd have thought with my artistic background and his love of the law that we wouldn't have much in common, but he loved music and art, and his research on past court cases fascinated me. We talked about everything and anything.

"Any news on the cease and desist letter?" Zoey asked, rising from the table with her empty plate.

"Not yet. They have ten days to respond. It's a waiting game."

At least with Stephen taking on my battle, it was easier for me to focus on work, or pretend to focus, and to stave off the panic. I now had forty of the new candy dishes in different stages of drying or painting. Still, on some days I became so angry at Fletcher and so hopeless about the future of my pottery that creating was impossible. I felt vulnerable, as if Fletcher had stolen a little piece of my soul.

So far, I'd put my logo on only three of the new pots. Because the more I thought about it, the more unsure I was that going through a lawsuit, if Fletcher didn't back down, would benefit me in the long run. Clinging to the old logo and being unable to work because of the emotions surrounding the case would only be self-defeating. But the few clients who preferred my superior pots would likely support me through a logo change. I could build again.

Except I hadn't yet designed a new logo I felt good about.

Zoey suggested it was because I hadn't given up hope on the current one, and she was probably right.

"I'll see you after work," Zoey said, gathering her purse and keys. "Do you know if Stephen's coming up this weekend?"

"He hasn't said anything." My heart did a funny little jump at the idea of seeing him again.

Zoey paused at the door. "Bianca, if things between you two . . . With Declan and I getting married . . . What I'm trying to say is, if you decide to move back to Phoenix, I'll understand."

"Because of Stephen? I barely know him."

"Sometimes a week is all it takes."

⚬⚬⚬

Several hours later found me taking the three candy dishes I'd made on Saturday from my kiln. They'd turned out better than I'd imagined, especially the intricate lids. The shape of each dish and the patterns I'd carved on them were the same, and each had vibrant glazes, but each hand-painted design was unique. I'd send pictures to my distributors, and if I was lucky, I'd have pre-orders for hundreds more over the next month. Fletcher would have nothing like them yet. I was back in the game.

A knock at the rear door leading from the garage drew my attention. The air conditioner was already installed, and Declan was putting in the insulation tomorrow, so I wasn't expecting anyone.

I opened the door, a grin spreading on my face. "Stephen?" How different I felt seeing him compared to our first meeting a week ago. "Come on in. You must be dying in that suit. It's already hot out there."

He stepped inside, his attention zeroing in on the new candy dishes. "Now that's something I'd like to put on my desk. It's big and in your face, but still . . . elegant."

"Glad you like them, because one is for you."

He examined a dish, opening the lid and peering inside. "Very nice. Much better than when I saw them last." He ran a finger over the surface of the glaze, and a shiver ran through me, as if he'd touched me instead. He set the dish on my worktable.

"So what brings you all the way here?" I asked. "Shouldn't you be at work?"

"Yeah, I was driving there but somehow ended up here. I have news—I guess I couldn't wait to tell you."

"What news?" My stomach clenched. He didn't look upset, but who drove three and a half hours to give the sister of a friend good news he could share easily over the phone?

"Ross emailed me late last night. His client has agreed to stop using your logo. He claims the similarity was unintentional, and that his client will pull your mark immediately from his future designs."

I stared at Stephen, unable to stop my smile from widening. "That's wonderful!"

"Well, he's still claiming the designs are his, and that he won't stop using them, but I've seen his stuff, and it's obviously inferior. The buyers will notice eventually, if they haven't already."

"The logo is the important thing, because it means quality—my quality. Oh, Stephen, thank you!"

The next minute I was in his arms, and his lips met mine. Passion flared, but there was also tenderness and hope and, somehow, a hint of the future. He pulled away after only a few minutes.

"I have to go to work," he said. "But I'm driving back out tonight. Late, since I'll have to make up for this morning. Can I see you tomorrow?"

Excitement curled in my stomach. "I'd like that. A lot."

And then, even though we both knew he had to leave, he didn't. Not right away. Instead, he kissed me again.

About Rachel Branton

Rachel Branton has worked in publishing for over twenty years. She loves writing women's fiction and traveling, and she hopes to write and travel a lot more. As a mother of seven, including a four-year-old, it's not easy to find time to write, but the semi-ordered chaos gives her a constant source of writing material. She warns her children that if they don't behave, they just might find themselves in her next book! She's been known to wear pajamas all day when working on a deadline, and is often distracted enough to burn dinner. (Okay, pretty much 90% of the time.) A sign on her office door reads: *Danger. Enter at Your Own Risk. Writer at Work.* Under the name Rachel Branton, she writes romance, romantic suspense, and women's fiction. Rachel also writes urban fantasy, paranormal romance, and science fiction under the name Teyla Branton.

For more information or to sign up to hear about new releases, please visit RachelBranton.com

Blind Spot

SARIAH WILSON

Chapter One

CINDERELLA WAS EITHER a liar, had incredibly low standards, or was the luckiest woman who had ever lived.

At the moment I was leaning toward the lying option. There was no way she'd gone on what was essentially a blind date and fallen in love with the perfect man the first night of the ball, and had really lived happily ever after.

Because the overweight, balding, sweaty man who sat across from me was no prince. And he was my eleventh Not A Prince in the last three weeks.

I blamed my mother for being the cause of my princess fixation.

As I studied my latest blind date as large drops of sweat blossomed on the top of his head like demented daffodils, making their way slowly down the sides of his face (what was his name again? Vincenzo? Franco? Fonzie?), I tried to pinpoint how exactly I had come to be in this position.

My mother, a professor of women's literature, had outlawed all things princess from my childhood home. I wasn't allowed to watch movies or read books that "warped my sense of reality and caused me to think a man would be my savior and my only path to a fulfilled life." What she hadn't seemed to realize was that by making those things forbidden, it had only made me want them more. I'll never forget the sheer joy, the absolute amazement I felt the very first time I watched the animated *Cinderella*. It was like my entire world had been altered. There was this magic, which I had been totally unaware of. And I needed more of it. I became a full-on princess junkie. I got as many hits as I could whenever I played at a friend's house, or stayed in from lunch and recess at school in order to mainline fairy tales while everyone else played outside.

When I was a teenager, while other kids in my age rebelled by sleeping around and drinking, I got a job at a company that organized princess parties for little girls. With my black hair, fair skin and hazel eyes, I was a total shoo-in as Snow White, even though Cinderella remained my favorite drug of choice. I was happy to dress up and spend entire afternoons pretending with a bunch of giddy little girls who loved princesses as much as I did. In high school I had no idea what I wanted to do, other than not to be in high school anymore. All I knew for certain was that if I didn't go to college, my mother would freak.

And I had no intention of dealing with that drama, because I had quite enough of it when she discovered what I'd been doing outside of school. But by the time she found out about my job, it was too late. I was a full-blown fairy tale addict. Oh, she cried and wondered how it was possible that I had turned out to be such a disappointment, how she should have done more, blah, blah, blah. She pointed out that it was impossible for me to ever actually become a princess, because I would somehow have to marry a prince, and there were hardly any of those left in the world. But I didn't care. I was happy.

I ended up at Sarah Lawrence College, where my mom taught, because I received free tuition. I discovered that I actually really loved learning when I got to choose what I wanted to study. I majored in medieval history, with an emphasis on royal families' genealogies. It was the princessiest thing I could find. And for my senior thesis, my advisor handed me a book that changed my life. It was about the royal family of a tiny European country called Monterra.

And they were the most fertile family I had ever heard of. Each king had anywhere from five to fifteen children, most of them boys. Princes. All real life princes. I can still recall how I had thrown open my laptop, my fingers shaking while I looked for information about the modern family. The reigning king had six living children, and half of them were mouth-watering men!

My mom had been wrong. Here was a country filled with princes. King Dominic had four brothers and a sister who all had enormous families. And the king had uncles who had fathered dozens of prince cousins. So many princes. All in one tiny little kingdom.

The odds of me becoming a princess had gone from zero to fantastic. I had to go to Monterra. Despite not wanting to turn into my mother, and with few other options available given my major, I planned to attend graduate school to become a professor or a teacher. And now there was only one place for me to follow my bliss. I applied and was accepted to the master's program at the university in Monterra.

With no scholarships and no way to qualify for loans in a country where I wasn't a resident, I sunk all of the money in my checking account into an international plane ticket and arrived with my suitcases and little else. I had no place to live. No job. I had been so totally focused on just getting there that I hadn't considered the realities of day-to-day living. Sitting on a bench in the main city of Imperia, realizing how foolish I had been, I started sobbing.

It was Tessa who found me. The first thing I noticed about her was how beautiful she was. Her hair was a rich black, her skin golden, and her light-brown eyes a startling contrast. And she is, to this day, the kindest person I've ever met.

"*Buongiorno. Ti sei perso?*"

"I don't . . . I don't speak Italian," I said in-between sobs. Something else I'd failed to consider in making this idiotic move.

"Oh. I said good morning and asked if you were lost." She spoke English flawlessly, with barely any accent.

"I'm not lost. Just stupid." For some reason the story

poured out of me, alongside my tears. I explained my impulsivity, leaving out the princess obsession part. She sat next to me on the bench, listening thoughtfully.

"And you have no money? No savings?" she asked.

I told her that the only savings I had were of the Daylight variety. I don't think she got it.

"This must be fate. I've been looking for a roommate. You could come stay with me. I'm Tessa, by the way." She offered her hand.

I shook it. "Maria. But everyone calls me Ria. Ria Phillips."

"Come, Ria Phillips. I have the feeling we're about to become the very best of friends." It was weird, but I had the same feeling. Like somehow I'd always known her.

She drove me to her apartment, which was on the top floor of a three-story building. It was on the outskirts of the capital city, but she explained that it was only a short bus ride to the university. Her apartment was ridiculously large and had three bedrooms, each with their own private bathrooms. My mouth dropped when she opened the front door. The living room's massive windows looked out over a pine tree forest and had a fantastic view of the Alps. The bathrooms looked as if they belonged in high-end spas. The furniture was modern and expensive looking. Tessa had mentioned she was a chef, and I figured she must have been the world's best chef to afford this kind of an apartment.

Part of me wondered why she had been looking for a roommate when she had a place like this. How was she not beating potential roommates off with a stick? I would have been willing to share my bedroom with two other girls, because it was literally big enough that I could have. Shouldn't people be lining up to live here? She let me pick which suite I wanted, and when I collapsed onto the ridiculously comfortable mattress, I realized I could have happily spent the rest of my life in that bed.

It seemed too good to be true. Some part of me worried

that maybe this was some sort of scheme meant to lure me in before selling me off, only there would be no Liam Neeson to rescue me when I was taken. But it might have almost been worth it if I got to keep sleeping on Tessa's Egyptian cotton sheets.

The move to Monterra, living in Tessa's apartment, everything that had initially seemed overwhelming soon became my new normal. I landed a part-time job at the university teaching undergrads in history courses, and worked as an English tutor at home. Tessa charged me hardly anything for rent, ignoring my protests that I should contribute more, and she often brought home delicious leftovers from the restaurant where she worked. Which made it easy for me to cover tuition and books.

I took over the majority of the chores in the apartment since Tessa hated to clean. I didn't much care for it either, but given how much she was covering financially, I had to do something to repay her for all her kindness. Plus, scrubbing floors and washing pots sort of fed my Cinderella fantasy.

And I adored Tessa. As predicted, she quickly became my best friend and my own Monterran fairy godmother. We loved the same TV shows, the same movies, and she shared my obsession with entertainment magazines. Eventually, I even told her about the princess thing. Which made her laugh a lot for some reason.

Once everything in my life settled into a comfortable routine, I decided I was ready to find my prince.

Problem was, I didn't know how to go about it. And by then the three princes in the ruling family were either married or engaged. To American women. Which meant I'd had a shot but missed it.

One of them, Prince Rafael, owned a software company, and had created a phone app called Love Is Blind. It was a way to meet guys, but there were no pictures. You decided whether or not you wanted to go out with someone based solely on their written description. Some part of me hoped that he had convinced his massive family to be beta testers, and that there was a cousin in there somewhere that I could meet. I tried to choose men who seemed to be obliquely referencing their royal heritage.

I had hoped for the best, but instead I went out on a series of progressively worse dates, often with men old enough to be my father. Much like tonight. And not one of them had turned out to be royalty.

Leaning back in my chair, I crossed my arms and tried not to sigh in disgust. Even if I wanted to blame my mother, the only person I had to blame for this mess was myself. Nobody else had made me agree to a bunch of blind dates from a dating app. I made sure to always have the men meet me at The Crown because, if nothing else, Tessa was in back with large, sharp knives.

Unfortunately, that meant the too-hot-for-his-own-good bartender, Paolo, would be watching over me with total amusement, a gleam in his eye and a straw between his perfect teeth. Physically, he reminded me of Tessa: the same dark hair and light brown eyes. Only his had little flecks of gold around the iris. Not that I noticed or anything. His shirts always seemed a bit too tight, as if he just flexed hard enough, the very obvious muscles in his arms and chest would rip the fabric to shreds. Although I knew I shouldn't objectify him, I would have very much liked to have seen such a thing happen.

Admittedly, I thought a lot more about Paolo than I probably should have. He was always smiling, and the bar was always, always crowded with women trying to snag his attention. Which he was more than happy to give them, his blinding smile lighting up the room. I had dated a man like him once in college. Too slick, too pretty, and too much of a player.

Plus, snobbish as it sounded, he was a bartender. I wanted to be with an adult. Someone with ambition beyond serving alcohol, partying and going home every night with a different girl. Not that I'd ever actually seen him leave with anyone, but I had to assume that it happened given the amount of cleavage that was regularly flashed at him.

"You are the student?" What's-His-Face asked me.

The student. Like I was the only person at the university. I sighed again. There I went, being a jerk because I was frustrated with this entire situation and couldn't figure out a graceful way to excuse myself. I couldn't even leave, given that Tessa was my ride home. And to be fair, my date spoke English much better than I spoke Italian. "I am a student. I'm pursuing my master's degree in medieval history."

His eyes glazed over. As if I'd said something he hadn't liked. He looked at me again with a dismissive expression, as if *I* was the one somehow failing to meet *his* standards. Despite the fact that I was at least twenty years his junior, had all my hair and wasn't even a little bit sweaty. I watched as his gaze drifted to the bar, to the scantily clad, gorgeous women who were currently trying to catch Paolo's attention.

"What is it that you do?" I asked, cutting my filet mignon. If nothing else, I at least got to eat Tessa's fantastic food. No wonder the owner paid her so much. I took a bite, and the meat was so soft it seemed to literally melt on my tongue. I closed my eyes for a second, savoring it.

"I am the dog catcher," the man said, and when I opened my eyes back up, I saw that he was still watching the bimbos at the bar.

I followed his gaze, and Paolo winked at me. Which made several of the women turn to cast me dirty looks. I redirected my attention to my plate.

"I am very much," my companion said, "the grandson of the *Duca di Siracusa* on *da parte di mia madre.* You are the lucky to be with me."

First the student, and now the lucky. Funny, but I didn't feel like *the lucky.* I was pretty sure that *duca* meant duke. Possibly because of his mother? Tessa kept trying to teach me Italian, but I was terrible at it. But if I had understood him correctly, I had finally found at least a quasi-nobleman, if not royalty.

That should have made me excited.

It didn't.

Instead it just seemed... pretentious. Yes, I am the last person who should say or think something like that given my life goals. But there it was. We'd been sitting here for ten minutes, and I already wanted the night to be over.

Tessa's food was the only thing keeping me from saying horribly awful things to The Dog Catcher. Low blood sugar tended to make me a tad crazy and mean. He was finally looking at me instead of "The Bachelor" contestant rejects, and I realized that I should say something. It took me a moment to find something neutral and not offensive. "That's nice."

He grunted his agreement and dove back into his food with a ferocity that was a bit terrifying. I scooted back slightly in my chair, taking my knife and putting it in my lap. Just in case.

My mom had been wildly overprotective, always convinced that I'd get kidnapped in a van or have my throat slit while doing laundry. It had made me, well, paranoid.

After a few more minutes of listening to this man smacking his lips and swallowing his food whole, with me wondering if he could somehow unhinge his jaw to shovel everything in even faster, he glanced at me again.

"Dinner is done," he announced. "Is enough? Now we go to bed?"

My eyebrows practically slammed into my hairline. Were we having a translation issue? Was he saying the evening was over, and we should go home, him to his bed and me to mine? I desperately hoped that was the case.

"What?" I tried to clarify.

"We go now. To do..." He made some appalling gestures.

Nope, no misunderstanding. And so not happening. Even though I was well-fed, the combination of shock, disgust and alarm created angry, rumbling tremors inside me. "Now look here…"

The next thing I knew, someone's nose was nuzzling my ear. For a second I was too surprised to react, not able to imagine who would do such a thing. Then I felt warm, strong lips pressing against the skin right under my earlobe, and those angry tremors turned into excited ones. I gasped as my muscles totally collapsed and my bones gave way.

Words were whispered against the skin of my throat. "Come, *tesora mia*, are you going to torture me all night? Will you ever forgive me?"

The only torture going on was what his fingers were doing to the back of my neck. It was so delicious, such an amazing feeling, that it took my hazy brain a good thirty seconds to figure out who was touching me.

It was Paolo.

Trying to rescue me.

Chapter Two

THE FEW TIMES Paolo and I had spoken, it had been of the bantering/insulting type. We had never gone out, ever, so he hadn't cheated on me or needed forgiveness. He must have seen my face and rushed over to protect me from The Dog Catcher. Or he was trying to protect The Dog Catcher from me, as Paolo carefully slid the knife from my relaxed hand.

What did he think he was doing? I was an adult. I could handle the creepy lecher guy on my own. I tried not to loll my head back as Paolo's fingers started kneading my neck.

"Sorry, I'm not the forgiving and forgetting type," I said through clenched teeth. But whether I'd clenched them out of anger or because I couldn't deal with the onslaught of sensations Paolo was causing, I wasn't sure.

And Paolo had definitely never put his lips and hands on my skin before, and it was driving me crazy. He moved his mouth lower, and I smelled his minty breath as it wafted up to my nose, which surprised me. I would have expected his breath to smell like alcohol. It didn't. He again kissed me at the base of my neck, which made my brain explode into a million rainbows, sending cold, prickly shivers down my spine while simultaneously warming my blood. How did he do that?

I had to push him back so I could concentrate again. "What... what are you..." I sputtered, finding that my mouth did not function, and that my skin was all flushed and hot from his touch.

"Come and find me at the bar when you have finished

315

with this one," he said with a nod, mischief and delight sparkling in his light brown eyes. "I'm always here, anytime you
want me."

He was basically implying to the entire restaurant that
we'd hooked up. I was not one of his bar groupies.

"Please excuse me," I said, standing up. I threw my linen
napkin on the table and followed after Paolo.

I grabbed the upper part of his arm, suppressing a gasp
when a current sparked between us. I wanted to blame static
electricity, but the floors were hardwood. I willed my hand not
to linger on his bicep as he turned, still wearing that charming
grin.

"What was that? What do you think you were doing?" I
asked, forcing my fingers to let go. I'd never stood this close
to him before, so I'd never realized how broad his shoulders
were. Or how despite the fact that I'd felt like an Amazon my
entire life, he had at least three inches on me. My mouth went
dry.

He moved even closer to me, dominating the space
around us in a heart-pounding way. He reached out and ran
his fingers down the length of my arm, leaving waves of fire in
his wake.

"Beautiful Ria." The way he said my name scrambled my
senses. He rolled the R on his tongue, and my legs went weak.
"I was trying to save you back there."

"I'm not a damsel in distress. I was handling it."

He looked over my shoulder. "Yes, you handled it. With
him walking out and leaving you with the check."

We were standing so close together that we should have
been touching, but weren't. Had Paolo always smelled this
good? Like... citrus, laundry detergent and hot-guy phero-
mones?

"What?" I said, in a breathy voice. How did his devotees
focus on anything when he smelled like this?

I turned to look over my shoulder and saw that what he'd
said was true. The Dog Catcher had left without paying his

half of the check. I sensed the second Paolo left to go back behind the bar, because I missed the warmth he radiated. I didn't like feeling bewildered and confused by my reaction to him. Rattled, I struggled with whether or not to say something to him about his botched rescue attempt. He'd had no right to interfere.

It was the sort of internal battle I regularly faced. My mom had done her best to bring me up to be a strong woman who didn't need a man. Although I never would have admitted it, I loved the idea of a guy like Paolo swooping in and saving the day. The mom-cultivated feminist part of me and the princess fantasy half were always at war. I both wanted to be rescued and resented the implication that I couldn't save myself.

It was exhausting.

"You know, I really didn't need your help," I said, elbowing my way through tan legs and fake boobs to reach the counter.

Paolo winked at me. And instead of annoying me, this time his flirtation made me feel all shivery. "It didn't look that way from here." I was about to tell him to get his eyes checked when he asked, "What will you have?"

"Oh. I don't know. Some sparkling water, maybe?"

"A girl after my own heart."

None of the women at the bar seemed to enjoy my intrusion. If looks could have killed, I would have been dead multiple times over. Even though I was not trying to flirt with him. I was trying to tell him off. That he was flirting with me was not my fault.

That I enjoyed it was.

I remembered his breath from earlier, how I hadn't detected any alcohol. "You prefer water?" I asked incredulously, watching as he pulled a chilled bottle from a fridge, popped the top and filled up a glass for me.

A shadow crossed his features and disappeared just as

quickly, replaced with a grin. "Of course. I treat my body like a temple."

I couldn't help it. I let out a laugh. "Open to everyone, day or night?"

He set the glass of water in front of me, rested his elbows on the bar and leaned toward me with a look so intense it made my breath catch. "I'd be open to you, day or night."

Grabbing my glass, I took a big gulp. What was wrong with me? The room suddenly felt unbearably hot. "How much do I owe you?"

"It's on me," he said with that smile. "Not literally on me. I mean I will cover the cost."

I had known what he meant. But now I was having vivid and inappropriate thoughts of him doused in water that made it difficult for me to swallow.

Which was probably why he'd said it.

My preference for water had nothing to do with working out or being healthy. Because I did not work out and found "healthy" to be a relative term. There was the genetic component that made drinking risky, but my freshman year in college was the main reason I never partook. Every girl in my dorm drank like somebody had told them there was a magical genie at the bottom of their bottle who would give them eternally tanned skin and perpetual beach waves in their hair. I saw how stupid it made everyone, and the danger they put themselves in by getting blackout drunk. I had never wanted any part of it.

"Are you dating that man?" he asked, drying off some tumblers with a white rag.

I could see why all of these girls were constantly vying for his attention. Because when Paolo spoke to you, it was like you were the only person in the entire universe that mattered. That he found everything you said fascinating and insightful. It made everything else disappear, including the weighty stares of everyone around us.

"No," I immediately said. "Blind date. But I'm thinking I might be done with those."

He nodded thoughtfully. "Excellent decision. I've seen some of the people you've dragged into the restaurant."

Ha. As if he had any room to talk. "At least I'm trying to seriously meet someone. What about you?" I gestured my hand to the right so he'd know exactly what I meant.

"I'm not dating anyone."

As if I couldn't have predicted that. "Translation? A series of meaningless hookups, because you can't be bothered with a committed relationship."

That shadow was there again. "I would like to be in a committed relationship. If I could find a woman of substance. Which is difficult when you keep fishing from the same shallow pond."

"That's a lovely thought. Women as fish. I'm sure the girls dig that."

He grinned again. "I'm serious. I'm looking for someone who is smart, kind, and beautiful, inside and out. A woman who isn't afraid of taking risks to get what she wants, because she knows exactly what she wants. A woman who won't fall at my feet and doesn't let me get away with things. Someone that will keep me on my toes. I want the kind of woman I can treasure."

My heart stopped for a full ten seconds, before it started thrashing frantically against my rib cage. Because even though I thought we'd been having an abstract discussion, he looked and sounded as if he was talking about me. But how was that possible? We didn't even know each other.

This was freaking me out. I mumbled a thank you for the water and hurried back to the kitchen. I told my waiter to bring me both checks so that I could pay for them, because it was almost closing time. While the bar was still in full swing, the kitchen was winding down.

I found Tessa in the back, humming to herself as she

rolled out dough. She glanced up and said, "What happened to you? You look like you saw a ghost."

"Paolo…" There was no explanation. What could I say? I thought Paolo was flirting with me and he's overwhelming and too handsome, so I'm hiding out in here?

"What about Paolo?" she asked the question so carefully that I put down my glass of water to study her. She had that "I'm innocent" tone to her voice and wore a neutral expression, but I knew her better than that.

Tessa always enthusiastically listened to all my dating exploits. She loved love. She also spent a great deal of time trying to marry off all of her kitchen staff. The chefs, the bakers, the waiters/waitresses, the hostesses and the guys at the bar. She would never give up if she knew I felt some kind of attraction toward Paolo.

Which I never quite understood, given her own typically dismal relationships.

"Nothing about Paolo," I assured her. "How are you doing?"

She knew exactly what I meant. "I'm fine. I haven't texted or called Giuseppe at all." Giuseppe was the latest in a string of bad boyfriends who had broken Tessa's heart. "In fact, you know that daydream of mine where a truck hits me, and after the police call him, and Giuseppe suddenly realizes that he's still madly in love with me and races to the hospital with a four carat diamond in his pocket, begging and pleading for my forgiveness?"

I nodded.

"Well, I haven't had it in at least nine days." She sounded so proud of herself. "Here. I need you to mix this by hand. It's the filling for the cannoli."

She put a metal bowl on the counter. Despite hating cleaning at home, her kitchen was always pristine. The countertops were so clean you could eat a dropped chocolate soufflé off of them.

Not that I knew that from personal experience or anything.

In addition to teaching me Italian, Tessa had been giving me cooking lessons. My entire life had consisted of microwaved meals, takeout, and food in cafeterias. Cooking was another one of those things my mother eschewed as house slavery designed by the patriarchy to keep women from the workforce.

I didn't know much about it, but even I thought mixing something by hand was weird. Still, Tessa was the chef. I extended my fingers, ready to stick them into the white liquid when she grabbed my wrist in alarm. "What are you doing?"

"Mixing by hand."

That made her laugh, and she handed me something silver. "This is a whisk, remember? Mixing by hand does not mean using your actual hand. It means using a utensil in your hand as you stir. Aren't you supposed to be the English expert?"

I sheepishly took the whisk and began stirring. This made much more sense.

And it was nice to have something make sense in my life. It was like the last few months had been nothing but an exercise in forcing me to reevaluate my life choices. Tessa came over and used a small spoon to taste the filling. "Almost."

She could eat anything, never exercise and not put on any weight. I'd easily gained ten pounds since moving in with her. Her ridiculous metabolism sometimes made it hard to be her friend. But then she'd make me zeppoles, Italian doughnuts, and we were fine again.

"What does *tesora mia* mean?" I asked.

Tessa was carefully and precisely cutting her flattened dough. "It means 'my treasure.' It's a term of endearment. Why? Who called you that?"

Her translation sent a pulse of unexpected heat through me. It shouldn't have, given that Monterran men used endearments all the time. It was because Paolo had said it. To me.

He'd said he wanted a woman he could treasure. And he was calling me his treasure. Was there a connection there, or did he say that to everyone? I couldn't talk it out with Tessa. If I told her what had happened, she'd never let it go.

The swinging doors of the kitchen were flung open, and one of the bar bimbos stumbled in on her high heels, loudly mumbling something in Italian.

"What is she saying?" I asked Tessa.

"I don't know."

The girl ran into a stand of pans, knocking a few of them to the ground with a loud clang. She looked like she was about to topple over, and I ran over to help.

"*Parli inglese?*" I asked her.

"Why does it matter if she can speak English?" Tessa asked.

"Because I speak fluent drunk." Since I'd typically been the only sober person in the room all through college, it had become my second language. The girl then began to mumble in a way I could understand. "She's looking for her car keys."

"That doesn't sound like a good idea," Tessa said, calling out for Paolo.

A few seconds later he was talking to Tessa in rapid Italian, but kept sneaking sexy little glances my way that gave me goosebumps.

And I swore I heard my name during their exchange.

I rubbed my hands up and down my arms, wanting the goosebumps to go away. Paolo was not the right guy for me. I heard him say in English, "I'll call her a cab. And I'll talk to Alfonso about over serving."

He put his hand around her waist, practically carrying her out to the front door. He shot one last grin at me over his shoulder. For some reason, watching him go made me regretful. He was sweet, helping the poor, lost alcoholic. Honestly, what was wrong with a man like Paolo? So what if he wasn't a prince? I'd just gone out with the grandson of a duke, and that disaster had been awful in every way imaginable (except for Tessa's food). But I'd had more fun interacting with Paolo for a few minutes than I'd had with anyone else for months.

Maybe it was time to grow up.

Tessa was forever trying to sell me on going out with her friends. "He does emergency rescue!" or "He works with a non-profit!" or "He works with the palace!" Admittedly, I'd been slightly interested in the last one. Because I'd deduced that I could use him to meet some royalty, which I immediately dismissed. Not only because it was selfish and evil, but also because there would be a level of expectation if I went out with one of Tessa's friends that didn't exist with some random guy I'd met online. If I didn't like my blind dates, I never had to see them again. But if he was a buddy of Tessa's? Odds were I'd be forced to interact with him in the future, given how much she loved to entertain.

And the fact that she focused solely on the jobs of the men she recommended wasn't lost on me. Because wasn't that all I'd been focusing on? The guy's job? Whether or not he was a prince? How stupid was that?

There was nothing wrong with a bartender. Or a firefighter or a volunteer or a member of the royal staff. Not to mention that I happened to not be a princess. I was a graduate student and part-time teacher/tutor. Why had I been so insistent that potential boyfriends be so much more?

Tessa had returned to finish her cannoli, proclaiming my filling to be "*perfetto.*" I watched her work for a couple of minutes. It was strangely soothing, and it let me think about where to go from here. Maybe I should take her up on her offer. She was such a fantastic person, so it would make sense that her other friends would be equally amazing.

"I think this is the longest you've ever been quiet, and it's starting to scare me," she teased.

Time to confess. "I think… I think I've given up on the whole prince thing."

Her eyes lit up as her hands went still. "Really?"

Not letting myself take it back, I nodded. "It was such a stupid thing to want, you know? I can't control who loves me, or who I love. I should be looking for a great guy. A…" Paolo's words echoed in my mind. "A man of substance."

"I know someone just like that. Let me set you up. And before you ask, he's a carpenter."

"Like Geppetto?"

She laughed. "As far as I know, he hasn't brought any wooden puppets to life. What do you think? Will you go?"

I needed this. I needed to move on from some childhood wish. I needed to let myself see what else was out there. "Set me up. Let's do this."

Tessa squealed, jumping up and down. "He is the absolute perfect guy for you. I can't wait for you to meet!"

Inhaling a shaky breath, I gave her a watery smile. Time to start adulting.

I'd been through complete nightmare blind dates.

Honestly, how bad could another one be?

Chapter Three

I SHOULD HAVE knocked on wood. Because as it turned out, another blind date could be pretty bad.

Tessa had insisted I leave everything in her hands. There was a restaurant over an hour away, straight up the mountain. One of her dearest friends from culinary school ran the kitchen, and Tessa assured me the food was incredible. Because it was the off season, the restaurant was only open for lunch. She gave me her car to drive, and I used my phone to find the place. Rain fell the entire way, as I drove past ancient forests and sheer rock faces. I thought of how hard it must have been to create this road straight through the mountain.

I had to pay careful attention, because the road twisted and turned, and there were many places I could have skidded and fallen off a cliff and died. As a result, I was almost twenty minutes late. Fortunately, Tessa had thought to stick an umbrella in the back seat, which meant all the water wouldn't ruin my hair and makeup. I ran inside, breathless and worried. I hated being late, and I was making a terrible first impression.

The dining room was completely empty. A waiter greeted me and showed me to a table for two near an eight-foot tall window. In any other weather but rain, I was sure the view would be breathtaking. But water blurred everything outside.

I was handed a menu, and my eyes kept drifting over to the front door. While I'd been surprised to find that I was the only one there, given the weather, it was understandable. But it also most likely meant that the next man to walk through the door would be my date. There were unsettling butterflies in my stomach.

Because Tessa had refused to tell me anything else about the guy beyond the fact that he was a carpenter. I didn't know if he was tall or short, hot or ugly, smart or dumb. I didn't even know his name. She had assured me it was more romantic this way. The princess part of me agreed, finding it to be like some kind of fairy tale. Two strangers meeting, knowing nothing about each other, and possibly falling in love.

But as the minutes ticked by, things were seeming less and less romantic. At first I wasn't upset. Hadn't I been late? The weather was terrible. He had an excuse. Then a half hour went by. And an hour. I tried my cell phone to call Tessa, but at this altitude there was no reception. I shoved it back in my purse. I could see the parking lot from where I sat, and I waited and watched.

Almost two hours after I'd arrived, the waiter brought me a dessert compliments of the chef, letting me know they were closing the kitchen. Humiliated, I ate it as quickly as possible, willing the rain to let up. The staff didn't allow me to pay, since I was Tessa's friend, but I left the waiter a big tip. In part so he wouldn't think I was completely pathetic, and because I felt bad for wasting everyone's time.

I had been on some dreadful dates before, but I had never been stood up. Ever.

The only thing that made me feel marginally a bit better was that at least he hadn't seen me and driven off.

Anger and embarrassment made my limbs shake. I stormed my way out to Tessa's minicar, slamming the door shut behind me. More than anything, I wanted to push the pedal to the floor. I refrained. With the roads so slick, throwing a tantrum might end with me being dead.

Instead I drove slowly, my rage festering. I had finally taken a chance, had put myself out there, and for what? To be stood up, feeling like a total idiot?

Better to live in a dream world, if this was reality. Angry tears flooded my vision, and I wiped them off my cheeks. I was not going to cry over some idiot.

The still rational part of my brain tried to talk me down. Tessa never would have arranged a date with the kind of guy who wouldn't show up. Something must have happened. There had to be a reason he hadn't come.

But the chaos beast inside me didn't care. It wanted to throw things and yell and bang my hands against the steering wheel. At the speed I was traveling, it was taking forever to get down the stupid mountain. A crack of lightning flashed just in front of me, and I screamed, slamming the brakes. The tires squealed, and the car skidded across the road, smacking into a tree.

It took me a few seconds to realize that I'd been in accident. My chest was heaving, and I felt like I wanted to throw up. My heart was pounding inside my throat, making it hard to breathe. I ran my hands over my ribs, wondering if the seatbelt had crushed them. But I hadn't been going that fast, and I hadn't hit the tree very hard. I seemed to be okay.

Grabbing the umbrella, I stepped outside to inspect the damage. My high heels dug into the mud, making it difficult to walk. I wished that I had brought a pair of tennis shoes. I let out a groan when I saw the whole front passenger side crunched inward. The repairs would be expensive, and I didn't have any insurance, because I didn't drive very often.

The rain thundered against the top of the car as I climbed back in. I turned the key toward me, and the headlights went dim. I said a little prayer, closing my eyes, and tried to start the ignition.

Nothing. Just a clicking noise.

"Please start. Please start," I muttered. I tried it again. And again. And again. But no matter how many times I begged the engine to turn over, it didn't happen. I was stuck. I pulled my phone out, realizing that it was nearly dead because I'd left the "Location" option on for the GPS. I turned the option off and discovered that the power cord in the car did not match my American phone.

What was I supposed to do? I started mulling over my options. I turned my headlights on. Maybe a police cruiser or fire truck would come by, and they would rescue me. Which seemed very unlikely, given that I hadn't seen a single other car on my way up or down the mountain. And the idea that some random person might stop to help me threatened to send me into full-on panic mode. I could literally hear my mother's voice telling me, "Never get into a stranger's car!"

I could walk back to the restaurant. Uphill. In high heels. Where they had already closed. Or try walking down the mountain and find some civilization.

And not a creepy mountain cabin where the owner collected chainsaws.

I sat in the car for over an hour, waiting. Routinely trying the ignition. I thought that the kitchen staff might drive home this way. But what if they lived in a different direction? Or their homes were closer to the top? I'd be waiting forever.

There was nothing else to do. I would have to walk. I grabbed my purse, putting my phone inside it. I zipped the purse shut, hoping that would protect my phone from the rain. Maybe when I was far enough down, I could call for help. I took the umbrella, got out of the car and started walking.

Even though the road wasn't muddy, it still felt treacherous. Every step I took made me feel as if I was about to slip. I almost never wore heels. Only on dates. Or when I was stood up.

Thunder rolled overhead, and I hoped that the lightning had passed. I checked my watch. I'd only been walking for twenty minutes, but it felt like twenty hours.

I caught sight of what looked like light in front of me. I squinted, trying to make it out.

Headlights. Coming straight toward me. *Please let it be a mom with three kids in her station wagon.*

My grandmother had once told me that bad things always happened in threes. Being stood up was the first, crashing Tessa's car was the second, and I had the sinking suspicion that a person on their way to kidnap and murder me would be the third.

If I survived this, I was going to call my mother and chew her out for making me so paranoid.

As it came closer, I saw that it was a white SUV. And the driver was not a mother with her children.

It was a man. He rolled his window down.

"Paolo?" I asked incredulously. "Am I hallucinating?" This had to be some figment of my imagination. It made sense. The last time I'd seen him at The Crown he'd been helping someone; now I was fantasizing that he had arrived to help me.

"I've been told that women dream about me, but I don't think I've ever made someone hallucinate before." There was that wink, that playful smile. He pulled his car to a stop, letting it idle in the middle of the road.

Not imaginary. I'd been gone so long, Tessa had probably been worried... and had sent Paolo after me? That seemed strange.

"What are you doing here?" I asked.

He blinked at me like I was the crazy one. "At the moment? Saving you again." He nodded to the passenger seat. "Get in."

Get in? All of my overdeveloped protective instincts, courtesy of my mother, told me to just keep walking. I didn't really know Paolo. What if he'd been lying in wait this whole time for a situation just like this one? So what if I knew where he worked? Serial killers had regular jobs.

"Let me check my calendar." I paused. "Nope. I definitely did not plan to be murdered today. I'm not getting in your car."

He blinked several times, as if he hadn't understood me. "Are you serious?"

"Very. You could be a rapist and a serial killer."

Now he looked insulted. "I am not."

"That's exactly what a serial killer would say."

"But you know me, *tesora mia.*"

I honed in on the Italian. "Your treasure? Treasure gets buried."

"No, treasure is treasured."

What was that supposed to mean? My pulse throbbed all through me, and I couldn't tell if it was fear, adrenaline or something else.

"You're wrong," I said. "I don't know you. We're acquaintances at best. And serial killers murder acquaintances all the time." I'd also probably watched too much *Dateline*. "I'm not letting you drive me to my doom."

He closed his eyes and muttered under his breath, and I saw how tightly he gripped his wheel. He opened his eyes back up. "Then you drive."

"So you can attack me while I'm helpless, because I'm concentrating on the road? No, thanks."

"Fine," he said through clenched teeth. He probably should be mad. I was being totally irrational, but I couldn't seem to stop myself. "I won't wear my seatbelt, and if I do anything that scares you, which I won't, you can crash the car into a tree or something to stop me."

"I'm not driving you without a seatbelt!" I protested. "I was just in an accident. What if we got in another one?"

His mouth hung open for a second before he responded. "You think I want to kill you, but you're worried I might get hurt in an accident?"

"Well, what if you're not a serial killer? Then I would feel really bad."

Paolo let out a groan that seemed to be a combination of anger and disbelief. "I'll wear my seatbelt, and you can tie my hands up."

"Tie you up with what?"

"I have some climbing rope in my trunk."

"Why would you have climbing rope in your trunk?" My

voice climbed higher in pitch with each word, as my eyes widened. "Do you know who keeps rope in their trunks? Serial killers!"

At that, Paolo got out of the car, slamming his door shut. I took a step back. The rain immediately drenched him, and even while freaked out, I admired the way his shirt melded to his chest.

"Just know," he said, "that I am resisting the urge to throw you over my shoulder and toss you in the backseat."

Despite how mad he sounded, his masculine words unexpectedly thrilled me. Something was seriously wrong with me.

"You feel like you don't know me?" he asked. "I have dinner with my parents every Sunday. I pay my taxes. I volunteer with search and rescue. I work as a sponsor for recovering alcoholics. I go to Mass every week, and I'm an Eagle Scout."

My inner mom voice protested. *Does he deliver puppies and fart rainbows, too? Too good to be true.*

He held out his hand to me. "Trust me, Ria. Please. Besides, I'm getting cold."

It was a combination of the tone in his voice, trilling the R in my name, and his shivering that played on my sympathies. Deep down I knew I could trust him, despite my overzealous fears. I put my hand in his, and he led me around to the opposite side, opening my door for me.

No guy had ever opened a door for me before. It was sweet. Even though I could have opened it myself. I shook out my umbrella and laid it on the floor, next to my feet.

When he got in, I said, "I'm trusting you. But for the record, if you kill me, I'm going to haunt you."

"Since we're putting things on the record, I never would have let you drive my car." He shook his hair, and water went flying everywhere.

"Why not?" I asked as we put on our seatbelts.

He shifted the car into drive and did a three point turn to

head us down the mountain. "I've heard about your road rage problem."

The only person I'd ever driven with was Tessa. She must have said something to him. But if my driving was that big a deal, why talk to Paolo about it and not to me?

"I don't have road rage. I have people-who-drive-like-morons rage."

"Which is why I wouldn't let you drive."

I crossed my arms. "That's sexist." My mother would have had a field day.

"It's not sexist. I just prefer living."

My stomach grumbled. I was starving. And wary. And cranky.

"Are you all right?" he asked, looking at me out of the corner of his eye. I wondered whether he'd heard my insides demanding food.

"Nothing a good lawsuit won't fix," I grumbled, leaning against the car door. Paolo was driving even slower than I had. Probably for good reason, considering I'd crashed.

"Do you know what your problem is?"

Did he not realize that he was making everything a thousand times worse? "Please grace me with your wisdom, oh enlightened master of observation."

He cocked one eyebrow at me. "You like me, and you won't admit it."

Chapter Four

"I'M SORRY YOU mistook my basic human decency for attraction," I replied, but it was all bark and no bite. Partly because I suspected he was right. He was obviously hot, and I did kind of like him. Hadn't he played a starring role in my decision to stop waiting for a prince?

And look at how well that was turning out.

"You have to admit that I look good on my white horse." Technically, it was a white SUV, but I didn't point that out. Because he did look good. Even if I didn't want him to.

"I don't have to admit anything," I growled, trying hard to pretend that I wasn't flirting back. Because I totally was.

"Oh!" He snapped his fingers as if he'd only just realized something. "I forgot. You're not very nice when you're hungry." He pulled the SUV over to the side of the road, putting on his hazards.

I felt a frantic moment of fear/excitement when Paolo took off his seatbelt and leaned toward me. At the last second, he turned his body to reach into the backseat directly behind me. He grabbed a backpack and pulled it into his lap. He opened it, rummaged around inside, and took out three chocolate-covered protein bars. He held them up next to his face, grinning at me.

"I hear food calms the savage beast." He handed all three of the bars to me.

He could have said anything he wanted at that point, hurled any insult, just as long as he fed me. I ate the first one so fast, I might have ingested some of the wrapper.

SARIAH WILSON

The sight of me hoovering up his food made him laugh. He reached out to tuck a stray piece of hair behind my ear, and I went completely still. Waves of electricity danced across the skin his fingers brushed.

"Don't you feel that?" he asked me, his voice almost a whisper. "Don't you think this is the beginning of something?"

The protein bar stuck in my throat, and I had to gulp it down. Was he really that intuitive? Could he tell that I wasn't as indifferent as I pretended to be? "I think this is the beginning of a beautiful mutual tolerance."

He threw his head back and laughed, and to my dismay, he also stopped touching me. Still chuckling, he put his seatbelt back on and resumed driving.

After I'd demolished all three of the bars, I asked, "Why do you have food in your car?"

"Eagle Scout, remember?"

"I thought that was an American thing."

He beat his thumbs against the wheel. "It's not just in America. Nice country, though. I lived there for a while. For university."

"Which one?"

Paolo hesitated, as if he didn't want to answer. "Princeton."

Princeton? What kind of bartender went to Princeton? And how strange was it that we'd gone to colleges that were only a couple of hours apart?

Before I could ask him about it, he kept going. "And to answer your earlier question, we have Boy Scouts in Europe, too. I joined because it appealed to me. I've always loved the outdoors. Rock climbing, hiking, fishing, boating, bicycling. What about you?"

"I like hiking. Or as I call it, walking."

He laughed again. He seriously had the best laugh. It made my heart glow brightly in my chest while simultaneously doing somersaults.

334

"You're back. Your evil twin is fine, but I much prefer the good one. Tessa wasn't kidding about the blood sugar."

Again with Tessa. What was my roommate telling him? Why was she telling him anything at all? My eyebrows knit together as my mind raced with possibilities.

"So you don't like the outdoors?" he asked while I wadded up the wrappers and put them in my purse.

"Not so much at the moment." Which earned me another smile. "I didn't have a dad growing up, so I never did that kind of stuff."

Paolo glanced at me in the rearview mirror. "I could take you."

Strangest part? I wanted him to. I opened my mouth, but words wouldn't come out. Which didn't matter, because he was already filling the silence. "I understand. My father was very, very busy."

I was still imagining us frolicking through forests and canoeing across lakes. It took me a second to adjust. "A workaholic?"

He pressed his lips together. "You could say that."

"Speaking of -aholics, my mom is a recovering alcoholic, too." When he'd been listing reasons I should trust him, I'd honed in on him saying he sponsored alcoholics. I leapt to the logical conclusion. "She stopped the second she found out she was pregnant with me, but my dad had already left by then, because he couldn't deal. She hasn't had a drink in the last twenty-three years."

I forced my mouth shut. What was wrong with me? I never told anyone about my mom. Ever. Not even Tessa.

"It's been 1,887 days for me."

I couldn't do that math in my head, but it sounded like a really long time. "I have a little addiction of my own." Those words just kept spilling out, and I had seriously come *this close* to telling him everything. And why? It wasn't like alcoholism was anything like my princess obsession.

He gave me the side eye, eyebrows raised.

"Not drugs or drinking or anything," I rushed to explain. "Just something I really loved and only recently have tried to let go of." Time to get the attention off of me and back to him. "You work in a bar every night? That must be tough."

Paolo shrugged one shoulder. "Tessa needs the help, and she doesn't have to pay me. I manage okay."

"Wait. Why wouldn't Tessa have to pay you?"

"I have other things I do for money, and I'm her brother."

Everything just stopped.

Her *brother*?

Now that he said it, I could definitely see the resemblance, but her brother? How had that never come up before? Tessa had some serious explaining to do.

"Did she not tell you?"

"No!" It made me wonder what else my roomie had kept to herself. And it made me realize how badly I'd misjudged Paolo. I had dismissed him as some guy who tended bar to party and pick up women. Instead, he was helping my best friend, while surrounded by drinks he probably craved more than anything and could never touch.

Absentmindedly scratching his chest, he slowed the SUV to a crawl. He leaned forward, and I turned to see what he was looking at.

"The road is gone," he informed me.

"Gone? How?"

"The rain washed it out." He shifted the car to Park, turning off the engine. "It happens."

We were practically on top of the missing road. That didn't sound safe. "Shouldn't we do something?"

"Right now, the best thing to do is stay put so we can be found." He grabbed his bag from behind my seat and pulled out a walkie-talkie, turning it on. He said something in Italian, and there was a scratchy response.

After he ended his conversation, he left the walkie-talkie on, and it made random noises, hisses and beeps.

"Shouldn't we turn around and go back up the mountain? How do you know we should just stay put?"

"I know because I volunteer with the search and rescue team. And there are several flash flood warnings for the area, so taking off on foot is a really bad idea, as is trying to go back up the mountain. Floods come down from the top, and we could be easily caught in one. The storm is too severe right now for a helicopter to get close, but as soon as it clears enough they'll airlift us out." He sounded so calm, seemed so sure, that it made my anxiety lessen.

"Another thing I didn't know about you." Tessa had really held back.

He was watching the rain fall against the windshield, and I used the opportunity to admire his profile. "It's why I was late to our date today. A village in the Bellavista Valley had to be evacuated. I tried to call you and Tessa, but it didn't go through."

A sharp, twisting anger began inside my chest, spreading through the rest of my body, consuming me. "You… you were my blind date, who stood me up for two freaking hours?"

Paolo looked at me in surprise. "Blind date? Tessa said you were expecting me. That you were excited to go out with me."

Rage made breathing normally a challenge.

But did I have any right to be angry with him? He had been out saving people. He had a good reason for not being there. All I could think about was how totally humiliated I'd been when he had stood me up, how scared I was when I got stranded thanks to my accident, and how even now my feet ached from walking down a mountain in high heels. And during all that it had never once occurred to me that *Paolo* had been my blind date.

Breathing in and out deeply, I tried to calm down. He slowly undid his seatbelt, eyeing me the same way you'd watch a rattlesnake. Moving carefully, worried about being struck.

He moved closer, putting his arm across the back of my

seat. "I'm sorry to have done that to you. I tried to call you." He slid his phone toward me, giving me the chance to verify. "But in my defense, I helped evacuate fifty families this morning."

Nope, no right at all to be mad. Playing the "I was saving people's lives" card totally robbed a girl of her self-righteous indignation.

I heard the click of my seatbelt being released. Then I felt him tugging on my arm, drawing me closer. "I intended to ask you out to dinner months ago, but Tessa told me to wait until you'd settled in." His hand cupped the side of my face, sending tingles into every single cell I owned. "I have been waiting a very long time, to have you all to myself. I would never have left you alone unless it was an emergency."

My throat had constricted. Somehow he'd maneuvered both of us so that I was pressed against his side. It was difficult to drag in air. Everywhere we touched seemed to erupt in flames. The little, golden-flecked fires in his eyes made it impossible to think.

The rain pounded on the car, encasing us in a hazy curtain of water. It was as if we were the only two people in the entire world. His gaze dropped to my mouth, and when I bit my lower lip in anticipation, I heard his breath catch. No question about it. He was going to kiss me.

I watched as he moved in closer and closer, the promise of what was to come making my heart beat slow and loud. I was so aware of everything around me. How the air between us felt heavy. The cute way his damp hair curled up at the ends. The sound of his breathing, that citrus and laundry soap smell filling my senses as his face drew near, his firm hands holding me in place.

And after what seemed like an eternity, his warm, strong lips finally pressed against mine for one... two... three earth-shattering moments, and it was like somebody had given me the key to Cinderella's suite inside Disneyland's castle. Only a million times better. Tiny lightning bolts coursed through me, sending jolts of craving and desire that almost knocked me backward. My pulse sped up, pushing me toward an imminent cardiac arrest. And he'd barely even touched me!

No question, I would be in serious trouble when he kicked this kiss up to PG-13.

Just as I reached for him, intending to put my arms around his neck, he suddenly stopped.

My eyelids flew open. Why, why, why? Why had he stopped? I ached for him to keep going. I had already decided that I officially wanted to spend the rest of my life kissing him, and he *stopped.*

"I shouldn't have kissed you," he murmured. "But you're adorable when you're angry, I couldn't resist." He traced the curves and lines of my face with his fingertips, and I intended to tell him to keep going, but his touch was turning my mind as blurry as our fogged-up windows. "Did I mistake basic human decency for attraction again? Or are you ready to admit you like me?"

That snapped me out of my haze. I moved back until I hit my car door. If I kept letting him touch me, I'd end up saying whatever he wanted me to say. And I still had some pride left, right?

Yeah, I wasn't believing it either. I totally liked him. Which was more than a little scary.

"So," I said, in a feeble attempt to change the subject, "you didn't come up here to rescue me. I can't believe you thought I would still be waiting for you. Four hours later."

"But here you are."

"Only because I got in an accident." Why did all of this have to be so amusing to him?

"But you're still here, *tesora mia.*" He put his hand on my knee, and I batted it away. Which made him laugh. Like he knew the real reason for my reaction. And it wasn't because I didn't want him to touch me, but because I did.

How could one person be so infuriating and irresistible at the same time? But mostly irresistible?

Paolo studied me. "We should get to know each other better. Tessa does nothing but sing your praises."

"She does the same with you. Obviously, she's easily impressed."

His seductive grin gave me both icy chills and hot flashes. "Or we're just that amazing." I started counting to ten, just to distract myself.

"Tell me about the men you're dating," he said. "Because, if you'll forgive me, your standards don't seem very high."

"As evidenced by me being here with you." I was teasing, and he knew it.

"Ouch!" he laughed. "You can't fool me. I know how sweet you are. Tessa told me about the Syrian refugee couple you're teaching English to for free."

I was going to kill Tessa. Even if that meant no more zeppoles.

As if he'd read my mind, he jokingly asked, "Do I need to feed you again?"

This had nothing to do with low blood sugar and everything to do with my frustration. I was sitting with the world's Olympic gold medalist in kissing, and we weren't doing what had earned him his medal.

I let out a sigh. I knew he had been teasing about the standards thing, and I wondered what he'd think if I told him the opposite was actually true. That my standards had been so high, I'd made myself miserable.

"Trust me, there's nothing to tell when it comes to the men I've been 'dating.' I think I should be off men for a little while."

"You don't like being *on* men?"

"Exhibit A, Your Honor." But I couldn't help it. I smiled. "What about you and your harem?"

"My what?" He looked legitimately confused.

"Your girlfriends at the bar? Do you have so many women, you can't keep track?" I wanted to sound light and breezy like him, but the barest trace of jealousy had crept into my voice.

And the smirk on his face let me know he'd heard it. "I'm not dating anyone. I haven't in a long time. I don't go out very much."

This from the man who every night had more women after him than I could count? "I think you and I do math differently."

"And I think…" He took my hand in his and squeezed it. I expected him to let go. Instead, he turned my palm over, lacing his fingers through mine in a way that felt both delicious and right. Like we should have been holding hands this entire time, because they fit so perfectly together. Then he started drawing lazy circles with his thumb on the back of my hand, and I felt it in my knees. "The only woman I'm interested in dating is you."

Chapter Five

WAS HE BEING serious? He was smiling, but he looked serious. He handed me another protein bar, which I opened with one hand and my teeth, because I suddenly didn't want to let him go.

Why was I fighting this so hard? Why was I being so ornery? I'd thought he was one type of guy, but now I knew he was nothing like I'd imagined him to be.

I still found it hard to believe that a guy who looked like him would want to be with a girl like me. Even when I'd dismissed him as "just a bartender," I'd always considered him to be unbelievably gorgeous. And very out of my league. Some subconscious part of me had probably assumed that if I let myself like him, he'd only break my heart, so I'd rejected him before he could. But in reality, he'd been nothing but open and honest with me, and it made my heart melt.

It scared me that I saw a possible future with him. That he seemed to be the kind of man I could fall in love with.

And that titles and daydreams of princes and everything else besides him and me faded away. None of the rest of it mattered.

I liked Paolo.

"Tell me about what it was like to go to school in the States," I said, wanting to distract myself from where my mind was headed.

Our conversation started there, and as it continued to rain we swapped college war stories like we were two veterans home from battle. I told him about my current studies and part-time work; he told me about his bajillion jobs. And it dawned on me that when I thought Tessa had been trying to set me up with all those friends, she'd only been trying to set me up with her brother. He was in search and rescue, volunteered with charities, bartended and did woodworking. It wasn't four different guys, it was just him. He did so much that it made me feel lazy, when I'd always prided myself on my work ethic.

We talked about our parents, how we'd both grown up with absentee fathers and how that had affected us. We talked about the American presidential candidates, and who should win the election. Whether Beyoncé should go on tour again. About how in the summer, the ancient forest beyond the rock faces surrounding us would host thousands and thousands of dancing, magical fireflies. Paolo promised to show me.

As we chatted, my remaining reservations and fears vanished. Like I'd flipped some internal light switch when I decided to let go of the fantasy and appreciate what I had right in front of me. Paolo constantly feeding me probably helped, too. We made each other laugh, and somehow we ended up with his arm around my shoulders, while his other hand still held mine. Right where I belonged. As if my body already knew what my brain had taken forever to figure out. He would routinely sneak small, short kisses. Enough to repeatedly thrill and excite me one second at a time. I got the sense that he didn't trust himself to do more than that.

Or he didn't trust me.

Which was probably smart, given that people were supposed to be on their way to rescue us and all I wanted was to drag him into the backseat and forget everything else.

It was, without a doubt, the easiest conversation I'd ever had. Totally effortless. As if we'd always been friends. It was like talking to Tessa. Only I was with a delectably hot man who was so kissable he made my lips tingle with want. There was no awkwardness, no weird pauses or silence. In fact, as we teased and questioned, we kept talking over each other. He seemed genuinely interested in discovering everything about me, just as I wanted to know everything about him.

Like I asked him if he'd ever been on a blind date before, and he reminded me that Tessa was his sister and he'd been on many.

"Which one was the worst?" I asked.

His hand had moved to rest on the back of my neck, his fingers kneading my nape. It was a struggle to keep my head vertical and not let it flop all over the place. I leaned against the headrest, needing the support.

"There was one woman who was a rabid vegan. She was... a little intense. To the point that she was planning on starting her own church, because she knew that God was against eating meat."

"Ha. If that were true, animals wouldn't be so tasty." That earned me a quick kiss against my jaw.

"And what was your worst?"

With no hesitation I answered, "Crusty Carmine."

He pulled back, both eyebrows raised. "Why would you call him that?"

"Does it matter? Is there ever a good reason to call someone crusty?" I shuddered, just thinking about it. "You can probably fill in the blanks. One of which should include pieces of Carmine landing in his soup. And then, his mom called me the following week to see how our date had gone, and to ask whether or not I planned on seeing him again."

"Wait, his *mother* called you?"

"Which I didn't know until Tessa got on the phone to translate for me. I think your sister laughed for three days straight. He was easily the weirdest person I'd ever met. And I've vacationed in Portland."

I realized Paolo's shoulders were shaking. I shoved his arm. "Stop laughing! It was very traumatizing!" But I couldn't really demand he stop when I was giggling.

"I know I shouldn't laugh. I have two sisters. I understand the correct response should be 'Men!' accompanied by an eye roll."

"Just sisters?" I'd already told him that I was an only child.

"And three brothers."

"Man, Monterrans have big families." I couldn't imagine growing up with a bunch of siblings. But Paolo probably couldn't picture growing up all alone, either.

He lifted my hand up and said, "Catholics," against my skin, which made me want to curl my fingers inward.

"Oh." That sounded more out-of-breath than I would have liked. "You said you go to Mass every week. Are you religious?"

"I believe in God, but I'm not sure about the other parts of it. I go with my mother because it makes her happy."

I rested the side of my head against his forearm. "Are you going to tell her?"

"That I think what she's doing doesn't matter? That I don't believe the same things she believes? No. It's a little like being employed by a large company, and doing everything you can to earn a promotion. But your coworker spends all his time telling you about how there's no such things as promotions, that management made up promotions to control you. It just makes you a jerk to tell people that what they believe in is wrong."

I liked the way he looked at things. "I always thought it would be nice to be religious. But my mother thinks all religions were invented by male patriarchies to enslave women."

He tugged on a lock of my hair and smiled. "I really need to meet your mother."

I had the feeling he just might.

His walkie talkie emitted a high-pitched shriek, followed by someone speaking a bunch of Italian too fast and quiet for me to make out.

"What's happening?" I asked

Paolo calmly reached over and opened the glove compartment. He took out a device that looked like a fat, see-through remote. It had fluorescent yellow coloring on it and the words "ACR."

"This is a personal locator beacon," he told me. "It will help them find us."

"What do you mean 'find us'? What's happening?" I was trying to mimic his calm, but I could instinctively tell something was seriously wrong. He was holding something back. I was starting to panic again.

"There is a flash flood warning, which means one is coming this way. We can't outrun it, so we're going to have to climb."

"Climb?" I repeated, looking at the sheared off mountain face next to the car, and then at my high heels. "There's no way."

But Paolo had already crawled into the backseat and was gathering equipment from the trunk.

For rock climbing.

Which I had only ever done twice before, when Tessa forced me to go to the gym with her. But that had been indoors, with appropriate shoes and clothing.

Before I knew it, Paolo had me get out in the pouring rain. I stepped into a rope harness, which he fastened into place, and then fastened to his harness.

"I just knew this day would end with me in ropes," I joked lamely.

But this time he didn't smile. That's when I knew things were even worse than I'd feared. That even though I'd initially imagined he'd wanted to off me, it had been Mother Nature planning to end my life today.

Paolo explained how the climbing would work, using words like "spring loaded camming device." I just stared straight up, not sure how this was going to happen. He handed me a helmet and helped me do the straps. Both of our helmets had lamplights on top, making it easier to see. He told me to kick off my shoes.

"You want me to climb barefoot?" I asked in disbelief.

He said my shoes were too slippery, and that I would actually be better off using my bare feet as I would be able to grip the rock.

"There's a ledge there," he pointed up, and I saw a small ledge above us, supporting a massive pine tree. "That's our goal." He had to yell the words to be heard over the storm. "It looks worse than it is. There are a lot of hand and footholds. You can do this."

Gulping, I nodded. "I trust you."

Then I scored my smile. "That's progress. Just do what I do."

Then he kissed me hard, the kind of kiss I'd wanted all evening. Where his earlier kisses had been gentle, tender and sweet, this was a blazing inferno fueled by desperation, need and concern. I could feel how worried he was behind all that passion and intensity.

"We need to climb." He went over to the rocks. I saw that it wasn't exactly straight up, and that there were boulders sticking out all over the place that I could grab on to.

"Now?" Didn't I get a countdown or something?

"Right now. I can hear the water coming."

Even though he was yelling, his tone was calm. Matter of fact. The way someone else might say, "The sky is blue."

Then he was scaling the mountain like he'd been born to do it. Thankfully, Tessa had taught me the basics. I could do this. I lifted my foot as high as it would go and once I felt secure, I reached up to find a hold to pull myself up. After only a few feet, I landed on something sharp and gasped from the pain. My feet would be cut up and bloody, but it was better than drowning. I just focused on finding something to grab on to, doing my best to follow Paolo through the blinding rain. I probably should have been scared of falling, but I knew he'd never allow that to happen. He stayed just ahead of me, watching me, making sure that I was okay. Just like he'd instructed, I did what he did. Put my hands and feet in the same places his hands and feet had gone.

I heard the water as it filled up the valley where just minutes before we'd been sitting in his car and talking. It sounded like a freight train. I didn't look down. Focusing on the pain in my hands and feet, I used that to keep me moving forward. Even though there were things to grab hold of, everything was slick and wet. My feet slipped over and over before I found each new spot to safely step. Just earlier I'd said I'd thought it would be nice to be religious. I was certainly religious now, begging God to let us live and to be rescued.

The roaring sound of rushing water echoed between the mountain walls. My heart pounded even harder in response. The silvery taste of fear filled my mouth.

Only a few minutes had passed, but it felt as if a thousand lifetimes went by before Paolo scrambled up and over the ledge. Once he had, the rope between us went taut. He yelled my name, and both of his hands reached for me. I grabbed on, and he pulled me up. He hugged me so tightly, I could barely breathe. My chest ached as I sobbed, my throat raw. The storm was so fierce, I didn't know if he could tell that I was crying.

Letting go of me, Paolo walked in a circle around the tree. He wrapped our climbing rope around the trunk. I sat close to the tree, the rock face blocking some of the wind. I put my arms around my legs, but it didn't hold off much of the chill.

He walked over to the edge, looking down at the dark water that seemed to be rising higher and higher. He was so amazing in a crisis. Calm and strong. While I felt like a total basket case.

My feet felt warm, and I touched them. I held my fingers up to the helmet's lamplight. Blood. The adrenaline was keeping the pain at bay for now, but I knew it was only a matter of time before the cuts became excruciating.

He crouched down next to me. "Are you okay?" he shouted.

The weather was worse up here. In addition to the Noah-esque rain, there were massive gusts of wind that we'd been protected from at the bottom, between the two canyon walls. My hair whipped around me and the strong blasts rattled the ancient, tall tree next to us. I was definitely not okay. But considering we were in the same boat, it wouldn't do me any good to tell him how cold, wet and scared I was.

"Still not the worst blind date I've ever been on!" I shouted back.

There was a loud crashing sound, and he immediately straightened. Next thing I knew, a massive branch fell from the tree, catching Paolo in the chest and knocking him backward.

Right off the ledge.

I tried to scream his name, but the rope yanked me forward, slamming me into the trunk. I had to save him. I couldn't let him fall. Not now, not when I'd just found him. Leaning back, I used every bit of strength I had left. I placed both feet against the tree, ignoring the stabbing sensations in my soles. I braced myself, pulling on the rope.

My tears returned. It was useless. I couldn't drag him back up, but I could keep him from falling.

I had no idea how long I stayed like that, repeatedly yelling his name. But then the rope suddenly went slack, and I crashed onto my bottom. My heart leapt into my throat. Had he fallen? But a moment later, I felt his arms around me, holding me close. I let out a cry of relief. He'd climbed back up. He was safe.

We were both safe.

He sat down next to me, pulling me into his lap, tucking me under his arm and sheltering me from the storm as much as he could.

Rain blinded me.

He kept murmuring something against my hair, and it took me a while to figure out he was saying *tesora mia* over and over.

I'd been so blind. I'd wasted so much time that I could have spent with Paolo. If tonight had shown me anything, it was that life was too short to fixate on things that didn't matter. I was so grateful that Tessa didn't share my blind spot and had seen the possibilities for me and her brother that I'd overlooked.

He kept saying I was his treasure.

But I was pretty sure he was mine.

Hours passed and morning came. The storm started to fade. The rain died down, and the winds stilled. The sun even decided to emerge. As if there'd never been a storm at all.

"Now what?" I asked in a croaky voice. The inside of my throat felt shredded. "If we have to climb back down, I'm not sure I can do it."

Paolo let out a grunt of pain as he finally released me. "Where do you hurt?"

"My feet and hands."

He moved to look at my feet, and began to pull out slivers of bark. "You did this for me." He said it incredulously, his voice filled with wonder and shock. I could only nod, a lump in my throat. Then he pressed a kiss to the rope burns on each of my palms.

He gathered me back up in his arms, again making that pain sound. "I will never, ever forget what you did to save my life."

"Technically, you rescued me first, and then I rescued you. That makes us even." My inner feminist was satisfied, and my inner princess was exultant. "Are you okay?"

"I think I might have broken some ribs. And yet this is still not the worst blind date I've ever been on, either."

For some reason that struck me as unbelievably funny, and I started to laugh. Paolo tried to join in, but his injured ribs made him groan. Then my stomach growled so loudly, I swear it had its own echo.

He pressed his lips against my forehead. "Would you like to go to dinner with me, and let me feed you some more?"

"When?"

"I was thinking later tonight. And every night after."

That sounded good to me. I kissed him as my reply.

"May I take that as a yes?"

"You most definitely may take that as a yes." I wanted to cuddle with him, but was trying to avoid his injuries. "But first we have to get off this ledge. And not by taking another header over the edge."

"I'm not worried about that. I think that's our ride now."

Shading my eyes with my hand, I heard the soft humming sound of helicopter blades. Soon they'd be so close, that they'd be as loud as that flood and the storm had been last night. "Just FYI," I warned him, "you may want to rethink your dinner offer. In case you hadn't noticed, I'm kind of a disaster."

"You're not," he said, putting his arms under my knees and around my waist. "And even if you were, in case you hadn't noticed, I'm pretty good with disasters."

With a loud groan, my insane, cracked-rib, soon-to-be boyfriend picked me up! He was going to hurt himself even more! I kept telling him to put me down, but he refused to let me stand on my injured feet.

As the helicopter headed toward us, it struck me as odd that it was painted entirely red. I'd seen rescue helicopters on the Monterran news, and they were always red, white and blue.

"Speaking of disasters," he said. "There's something I have to confess."

I shielded my eyes to look at him. It was the first time I'd ever seen him looking so uneasy. Even when we had to climb to save our lives, he'd been worried and serious, but calm. It had to be something really terrible.

"Are you married? Because I will do more than just haunt you if you are married." It was the worst thing I could imagine. That or a terminal illness.

"No. I'm not married." I couldn't have described how relieved I felt. "But… that helicopter, that's my security team."

"Security team?" I repeated. "Why would you have a security team unless…"

"I'm a prince." He said it like it was a bad word. "My father is one of King Dominic's younger brothers."

I decided I was hallucinating. I was lying in a coma in some hospital, and my brain was making this up. There was no way this was real. I pinched myself on the arm. "Ow!" I yelped.

"Did you just pinch yourself?"

"Obviously. Because it sounded like you said you were a prince."

He swallowed, hard. "Yes."

Even though this was happening, I still couldn't believe it. "Why didn't you tell me?"

"Every woman I meet is interested in the crown and the money. Even at Princeton, everybody knew who I was. A tiny part of what made you appealing was that you had no idea who I am or who my family is."

His family. "That means Tessa's a freaking princess?"

"A very rich princess. Who owns not only your apartment, but the entire building. And we co-own the restaurant together."

No wonder Tessa had laughed when I'd finally confessed my princess obsession.

And no wonder she hadn't seriously pushed her brother on me until I'd called off my prince hunt.

Because she had a real life prince that she thought was perfect for me, but she didn't want me dazzled by his title or distracted by his crown. She wanted me to love Paolo the way she did—for himself.

For the treasure that he was.

Once he and I had both recovered, I'd tell him all about his sister's scheming and my crazy royalty infatuation. Hopefully by then I would have proven to him that he was who I wanted. That I was falling for Paolo, and not his prince-hood.

The helicopter had almost reached us when he asked, "Are you okay with this? Do you think you'll be able to handle me being a prince?"

That made me laugh. "I think I'll find a way to manage."

Bestselling author **Sariah Wilson** has never jumped out of an airplane, never climbed Mt. Everest, and is not a former CIA operative. She has, however, been madly, passionately in love with her soulmate and is a fervent believer in happily ever afters—which is why she writes romance. She has published many happily ever after stories. She grew up in southern California, graduated from Brigham Young University (go Cougars!) with a semi-useless degree in history, and is the oldest of nine (yes, nine) children. She currently lives with the aforementioned soulmate and their four children in Utah, along with three tiger barb fish, a cat named Tiger, and a recently departed hamster that is buried in the backyard (and has nothing at all to do with tigers).

Her website is: www.SariahWilson.com

Printed in Great Britain
by Amazon

52639601R00205